This is a work of fiction. The characters, incidents, and dialogues are products of the author's imagination and are not to be construed as real. Any resemblance to actual events or persons, living or dead, is entirely coincidental.

ЯED

Copyright © 2014 by: Jennifer Anne Davis

For information address:

Clean Teen Publishing
PO Box 561326
The Colony, TX 75056

www.cleanteenpublishing.com

Typography by: Courtney Nuckels
Cover design by: Marya Heiman

ISBN: 978-1-940534-71-8

To Landon
The second in my own personal trilogy
I love you to infinity and beyond

Content Disclosure

For more information about our content disclosure, please utilize the QR code above with your smart phone or visit us at www.cleanteenpublishing.com.

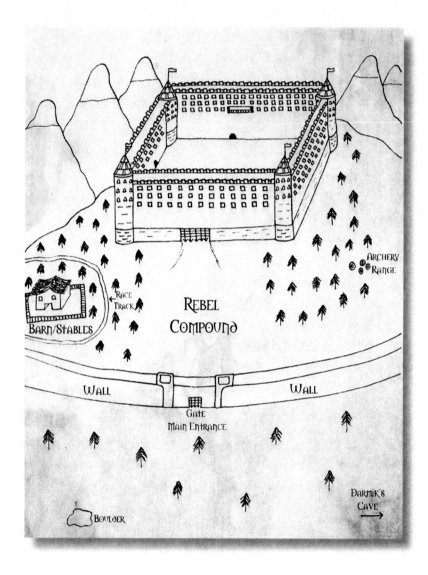

ARCHERY
RANGE

RACE
TRACK

BARN/STABLES

REBEL
COMPOUND

WALL   WALL

GATE
MAIN ENTRANCE

DARMIK'S
CAVE

BOULDER

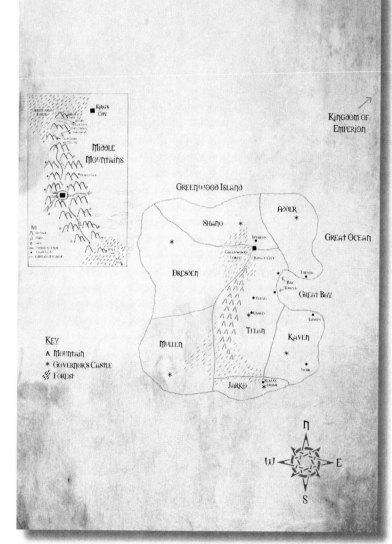

KINGDOM OF EMPERION

GREAT OCEAN

GREENWOOD ISLAND

ADDLR

SHANO

WEBBEN

DRESDEN

GREENWOOD FOREST

KING'S CITY

TRESEK

BAY TOWNS

GREAT BAY

TELGO

LUMEN

USAVO

TELAN

KAVEN

MULLEN

NOIR

JARKO

BLAIR'S HOME

KEY
⋀ Mountain
✳ Governor's Castle
🌲 Forest

Middle Mountains

GREENWOOD FOREST

KING'S CITY

KEY

N
W — E
S

PROLOGUE

Mako

Revenge was so close that Mako could almost taste it. He would make Barjon pay for murdering his family and destroying Greenwood Island. However, Princess Amer was the key to everything and, right now, she stood on the gallows with a noose cinched around her neck.

Mako shifted in the tall, thick tree, his green and black tunic camouflaging his entire body. He remained perched among the leaves and branches fifty yards away from the gallows. There were only a few trees on the grounds, and he felt exposed. He would have preferred to be on the wall surrounding the castle, but had been unable to infiltrate the guards. He needed to be elevated to make the shot, and the trees were the next best thing. His legs ached from standing in the tree all night, but he didn't dare stretch for fear of catching someone's attention.

A soldier began tapping a single beat on a drum, the haunting sound echoing throughout the courtyard. Hundreds of people were crammed together in front of the gallows to watch Amer's execution. On the castle's balcony, Barjon was sitting on a royal-blue, high-backed chair. The curtain behind Barjon shifted, and Lennek strolled out and leaned against the railing. He smiled down at Amer with a smug expression on his face.

Mako's hands itched to squeeze Lennek's throat until the life drained out of him. He forced his temper in check. It was only a matter of time before Barjon and his sons would get what they deserved.

The clouds were growing thick and heavy as a storm moved in. Mako glanced back down at Amer. Her body shook from fear. He couldn't believe how much she looked like her mother—the same blonde hair, blue eyes, and bone structure. Seventeen years ago, Mako swore to Queen Kayln that he would protect the princess, and he intended to keep that promise. Rage built inside of him. He had to stifle the memories of everything that transpired on that horrific day. He would not allow Amer to meet the same fate as her mother or his wife and baby daughter.

Scanning the courtyard, Mako searched for Darmik and immediately found him sitting atop a black horse surrounded by soldiers. Darmik had been tracking some of Mako's men—had even fought and killed a few, so he had to assume Darmik was prepared for a rescue attempt. Yet, there weren't as many soldiers positioned in the courtyard as he expected. Mako had a few of his own men down among the crowd, ready to move the people when necessary.

The drum beat wavered and ceased. An eerie silence descended over the courtyard. Mako steadied the longbow, sweat dripping down his forehead. Pulling back the stiff string, he nocked an arrow and waited for Lennek to give the command, signaling the execution. Timing was crucial.

The longbow had a heavy draw weight. Mako couldn't hold the position much longer. He focused on Lennek, watching his body. Two of Mako's men were hidden in other trees, each armed with a longbow. Jantek was twenty-five feet to the right, Donok thirty feet to the left. The plan was for Mako to take the first shot, Jantek to take the next immediately after, followed by Donok a second later. Mako would take a fourth shot if necessary.

Lennek raised his right arm and shouted, "Now!"

Mako forced himself to wait a fraction of a second before releasing the arrow. The rope around Amer couldn't be too slack. The rope's width, the time it would take for the arrow to travel to the target, and the wind speed were minute details that meant the difference between life and death.

He released the arrow. It was a beautiful shot, but he had no time to admire its delicate arch through the air.

Amer began to fall. Mako nocked another arrow.

His first arrow struck the rope, slicing it, but not all the way through. Jantek's arrow sailed through the air and pierced it again; Donok's arrow hit the rope right behind Jantek's. Amer's weight pulled the rope—it was about to go taunt, breaking her neck. Mako had already released a second arrow.

The rope severed.

Instead of Amer's body dangling, she fell through the narrow opening, smacking her head against the wooden platform with a loud thump. She landed on the ground beneath the gallows, not moving. People in the courtyard screamed, thinking they were under attack. In the midst of the confusion, two of Mako's men, dressed in stolen army uniforms, ran under the gallows and grabbed Amer.

·ONE

Rema

Rema wanted the last thing she saw to be of something beautiful. Scanning the crowd of unfamiliar faces, she spotted Darmik dressed in his commander's uniform off to the side of the courtyard atop Nightsky. He must not have ever loved her—their entire relationship had to have been some sort of game. Hurt and betrayal raged inside of her. Not wanting to die like this, Rema focused on his horse—the only connection to her home in this dreadful place. As if sensing her, Nightsky's head turned toward Rema. She stared into his dark, knowledgeable eyes. Tears blurred her vision, but she couldn't look away. Images of Uncle Kar and Aunt Maya filled her with a sense of peace.

Lennek yelled, "Now," his voice echoing in the courtyard.

The floor beneath her feet moaned as it opened. There were several odd "whooshes" by Rema's ear.

And then she fell.

Rema's stomach dropped. She dove from cliffs enough to know the sensation of falling. This was much the same, only, instead of cool water, her body slammed into something hard. There was an immense amount of pain.

So this is what death feels like.

Her world went black.

Two

Darmik

There were no signs or indications of a rescue attempt. Darmik scanned the courtyard again. Nothing was amiss. It didn't make any sense. If Rema was the rightful heir to the throne, as the rebels claimed and her tattoo indicated, then surely the rebels would at least attempt to save her.

Lennek gave the command. The soldier manning the gallows pulled the lever, opening the floor beneath her.

Maybe Darmik was wrong. Maybe she was just a girl. Rema's eyes found his for a brief second, and then she turned away. His heart sank. He couldn't allow her to die. Darmik had never disobeyed an order before. But if Rema was just a merchant's niece, she didn't deserve to be executed for kissing him. He was responsible for her predicament, and wanted to save her. Reaching down, Darmik grabbed the knife strapped to his lower leg. When he righted himself, her body was already falling. Darmik's hand tightened around the hilt. He was about to throw the dagger to slice the rope, but four arrows sailed through the air, severing it before he had a chance.

Swiftly scanning the direction the arrows came from, Darmik saw a man shimmying down a tree. Was there a rescue attempt in place? Darmik frantically searched the courtyard, looking for anything amiss.

Rema's head smashed against the wooden platform, a horrible, wood-splintering sound, and she landed on the ground with a thud. Two soldiers ran under the gallows, grabbing her body. Darmik didn't recognize either of the men. They weren't his soldiers.

There was a rescue attempt in place! He took this as confirmation—Rema was the heir. Nudging his horse forward, he headed straight for the gallows. People yelled and ran toward the exit. He had no idea where Rema was amidst the chaos.

Darmik turned back to face his squad, about to order them to close the courtyard gates, when he saw two soldiers sprint to the entrance of the army's secret tunnel carrying someone. It had to be Rema.

"Stop them!" Darmik shouted, pointing his dagger at the tunnel. He couldn't believe he'd almost rescued Rema himself. When it came to her, he lost his wits, and he needed to remain focused if he wanted to stop the rebels.

The squad of soldiers took off after the rebels, Darmik not far behind them. He stormed inside the dark tunnel, unable to see anything.

Horse hooves pounded on the dirt. Sparks from swords clashing shone in the blackness.

A soldier screamed, "It's an ambush!"

From the sound of things, there were well over

two dozen men fighting in the tunnel. Darmik lowered his body in the saddle and rode straight through the fray. If he and his men were under attack, then the rebels probably had Rema through the tunnel and were already well on their way to freedom. These rebels were meant to slow his pursuit of her. A hand grabbed his leg, and he jabbed his dagger hard and low, embedding it into a man. Pulling the weapon free, Darmik continued.

When he reached the end of the tunnel that exited outside the city walls, thunder boomed. Scanning the horizon, there was a single horse and rider traveling straight through the field instead of for the cover of the forest. A limp body lay in front of the captain on the horse. The body looked like Rema. Darmik nudged Nightsky and the horse took off. Leaning low, he chased after the rebel, confident he could close the mile gap between them. Given the number of soldiers he had stationed in the nearby area, it surprised him when no one came to aid in the chase. Since the rebel wore a captain's uniform, Darmik's men were tricked into letting the rebel flee without question. He was on his own.

The rebel finally entered the forest. There was no way Darmik would be able to overtake the rebel and Rema amid the dense trees and thick vegetation. Having limited options, he stopped his mount, pulled out his bow and arrow, and shot at the man's horse. The arrow struck the animal's thigh, causing the horse to rear up. The man reigned in his mare and dismounted, gently lowering Rema to the ground. She lay on the forest floor, unconscious.

About ten feet away from the rebel, Darmik

dismounted and unsheathed his sword. The rebel appeared to be in his late forties and was large and muscular, with a look of determination across his face. He, too, wielded a heavy sword capable of amputating a body part. Darmik slowly approached the man, and then made the first move, sliding his right foot forward. He kept his elbows inward, and sliced toward the rebel's sword arm. The man twisted and blocked the strike. Moving his body to the left, Darmik raised his sword and struck at the rebel's thigh. Again, the man blocked the blow and countered with one of his own.

Rema screamed in agony. Blood covered the side of her face and the front of her dress. The cut rope was still wrapped around her neck, entangled with her key necklace.

"Where are you taking her?" Darmik demanded. Rema's betrayal still stung, yet he didn't want her to die. It was infuriating the way she made him feel.

"She is none of your concern," the rebel replied, moving in front of Rema.

"You think you can just ride off with Rema and what? Restore her to the throne?" Darmik kept his face blank. He advanced toward the man, both hands holding his sword out in front of him.

Rema pulled herself up against a greenwood tree, fresh blood oozing from the cut on her forehead. When she saw Darmik, her eyes widened and her shaking hands flew to her neck, touching the rope still clinging to her.

"It's okay," the rebel gently said, his eyes steady on Darmik as he spoke to Rema. "I'm here to protect you. I will not let anyone hurt you, especially *him*."

Rema peered at the rebel with a confused look on her face.

"Does Rema know who she really is?" Darmik demanded. But why would the rebels keep her in the dark? From a strategic standpoint, it didn't make any sense.

"What do you mean?" Rema asked.

The rebel's face hardened as he advanced toward Darmik, raising his sword, prepared to strike.

"Wait," Rema said, her voice weak. "If you're really here to help me, then do not hurt Prince Darmik."

The rebel stumbled when he heard the request. Darmik couldn't help being shocked as well, especially after the way he had treated her since her arrest.

"Ahh," she cried glancing down at the blood covering her hands and filthy dress. Darmik feared she would pass out.

The rebel lowered his sword. "She's losing too much blood. We can stay here and fight, or I can get her to a healer."

Darmik cringed as Rema's head fell forward and her entire body slid to the side, unconscious. He raised his sword, preparing to strike the rebel.

The man took a step away from him. "If she wants you unharmed, I can only assume you want the same for her?" His eyes locked on Darmik's, like he was trying to read his thoughts.

Darmik did not want this rebel to know he had feelings for Rema. That information could only be used against him, and he didn't want to give the rebel any leverage. "No," he said. "My interest lies in finding your base camp and destroying you. I don't care what happens to her."

The rebel studied him for a moment. "I have a healer not far from here," he finally said, lowering his sword. The rebel seemed intent on keeping Rema safe. If Darmik defeated him, then what would happen to her? If Lennek got his hands on Rema, he would destroy her.

"Go then." Darmik dropped the point of his sword to the ground, taking a step back.

The rebel gave a curt nod before sliding his sword back in its scabbard. He picked up Rema, setting her atop Nightsky.

"Since you've injured my horse, I will also need yours." After tying her to the animal, he mounted his own. Darmik watched them ride away as heavy rain began to fall.

THREE

Rema

Rema's eyes flew open. Was she dead? Her head throbbed. *No*, she thought, *death wouldn't hurt so much.* She lay on a straw bed in a small, dark room. It had to be the dungeon, although it lacked the putrid smell of human waste mixed with decaying rats.

She tried to remember how she got there. The last thing Rema remembered was standing on the gallows with the noose around her neck. She recalled focusing on Nightsky's big, black eyes, then she fell, her body slamming into something hard and her world going black.

Did the rope break? Tears slid down her cheeks. If so, would she be rehanged? Rema couldn't go through that again. The faint sound of angry voices resonated outside the small room as she strained to listen. Were soldiers coming for her now? Was it time for the king to remedy her botched execution?

Rema tried to sit up, but an explosion of pain rippled through her skull. Her world went black again.

ॐ

When Rema came to, she heard Aunt Maya and Uncle Kar talking to a female voice she didn't recognize. She wanted to shout out to them, but stopped herself just in case. Maybe, she shuddered in horror, her aunt and uncle had been arrested and imprisoned here in the dungeon with her.

Rema knew that if she tried to sit up, she'd pass out again. Her body felt as if a horse had stepped on it. Reaching up, she stroked a bandage wrapped around her forehead. Where her fingers touched, a fire burned. If she were in the dungeon, then why would they bother to dress her wound? Maybe Lennek didn't want her to bleed to death—that was the most likely cause. He'd want her conscious when she was hanged.

Someone bumped against the wooden door. The holding cell she had previously been in had iron bars for one of the walls, not a normal wooden door like this one. Looking around, Rema realized a brown, wool blanket covered her. Next to the bed sat a table with a washbasin, the water red. A washcloth splotched with blood hung on the edge. Several small bowls similar to ones Aunt Maya used to mix medicine surrounded it. The faint smell of mint hung in the air.

The door opened, and a woman entered. A dull, gray light illuminated the room. "You're awake," the woman said, smiling. She wore a long, plain black dress and her brown hair was pulled back into a bun.

"Who are you?" Rema asked, her voice hoarse. She wanted to ask about her aunt and uncle, but was afraid to say anything about them until she knew what was going on.

"My name is Nulea. I am a healer." The woman pulled out a chair and sat next to the bed.

Nulea had a friendly smile, and she didn't seem threatening in any way. However, Rema still had no idea what was happening.

"Rest assured," Nulea said, "you're safe now." She had pale, white skin, similar to Rema's, not tan like most of the people on Greenwood Island. Nulea reached toward her.

Rema jerked backward, then wished she hadn't when the pounding in her head increased.

"Try not to move," Nulea said. "You have a nasty gash on your forehead. You lost a lot of blood and have been unconscious for some time. I had to stitch you up and put catnip on the wound."

Nulea reached out toward Rema again, inspecting the bandage. Her sleeves slid to her elbows, revealing two bare wrists.

"Where is your mark and band?" Rema asked. She had never seen someone without a tattoo or identification band before. Each child born in the kingdom was tattooed on their left wrist with their region's emblem, and every person in the kingdom wore a band on their right wrist stating their name, age, and marital status. The law was simple—the army would execute anyone found without either one.

"I don't have them," the woman answered. "You still have some bleeding." Nulea smiled, a dimple on her right cheek showing. "You'll have to stay here for a few days until you're stronger."

"And where exactly *is* here?" Rema asked.

Nulea's eyes darted to the far end of the room where a hearth was situated. "I better get a fire going so you don't catch a cold."

"Please," Rema tried again, "am I in the king's dungeon?"

"No," Nulea answered. "You are *not* in the dungeon. Like I said, you're safe." She knelt and pushed the logs around, finding some embers and nursing the fire back to life.

"How did I get here?" Rema asked.

"Mako brought you. He'll explain everything to you in a bit." Nulea stood.

Rema knew that name. Her hand flew to her neck, still burning and tender from the thick rope. The rope was gone, but the necklace with the ruby key was still there. The secret message locked inside told her to trust in Mako.

"Are you hungry, dear?" Nulea asked.

Rema was in so much pain that food was the last thing on her mind.

"I'm fine, thank you."

"I'm going to let Mako know you're awake." Nulea slipped out of the room, closing the door behind her.

Rema was once again alone. Where was she? If only she felt strong enough to stand. She wanted to look around, just to make sure this wasn't some sick joke, and she wasn't really in the dungeon.

The fire crackled. The light from the flames provided a better view of the room. The walls were a dark, gray stone. Two closed, wooden shutters hung side by side on one of the walls. They shook, the wind pounding against them. That was a good sign. If the shutters opened to the outside, then Rema wasn't underground.

She fingered the necklace. *Trust in Mako.*

***

The door banged open, startling Rema awake. Perhaps everything that had occurred during the past few hours had been a dream, and soldiers were coming to take her to the gallows—only this time the rope wouldn't snap.

Two figures rushed toward Rema. She rubbed her eyes, adjusting to the dim lighting.

"Rema!" Aunt Maya exclaimed. She fell to her knees next to the bed and clutched Rema's hand.

Uncle Kar stood right behind Maya, a smile plastered across his face.

"What are you two doing here?" Rema asked, reaching her free hand out to her uncle.

He came closer and grabbed it. "We're here to see you!" he said.

Aunt Maya let out a sob. "I never thought I would see you again." She kissed Rema's hand, and then held it against her wet cheek.

"I never thought I'd see you two either!" Rema cried. "Are you both all right?" They looked like she remembered them—gray hair, dark brown, weathered skin like a well-worn saddle. Neither had any visible cuts or bruises, but she did notice her uncle stood slightly hunched.

"We're fine," Kar responded, squeezing her hand. "How about you?" He pointed toward her forehead.

With the excitement of being reunited with her aunt and uncle, Rema had forgotten about her pounding head.

"I'm alive," she whispered, still afraid it was all a dream. One minute she had a noose tied around her neck, and now she was safe with her aunt and uncle. It seemed impossible.

Nulea entered, holding a metal cup with steam rising from it. "Kar, Maya, I thought we agreed to let her sleep."

Kar chuckled, the sound filling Rema's heart with warmth. "Well, you requested we let her sleep. But when word came that she had regained consciousness, we had to see her for ourselves." He looked down to Rema, his eyes sparkling. She couldn't remember the last time she'd seen him so happy.

"I have a cup of steeped listerblossom infused with willow bark for Rema to drink," Nulea said. "This will help ease the pain." Kar and Maya each took one of her arms and helped prop her against the wall. Rema winced from the painful throbbing in her head. The healer handed her the cup. "I'll let you have some time alone."

"Is Mako coming?" Kar asked.

"No," Nulea responded. "Once I informed him she was awake, he left. I expect he'll return later tonight once he's sure no one followed him." Nulea closed the door on her way out.

"Who's Mako? Where are we? And how did I survive my execution?"

Kar and Maya exchanged a brief look.

"You should rest," Maya said.

Rema grabbed her aunt's hand. "Please don't leave me in the dark like this. So much has happened. I want to—"

"I promise we will tell you everything," Kar said. "But now is not the time."

Rema wondered why no one would answer her questions. She tried to catch Uncle Kar's eyes, but he wouldn't look at her. Rema sighed and drank the bitter tea, thankful that she was alive.

FOUR

Darmik

Crouching behind the moss-covered boulder, Darmik peered toward the steep hill once again. All was still. He slid to the ground and crawled forward on his hands and knees until he was closer to the area in question. Rocks and vegetation covered the hills, making it difficult to find any openings or large crevices. Noticing an area between two narrow boulders covered by a thick, broken branch from one of the nearby trees, Darmik had a gut feeling the branch hid an entrance to a cave.

The rain lessened to a light mist, and the sky was turning dark. Darmik had been tracking the rebel and Rema since he let them go and watched them ride away. Even though it had only been a few hours, it felt like days, his decision weighing heavily upon his conscience. When Darmik initially discovered that Rema was the long-lost princess, it infuriated him. He had assumed she knew her identity and was deceiving him the entire time in order to regain the throne. However, after seeing her confusion at her sentencing, Darmik wasn't so sure she knew who she really was. It seemed reasonable to assume a rescue attempt would be made. But Darmik hadn't expected that the timing would be so close—Rema had almost died. Then, when he'd caught up to the rebel, Rema again acted as if she had no knowledge of her heritage.

Darmik shook his head, forcing himself back to the task at hand. He needed to investigate the area now, before it was dark. Focusing on the forest floor, he noticed the scattering of leaves. He brushed a three-foot section clear, and discovered hoof prints and footprints captured in the damp earth. Because of Darmik's training at Emperion's elite military school, he could tell this rebel learned to hide his tracks from an expert. For the past couple of hours, he followed one false lead after another, trying to track where the rebel took Rema.

Pulling out his dagger, Darmik stood and approached the large, broken branch. Moving it would be difficult because of its weight, and it would make a lot of noise. Instead, he chose to duck underneath it. He moved aside the leaves and found a black hole approximately four feet in diameter. He broke off a small, damp branch, wrapped some dry ferns around the top, and lit it on fire. Using the makeshift torch, Darmik crouched low and entered the cave.

Inside, Darmik squatted down and studied the area. The markings on the middle of the dirt floor looked like a blanket had once been laid there. There were several drops of blood on the ground. Something shiny caught his eyes. He picked it up and held it to the light from his torch. It was a needle, the thin thread still attached and the tip coated with blood. The image of Rema screaming for him to help her assaulted his mind.

The rebel must have brought Rema to this cave so the healer could tend to her wounds. Glancing around, there was a stack of wood in one corner and bread and vegetables in another. This had to be one of several rebel camps. Knowing that Darmik was tracking them, the cave was probably abandoned once Rema became stable.

Darmik still couldn't believe he'd let her go, with his horse no less. But what other option did he have? If he stayed and fought the rebel, Rema would have died and then he'd have no way to find the rebels. However, wouldn't her death have ended the rebels' cause? Darmik wasn't sure. And it didn't matter. He had to find her—and find her he would.

All of his training had ingrained in him the necessity of following the order of command. But the right course was no longer clear. War raged inside of Darmik. Trell had made him promise there would be no unnecessary killing. Darmik's duty was to protect the kingdom, and he was also obligated to his father. But these elements in the puzzle did not seem to fit together.

Darmik came to realize that even if he had stayed and fought the rebel, he wouldn't have taken Rema back to the king and Lennek to be executed. Seeing her hanged forced him to face his feelings—he still loved her. So he did the right thing by allowing the rebel to take Rema. Now all he had to do was follow them, although tracking them was proving to be more difficult than he imagined. And once he found them, what was he going to do?

Exiting the cave, Darmik finished sweeping aside

the leaves covering the forest floor. He discovered several sets of boot prints. One set in particular sunk in deeper than the others did. This rebel was mostly likely carrying Rema. Moving in that direction, he looked for anything indicating horses had been in the area. There was nothing. Darmik decided to follow the direction of this particular pair of boot prints. After a few minutes, the prints led to rocky terrain—impossible to track any further. If the rebel continued in this direction, then he traveled down the hill, away from the Middle Mountains, which made sense. No one lived on the Middle Mountains. The mountain range loomed higher than any other part of Greenwood Island, going so high as to ascend into the clouds. The weather so severe that no one could survive.

Darmik came to a narrow stream that carried snowmelt from the frigid peaks above him. He took a drink and splashed the icy water on his sweaty face. Night closed in; he needed to find a place to stay and something to eat. He decided to go back to the cave, remembering the food. Besides, it seemed unlikely the rebels would return.

Once inside the shelter, Darmik started a small fire and ate some bread. Afterwards, he lay down on the dirt and tried to sleep. Tomorrow he would continue in the direction of the footprints. But what if that was what the rebel counted on? After all, the man clearly demonstrated that he had exceptional training, maybe even on par with Darmik's. Perhaps the rebel expected Darmik to follow him, and he intentionally led him away from his true destination? That's exactly what Darmik would do if he were in the rebel's shoes.

If the tracks led away from the Middle Mountains, then did the rebel travel up into the mountain range? Darmik was in no position to go into such treacherous territory. He needed reinforcements, proper clothing, and a traveling partner. A plan formed. Tomorrow, he would return to the castle and seek out Neco—his closest friend and most proficient soldier. Together, they would climb the Middle Mountains and find the rebels.

FIVE

Rema

Rema awoke after a long, uninterrupted sleep. Pleasant smells filled the air, and warmth replaced the feeling of fear—her constant companion for weeks. The dim lighting suggested morning had arrived. The howling wind beat against the closed, wooden shutters. Rema glanced at a noise from the end of the room. A girl was bent over the hearth, trying to nurse the fire back to life.

Stretching her legs, Rema let out a yawn, happy to be on a straw bed instead of the fecal-infested one in the dungeon where she had awaited her execution. Her life had dramatically changed.

"Good morning," Rema said to the girl.

The girl stood and smoothed down her simple wool dress, coming closer to the bed. "Morning. I'm glad you're awake, miss. You've been asleep an awfully long time. How do you feel?" She pushed her long, chestnut hair away from her brown eyes while studying Rema thoughtfully.

"Where exactly are we?"

"You're at the infirmary. My mother, Nulea, has been tending to you."

"And what is your name?" Rema asked, noting that the girl shared her mother's pale skin. She looked to be about sixteen.

"Vesha," she answered. "I assist my mother with patients when she needs the help." She raised her arm, pointing to the hallway outside where, presumably, more rooms were located.

The sleeves from her dress inched down slightly, allowing Rema to see Vesha's wrists. Like her mother, she did not bear an identification band or tattoo. Uneasiness settled over Rema. She had to be on Greenwood Island— no one ever left. The nearest kingdom was Emperion, located on the mainland, and the journey took weeks.

"What region are we in?" Rema asked. King's City sat on the borders of Dresden, Telan, and Shano. But, feasibly, they could be in any of the seven regions within the kingdom.

"I better go tell Mother you're awake." Vesha quietly left the room.

If Rema was indeed somewhere safe, like everyone insisted, then why couldn't their location be divulged? What was going on?

If only she could make it to the shutters and peek outside. Then she could see if she was in King's City or in some small, remote village. Moving as slowly as possible, Rema rolled onto her side and pushed her body up. Her head swam, and it felt as if the room was spinning. She sat still, waiting for her body to acclimate.

The door swung open, and Nulea entered, carrying

a tray of food. When she saw Rema sitting up, her eyes widened and she rushed to put the tray down on the table next to the bed.

"You need to lie still," she scolded. "Your body isn't ready to move around yet." Nulea lowered Rema back to the pillow. Crossing her arms, she stared at Rema. "I can tell you're a stubborn one. I'll be back."

She returned a moment later with Vesha, who was now wearing a thick, black tunic with trousers and some sort of brown leather gear over her clothing.

"My daughter will stay with you until you are better."

Vesha sighed. "Mother, I have training."

"Training for what?" Rema asked.

Nulea glanced sideways at her daughter, the corners of her mouth tightening. She shook her head ever so slightly before turning her attention back to Rema. "I need to check your bandage." Nulea sat next to her. "Hold still while I remove the dressing and apply some medicine to the wound. Vesha dear, don't just stand there. Go change. You'll be here with Rema for a couple of days."

Vesha's face reddened, and she stomped out of the room.

"I don't want to be a burden," Rema said. "She doesn't need to sit with me."

"Shh, I told you not to move. That includes your mouth." Nulea smiled while unwrapping the bandage on Rema's head.

"Sorry," Rema replied.

Nulea gave her a stern look, and Rema snapped

her mouth shut. Once Nulea was done tending to her wound, and before she left, she reiterated the importance of resting and staying in bed.

When the door opened again, Rema expected to see Vesha. However, a man in his forties stood at the entrance to the room. His tall frame and muscular body took up the entire doorway. Brown hair and a beard covered his face.

The man looked vaguely familiar to Rema, and she tried to recall where she'd seen him before. "Didn't you buy horses from my uncle on occasion?" she asked.

"Yes," the man replied. His brown eyes penetrated into hers. "My name is Mako."

Rema shuddered. This was Mako—the one mentioned in her necklace.

"May I come in?" he asked.

Rema nodded.

Mako carefully crossed the room and sat on the small, wooden chair next to her bed. His eyes looked tired, like he hadn't slept in days. He wore simple brown pants and a heavy wool tunic. When he folded his hands on his lap, Rema noticed his knuckles were bruised and his left wrist bore a bloody cut where an identification band should've been. Mako's eyes sought hers, and he smiled.

"What do you remember of your rescue?" he asked in a soft, gentle voice.

"Not much," Rema said. "I remember standing on the gallows, waiting to be executed. Then I woke up here. Everything in between is unknown to me."

Mako stared at her with an unreadable expression.

"Are you going to tell me how I got here?" Rema asked. "It seems some great mystery that no one is willing to reveal." She was getting anxious, and wanted answers to calm her nerves.

He grinned. "It's no great mystery, but it is a secret. And I'd like to keep it that way." Rema opened her mouth to argue with him, but Mako held up his hand and continued, "We are in a fortress that was built a century ago. No one knows of its existence. After the takeover, a group of survivors came here. We've managed to start a new life, separate from the monarchy."

Several questions swam through Rema's mind. "I don't understand. If it was a secret location, then how did people find it? How did you know about it?"

Mako flexed his fingers, looking uncomfortable. "When you are feeling better, I will give you a tour of the compound and explain everything. For now, I just want you to focus on getting well."

Rema was anxious to see what waited outside the walls of her tiny room, but for now, she'd settle for having some of her curiosity answered.

Rema asked, "Can you at least please tell me how I got here?"

"Yes." Mako smiled down at her. He seemed a bit shy. Rema liked that he was soft spoken. There was something comforting and peaceful about this man.

"I shot an arrow through the rope around your neck, and you fell. One of my men grabbed you and escaped from the grounds through a secret tunnel. I met the two of you just outside the exit with a horse. My man handed you over to me, and then I brought you here."

Rema lay there, stunned. "But why?" she stammered. "Why would you help me? I'm no one of importance, and you've committed an act of treason!"

"We'll have plenty of time to discourse on the matter later, in more depth. Before I go," Mako said, looking away from her, "I have a question for you. You lived in the castle with the king and princes for several weeks?" He turned back toward Rema.

"Yes," she answered, surprised by the change in topics. She was still wondering why he rescued her in the first place. Did he owe a debt to Kar and Maya? Was this his way of repaying them? Her head started pounding, and she winced.

Mako handed Rema a silver cup containing some sort of pungent-smelling liquid. She drank it, the contents soothing her at once.

Vesha entered the room. "Oh, sorry to interrupt. I didn't know you were in here. My mother ordered me to sit with her."

"It's okay," Mako said. "Can you do something for me?" Vesha nodded. "Find Savenek and let him know we've returned. Tell him I need to speak with him in my office, immediately."

Vesha nodded and left.

When the door closed, Mako turned his attention back to Rema. "When you stayed at the castle, did you spend a lot time with either of the princes?"

Why in the world did Mako care if she spent any time with Darmik or Lennek? "No more than was absolutely necessary."

Mako stood and moved to the hearth, his back to

her. "On the way here, I had an altercation with Prince Darmik." He glanced over his shoulder.

Rema jerked and Mako nodded, as if he had expected her reaction.

"Is Darmik all right?" Even though she knew he didn't love her, she still didn't want him hurt, or worse, dead. Her hands clutched into fists, waiting for Mako's answer.

"We briefly fought," he responded, "but you were bleeding profusely. Darmik noticed and backed off, so I could get you to a healer."

"What do you mean...*he backed off?*"

Mako turned to face Rema, his hands clasped behind his back. "He stopped fighting and lowered his weapon."

That surprised Rema. She was stuck in that hellhole of a dungeon for over a week, and Darmik showed no signs that he cared what happened to her. Even at her sentencing, he barely looked her way.

Her eyes filled with tears. "I have no idea why he would let me go." Perhaps Darmik only wanted her healed so he could capture her, returning her to the castle in order to watch her execution.

"I'm guessing he wanted to track us, thinking that I'd lead him to our base camp." Mako smiled. He seemed to do that a lot. "At first, I was afraid that you two had formed a friendship."

Rema's face heated up. She tried hard not to reveal any facial expressions. She didn't want Mako to know she once had feelings for Darmik. Mako stood staring at her, waiting patiently for an answer.

Clearing her throat, Rema said, "No." She couldn't prevent her voice from quivering. "My head hurts. I need to rest," she lied. She wanted to be alone to sort through her feelings for Darmik.

After Mako left, Rema couldn't prevent the tears from coming. The door creaked open, and she squeezed her eyes closed.

"Are you all right?" Vesha asked. "Do you need me to get my mother?"

"No. I'm fine," Rema said. "I'm not crying because of my head." She wanted to tell the girl that she was crying because her heart was broken. She thought Darmik loved her, but he was only using her, and she had fallen for it. However, Rema couldn't confide that in someone she just met.

"Sometimes I cry because I'm not allowed to leave the fortress," Vesha whispered.

"What?" Rema exclaimed, looking into Vesha's brown eyes. "You can't leave?" The girl shook her head. Fear coursed through Rema's body. Why couldn't she leave? What sort of place was this? "You mean, you've never been anywhere?"

"No, never."

Rema laughed. Vesha's eyebrows bent inward. She opened her mouth to say something, but Rema cut her off. "I'm only laughing because we're like two peas in a pod. I wasn't allowed to leave my home either. Until Prince Lennek came for me. Then he locked me up in his castle and didn't allow me to go anywhere." Her hands squeezed the blanket. Vesha's eyes widened with shock.

Rema patted the bed, inviting Vesha to sit next to her.

"It's difficult having no control over your life, isn't it?" Rema asked.

"You have no idea." Vesha sat down, the mattress sinking under her weight.

"You'd be surprised. Would you like to hear my story?" Rema asked.

"I've been dying to know more about you. I've never seen anyone with blonde hair and blue eyes before." Vesha ducked her head. "But I was told not to ask you any personal questions."

Rema felt like she could trust Vesha—almost as if they'd known each other all their lives. She went on to reveal all the events that happened over the course of the past season. About how she was supposed to marry Bren, her best friend, but Lennek killed him. How Lennek forced her to accept his marriage proposal. How she was taken to the castle and locked in a room there. Then she told Vesha about being thrown in the dungeon and the almost execution. Rema was very careful to leave out all parts relating to Prince Darmik.

"Wow. That is so exciting."

"No," Rema said, "it was terrifying."

"But at least you got to experience something. All I do is help my mother and train. That's it. My mom thinks that because I'm a girl, I can't go on missions or run errands. But she's wrong. I can do those things."

"What are you training for?" Rema asked, curious about the brown, leather things she saw her wearing earlier.

"I'm not supposed to say. When you're better, Mako is going to show you around the fortress and explain everything."

"It sounds like I'm back to my old life of not being allowed to do anything or see anyone." Rema signed. "But at least we're safe, right?"

Six

Darmik

ing's City loomed ahead. Darmik steered Nightsky toward the secret tunnel, hoping to make it inside the military compound before the king discovered his presence. Darmik was thankful that he had found Nightsky; otherwise, he would never have made it to the city so quickly. After he had left the cave, he headed away from the Middle Mountains, in the direction of the footprints, just like he thought the rebels wanted him to. When he reached a small village, Darmik found Nightsky tied to a post on the edge of the town. Now he knew, without a doubt, that the rebels went in the opposite direction, somewhere up in the Middle Mountains—which was insane, but it made sense as to how they managed to stay hidden from the King's Army.

Entering the tunnel, Darmik saw evidence of his earlier scuffle with the rebels. The dirt floor was roughed up, but at least the dead bodies had been removed. He wondered how the rebels discovered the tunnel in the first place. He'd have to look into that matter later.

After stabling his horse, he went straight to

his office, where he found several messengers eagerly awaiting his return.

Before anyone could speak, Darmik held up his hand, stopping them. "Where is my elite squad?"

"Commander," a soldier stepped forward, "they're out looking for you."

"Raise the flag," Darmik ordered. Neco wouldn't return with the squad unless he knew Darmik was in the compound. If the royal-blue flag with the silver crown was flying outside, then Darmik was on the premises. "When they return, see that Neco comes straight here. Dismissed."

"Commander, do you want our reports first?" another soldier asked.

"No," Darmik responded. "I'll hear them later. Everyone out. Oh, and you," Darmik pointed to his personal runner, "see that Captain Phellek comes to my office as soon as possible."

Once everyone left, Darmik rummaged through his desk, locating various maps. He pulled out several that showed the area surrounding the Middle Mountains. One marked the lower perimeter of the mountains; however, none revealed the actual terrain farther up.

There was a knock on the door, and Captain Phellek entered.

"Have you been in charge since I left yesterday?" Darmik asked.

"Yes, sir. The king ordered all rebels to be killed on sight. Prince Lennek has demanded that Rema is to be brought before him, and she's to be alive."

Darmik figured as much. "I have a special

assignment for you."

"Of course, Your Highness."

Darmik sat down and indicated that Phellek should do the same on the chair opposite his.

"*No one* is to know," Darmik said, hoping Phellek would understand he meant King Barjon and Prince Lennek.

"You have my word," he promised.

Darmik considered Phellek as a father figure. When he was just a boy, Phellek took him under his wing and trained him. The man even gave him his prized sword. There was an unspoken respect between the two of them, and Darmik felt confident Phellek's loyalty was to him, not the king.

"My flag has been raised. I expect my elite squad to return at any moment. As soon as they do, I'm going to set out with the First Company for the village towns in Telan near Greenwood Forest, under the assumption the rebels are located somewhere around there."

Phellek nodded. "How can I be of service?"

"Neco and I are actually heading out on a secret mission. No one can know we're gone. I'm pretty sure I've located the rebel base camp, and plan to do some reconnaissance. In order for this to happen, people need to believe I'm leading the First Company to the village towns, and that we are actively searching the surrounding areas. Do you understand?"

"Yes," Phellek said.

"I am going to choose a man of similar height, build, and age to replace me and lead the First Company to Greenwood Forest. I need you to lead my elite squad on a separate secret mission to find a man by the name of Trell. He lives in Werden. Bring him back here without anyone knowing. Keep his presence a secret. Can you do this for me?"

"Of course."

A young messenger boy entered the office. "Commander, your elite squad has been spotted outside the city."

Darmik nodded, dismissing the boy. "Go ready yourself. You ride out today."

Phellek nodded. "May I ask something of you in return, Darmik?"

Darmik noticed the lack of his title. Phellek only used his name informally when they were alone, and rank was not an issue. "What is it?"

"On your quest with Neco, watch yourself. You may be able to move without notice and much faster than with your squad, but the rebels won't hesitate to kill you. And you won't be able to stop them if you're outnumbered. Your title of Commander and Prince means nothing to them." Phellek reached out, resting his hand on Darmik's shoulder. "This is war. Even you are not invincible."

Darmik stood. "Thank you for your concern. I will be extra cautious."

"The kingdom can't survive without you. The king would destroy it. You are our only hope."

Darmik stuck out his arm to shake Phellek's hand. Phellek hesitated, knowing that a prince never shook hands like commoners did, but Darmik wanted Phellek to know how much he respected him and valued his opinion.

"You have been the father that mine could not be. Thank you."

Phellek took Darmik's hand. "And you've been the son I wish I'd had." Phellek turned and left. As soon as he was out of sight, Darmik rolled up the maps and stashed them in a bag. He needed to go to the weapons' room and the supply center.

"Prince Darmik," Arnek said, strolling into the office. "So you are, indeed, here. Prince Lennek saw that the flag was raised. The king wants to see you in the Throne Room. Now."

Darmik loathed Lennek's personal steward. "The next time you enter my office without knocking first, like all servants are required to do, I'll kill you. Understand?"

Arnek flinched, but recovered quickly. "I'll escort you there, Your Highness."

"I have a few things to do first. Tell my father that I will be there momentarily. You're dismissed."

He knew he couldn't keep his father waiting long, but Darmik had to pack before his squad arrived.

❧

Darmik entered the Throne Room still wearing his clothes from yesterday. At the end of the royal-blue runner was the marble dais, King Barjon sitting in the Throne Chair. Two royal guards stood on either side of the king, blending into the velvet fabric hanging from the ceiling behind the king's chair. Other than that, the room was empty. The king must have already concluded his business for the day. Walking past the marble columns toward his father, Darmik kept his eyes and ears open for Lennek. His brother would not be happy with him for Rema's escape.

At the bottom of the dais, Darmik lowered to one knee and bowed his head. "Your Majesty."

The king did not respond. Instead, he sat there with his dark brown eyes boring into Darmik's.

A side door flew open, and Lennek stormed into the room, his royal-blue cape floating behind him. He stopped next to Darmik, who was still kneeling, and kicked him in the stomach. Darmik fell over, surprised by his brother's physical aggression.

Peering up into Lennek's enraged face, he said, "Easy brother. Let's not forget I'm on your side, and you need the army. You can't afford to attack me."

"Silence," the king ordered, "both of you."

Darmik rose to his feet.

Lennek stood next to him, his arms trembling with rage.

"Darmik," the king said. "Can you please explain to me how Rema escaped from her execution? Not only was a noose tied around her neck, but you were in the courtyard along with at least a unit of armed soldiers. How did she get away?" The king leaned forward in his chair, his hands clutched onto the arms of it. His eyes narrowed at Darmik, as his nose twisted in disgust.

"It's all your fault!" Lennek screamed. "You let the whore get away!"

Ignoring his brother, Darmik took a step toward the king. "Your Majesty, she was rescued by a small band of rebels. I have tracked them to the village towns located in the northern end of Greenwood Forest. I am preparing the First Company as we speak."

"And do you intend to apprehend her and the rebels?" the king asked, like he was speaking to a small child.

Darmik needed to tell a believable lie. "No, Father. I intend to kill the rebels on sight, and bring Rema back here for her proper execution, as Prince Lennek so desires."

The king leaned back in his chair. "Are you capable of handling this matter?"

Darmik bit his tongue to stop a nasty reply. Even though he was used to this behavior from his father and brother, it still hurt.

Lennek sneered. "Darmik's not capable of handling anything. He's already proven that. I say we release him from his position as Commander."

"Enough," King Barjon ordered. Darmik knew his father was aware that the soldiers were loyal to and trusted Darmik. Any shakeup in the ranks would have to happen at a more peaceful time. His father couldn't afford to lose his most powerful weapon right now.

"Darmik, you will lead the First Company to Greenwood Forest. Find Rema and bring her here. Kill the rebels and end this ridiculous spectacle," King Barjon ordered. Lennek started to object, but the king raised his hand. "Once Rema is brought here, Lennek, you may decide her fate."

"Can it be a private execution?" Lennek asked with a malicious gleam in his eyes.

"I don't care what you do with the churl, so long as you finish her. As for you, Darmik, fail in this matter, and you will be relieved of your position. Are we clear?"

"Yes, Your Majesty." Darmik's father never threatened his position before.

The king nodded, dismissing him. Darmik hurried back to the military compound, hoping his elite squad was packed and ready to go. Time was crucial.

Upon entering his office, Darmik saw someone sitting in a chair, his back to him. The man's hair was cut short, his long, lanky legs crossed in a careless manner. Darmik closed the door.

"So, you're finally back from, well, I don't know where exactly, but I assume you know where Rema is?" Neco stood.

"I have a good idea," Darmik responded.

"Are we going after her?"

Darmik stared at his friend. There was something in Neco's eyes that told Darmik he wasn't fooled by him—he knew Darmik cared for Rema.

"All you need to know is that this is top secret. Pack for winter weather and climbing. We leave through the tunnels in thirty minutes."

Neco smiled. "This sounds…interesting."

Half an hour later, one of Darmik's men from his squad, disguised as Darmik with his cape, hat, and sword, led the First Company through the streets of King's City. In the midst of the chaos, Captain Phellek led Darmik's elite squad toward Werden, and Darmik and Neco slipped through the tunnel, exiting the city walls.

SEVEN

Rema

Dreaming no longer held the escape it once did. Instead of beauty and adventure, the darkness was now filled with evil, violence, and betrayal. Fear consumed Rema every time she closed her eyes. What if, when she woke up, she was standing on the gallows? She could still feel the rope around her neck.

Lying in bed, Rema's fingers skimmed her tender neck, thankful the noose no longer entangled her. The pounding in her head was now only a dull pain and easily manageable. Based on her calculations, she had been there for about a week. And she still had no idea where *there* was. Rema yawned and sat up. Her room was empty. Glancing around, she noticed the door slightly ajar.

Suddenly, the shutters rattled from the howling wind. She never heard such loud, violent wind before. When she exhaled, the air turned white. It wasn't the winter season yet, but it felt cold enough to snow.

"Where have you been?" a young-sounding male voice asked.

Startled, Rema looked toward the door. Being

opened only a couple of inches, she was unable to see anything in the morning light of the gray hallway, but she could hear the male's voice clearly as he stood on the other side of the door.

"Helping my mother," a second voice responded. It was Vesha. There was a soft shuffling noise, like fabric rustling.

"You shouldn't miss training. It needs to be your priority. Especially now."

"Lower your voice," Vesha whispered. "Trust me, I know the importance of my training. But I'm tending to a patient. It'll only be for a week or so."

The male voice chuckled. "I don't think I've ever seen you in a dress before. You almost look like a girl."

"Shut up, Savenek. My mother insists I wear this while tending the sick. Now get out of here. I have work to do."

He laughed. "I'll see you tomorrow at sunrise. We can get in a quick workout before you come here. No excuses." A set of footsteps faded away.

Rema threw back a half-dozen wool blankets, including a heavy fur one. When her feet hit the stone floor, she gasped from pain even though she was wearing socks. The floor was as cold as ice. Rema tiptoed toward the door, wanting to catch a glimpse of what was outside the room.

She was about halfway there when the door flew open. "You're awake," Vesha said, stepping inside. Her cheeks had a red hue to them. "What are you doing? You can't get up yet." Vesha set down the tray of food she was carrying and helped Rema back onto the bed, covering her with the blankets.

Rema propped herself up, her stomach growling.

"I feel fine," Rema said. "You have to let me out of bed at some point."

Vesha stared at her as if she'd sprouted an extra head. "Well, until my mother says it's okay for you to walk around, you'll stay there."

Rema sighed. Her legs were going to stop working if she didn't get some exercise. This was insane.

Vesha placed the tray next to Rema, went to the hearth, and added a couple of logs to the fading fire.

"So," Rema said, taking a bite of her porridge. "Who's Savenek?"

A log slid through Vesha's fingers, falling onto the stone hearth with a bang. She picked it up and threw it into the fireplace. "Um," Vesha stammered, while standing and pulling her sweater tightly around her body. "Why do you ask?"

"Just curious." Now that Rema was feeling better, she was noticing small things that seemed out of place. Like the fact that Vesha was wearing a heavy, thick wool dress covered by a sweater, a knitted hat, and gloves when the winter season hadn't hit yet. And the food. Rema was fed nearly the same thing daily: bread, porridge, cheese, and meat. In other words, simple, bland foods.

Not looking Rema in the eyes, Vesha said, "I need to check on a couple of other patients. I'll be back in a bit."

Rema was tired of not knowing anything. Perhaps if she asked non-threatening questions, Vesha would open up and reveal something of importance. "How many sick people are here?"

Vesha hesitated. "Well, there's only one sick person. Most of the people in the ward are injured."

"Are you training to be a healer? To take over for your mother?"

"No. But my mother needs the help. I'm only one of two that can do stitches and set broken bones. Until someone else takes an interest and learns, the duty falls to me." Vesha finally smiled. "Why? Do you want to be a healer?" Hope filled her face.

Rema had absolutely no interest in tending to those injured or sick. The thought of blood reminded her of Bren, and she shuddered, trying to block out the memories of his death.

She focused on Vesha. "How are people getting injured?" Rema asked. "Are we near the mines? What town are we in?" Perhaps the brown leather gear she saw Vesha wearing earlier was for mining.

Vesha laughed. "You must be feeling better. I don't have the time to answer all of your questions, but don't worry, Mako will explain everything when he returns."

⊗⊘⊚

The days quickly fell into a boring, predictable routine. Vesha arrived each morning with Rema's breakfast, followed by a visit from Aunt Maya and Uncle Kar. Once Rema was cleared to get out of bed, Nulea allowed her to stand and walk around her room, but only when she was accompanied by someone else. After a simple lunch, Vesha always returned to spend the afternoon with her.

Every time Rema was alone, she tried to get out of bed and walk around on her own. When her head was well enough not to cause her additional pain, she was finally strong enough to do it.

At the end of the second week, Vesha watched while Rema got out of bed and sat in the wooden chair without assistance.

"Well, I suppose Mother will say you're well enough to leave the sick ward. I think your room is ready."

"Will I be staying with my aunt and uncle?" Rema asked.

Vesha sat on the edge of Rema's bed. "No, I believe Maya and Kar are leaving soon."

They hadn't said anything to Rema about leaving. Why would they want to go anywhere? And why were they leaving without her?

"I think they need to do something with their horses," Vesha said, as if sensing Rema's concern.

Maybe they were getting Snow! Rema wanted nothing more than to see her horse. "I can't wait until I'm well enough to ride. I haven't been free to ride alone since that day Prince Lennek took me."

Vesha wrinkled her face in disgust. "Do you know why Lennek wanted to marry you?"

Rema laughed. "No, I don't. But I'm thankful I didn't have to marry him. He was even worse than the rumors portray him to be."

"What about that boy you mentioned, Bren? Did you love him?" Vesha fidgeted with the corner of the blanket.

Rema didn't like talking about Bren. His death was still fresh in her mind. Glancing up at the wood-beamed ceiling, Rema tried to focus on a happy memory of the two of them and not his gruesome death—Bren riding his horse, trying to beat her as they raced through the forest, laughing.

"Yes, I loved him. But only as a friend. At first, I was afraid to get married, to tie myself to another person. Now, I can see we would have been happy. And who knows, perhaps our friendship would have grown into that kind of love." Rema remembered walking with him outside the horse pasture, when he told her why he wanted to marry her. Whispering, she said, "I think he already loved me."

"How could you tell?" Vesha asked, leaning toward her.

"I don't know," Rema said. "It was the way he looked at me. I could feel it."

"Oh." Vesha stared down at the blanket clutched between her hands, her cheeks red.

"Is there someone you fancy?" Rema asked, suspecting that there was.

Vesha's eyes darted first up to Rema's, and then quickly away.

"You can tell me," Rema said. "I promise I won't tell anyone." She moved to the bed, next to Vesha. She took Vesha's hands and held them tight. "Sometimes it helps having someone to confide it. I have no one here. I'm hoping we can be friends. Even after I'm out of the sick ward."

Vesha squeezed Rema's fingers. "I'd like that. But

you can't tell anyone." Rema nodded. "There is someone, but Mother would never approve."

"Why?"

"Mother insists I marry someone sensible. Like the blacksmith's son. But he's as dull as a doorknob." Vesha shook her head.

Rema laughed. "So who do you fancy?"

Vesha let out a large breath. "I'd rather not say. I'm not sure he feels the same way for me. We're friends, but I think that's all."

"When I get out of here, you will have to point him out to me. I'll watch how he looks at and behaves around you. Perhaps he is interested, but he's shy." Rema wondered if it was the boy she heard Vesha talking to in the hallway. What was his name? Savenek?

Smiling, Vesha said, "I don't know about shy. But he's never fancied anyone before. He's so focused on training that he doesn't have time for anything else."

"What profession is he training for?"

Vesha abruptly stood. "I need to check on another patient." She hurried away.

As the door closed, Rema's thoughts drifted to Darmik.

Prince Darmik, Commander of the King's Army. Handsome, confusing, and infuriating. At one time, she thought he loved her. Then when Lennek saw them kissing, and Darmik acted like he didn't even know her, Rema knew she was a part of some sick joke concocted by the brothers. Otherwise, Darmik would have said something or helped her in some way—not looked at her with hatred and disgust.

"It almost worked," he had told her. She wasn't sure what he was referring to. He never contacted her once while she was imprisoned in the dungeon. When she saw him at her sentencing, he still looked at her with hatred in his eyes. And he had backed Lennek up, agreeing that she had acted treasonously, which led to her being found guilty and sentenced to death.

Technically, she did kiss Darmik while engaged to the Crown Prince. Or, Darmik kissed her. In theory, the act could be considered treasonous. However, at the time, she was being forced to marry Prince Lennek. And Lennek was sleeping with half of the women at court—both courtiers and servants alike. So, in Rema's eyes, she wasn't guilty.

The kiss was beautiful and stirred feelings inside of Rema that she never felt before. Darmik must not have felt anything; otherwise, he wouldn't have allowed her to be executed. Instead, he sat atop Nightsky, watching Rema on the gallows with the noose tied around her neck. If he loved her, he would have fought for her.

But then she was rescued, and Darmik let Mako flee with her. What did that mean? Was it simply so he could track the rebels? Frustrated, Rema stood and stretched. It didn't matter, she told herself. That chapter of her life was over. It's not like she had a future with Darmik anyway.

She would take the memories of their time together and hold onto them. Now she needed to forget the hurt and anger and move on.

The howling wind slammed against the wooden shutters. Listening for voices in the hallway, Rema didn't hear any. She rushed over to the shutters, placing her hands against them. They were freezing cold and violently rattling. She unclasped the lock and they flew open, almost smashing her nose. The wind whipped across Rema's face, making her gasp and her eyes tear.

The fortress had to be old, since the room didn't have a glass window, especially in this weather. Rema moved against the wall, and then carefully glanced outside. It was like the building was suspended in air—there were clouds below her. Where in the kingdom was she? Holding onto the ledge, Rema looked straight down against the building. Directly below, she saw the tops of trees shrouded in clouds. Rema grabbed onto a shutter and threw her body against it, pushing it back in place. After slamming the other one closed, she quickly locked them together, her hands numb with cold.

It was time for answers. She wasn't going to sit in the room any longer waiting for Mako to return. Her body had recovered enough to move about, and everyone insisted she was safe there—that she was no longer a prisoner. She should be allowed to move about freely.

Rema went to the door and placed her hand on the brass knob. Taking a deep breath, she pushed it open and stepped out into a dark hallway.

EiGHt

Darmik

Darmik and Neco lay on their stomachs, camouflaged with leaves, observing the small village town below them.

"Nothing out of the ordinary," Neco commented.

"Yes," Darmik agreed. "When the First Company arrives later today, I suspect they will be stationed just north, over there, in that open area."

"Do you want to use this town as our marker?" Neco asked.

"Yes," Darmik said. "We'll start climbing the Middle Mountains here." This was the village where he'd found his horse. Darmik was sure they were in the vicinity of where the rebels entered the mountain range.

No trails were visible. The forest was dense, but the ground was clear, and traveling over the terrain would be fairly easy. Darmik slid away from the edge overlooking the village. When he was certain he was out of eyesight, he stood.

"How do we know where to go?" Neco asked, scanning the massive mountain range looming before them. Everyone knew the stories about the infamous, rugged terrain. No one lived there. The steep mountains were so large that they disappeared into the clouds.

"We don't," Darmik said. "That is why it's just the two of us. We need to move quickly if we want to pick up the rebel's trail."

Darmik doubted there was one—the man had proved to be more than competent. But he was sure he could figure it out. He just needed to think about what he would do in the rebel's position.

They gathered their sacks, slung them over their shoulders, and began their journey into the mountain range where no one came out alive.

☙❧

At first, the terrain was easy. As night neared, the land steepened and the ground turned rocky. They were still surrounded by thick, tall trees. Confident they were well hidden, the two set up camp for the night.

The next day, after a quick breakfast, they continued. The trees began to thin, and the ground turned to solid rock. They walked at a brisk pace the entire day, having little conversation.

The friends journeyed for several days, steadily climbing north. Now Darmik knew why the rebels left his horse at the village. It would have been near impossible for one to travel over this terrain on horseback. But how did the rebel carry Rema? Darmik knew he was missing some vital piece of information. Something was wrong.

"Having doubts?" Neco asked, as they were forced

to use their hands to aid in climbing. All trees vanished, and it looked like they were in a wasteland. No wonder people claimed no one lived up here. It seemed there was nothing to sustain life.

"Maybe we should travel a different direction, instead of going any higher," Neco said.

Darmik grabbed onto another rock, pulling his body upward. His hands ached. Luckily, he wore leather gloves, but his fingers were still blistered and sore from climbing.

"Let's find a place to stop and rest," Darmik said. He swung his left hand up, grabbing ahold of a sturdy rock, hoisting his body higher. There was no way the rebel traveled this way, especially with Rema. Maybe Neco was right; they should focus on another direction instead of going any higher. "Neco?" Darmik called after hearing the tumble of many stones.

Neco didn't respond.

Darmik twisted in order to see his friend below him. Neco hung by his right hand, his body dangling against the rocky mountain.

"Don't move," Darmik said as he climbed down next to Neco.

"No intention of going anywhere," Neco said between clenched teeth. "Just be careful. When I went to grab on, the rock shifted." His face was red from straining to keep his grip.

Darmik maneuvered his body just below Neco's and slightly to the side of him. The rocks in this particular area felt loose all of a sudden.

"Any chance you can hurry?" Neco grunted. "My

hand is about to slip, and I'd very much like not to bounce against these rocks to my death."

Sweat trickled from Neco's face.

Darmik found two sturdy areas for his feet. After wedging them in, he leaned his body against the rocky mountainside and released his hold. Moving carefully, he raised his arms. When he was confident he had his balance, Darmik took hold of Neco's ankles.

Neco let out a sigh of relief. His hand slipped from the rock, and the full weight of his body rested in Darmik's hold.

"Whatever you do, don't lean back," Darmik grunted. "Keep the front of your body against the rocks."

The air felt thin and scarce. Darmik's arms shook. He couldn't hold this position much longer. But he wouldn't let his friend die.

"Now, very slowly, find two rocks to grab onto."

Neco's body was shaking. Taking a deep breath, Darmik focused on keeping his friend alive. He wouldn't let go or allow him to fall. It was Darmik's responsibility, and he would see him to safety.

"Okay," Neco said, "I've got a good grip. You can let go."

Darmik released his friend, and then found his own rock to grab onto.

"I strongly suggest we find a spot to make camp for the night," Neco said.

"I agree." Darmik and Neco had been in some close calls before, but this one was a little too close. All the strength drained from Darmik's arms. The terrain ahead would most likely only get worse. "Let's go back down until we find an area to rest."

Without further conversation, the pair backtracked down the steep rocks. After about an hour of climbing through hard wind, they found two large boulders with enough space between them for Darmik and Neco. They decided to use that area for the night. It was too small to lie down or build a fire, but it provided enough room for them to sit side by side. And that was all Darmik wanted right now—to be on solid ground, even if it was only temporary.

୧ୡୢ

When Darmik awoke, the wind howled around him and he was freezing cold. Pulling his knit hat over his ears, Darmik suddenly understood how ill formed his plan was. He was so wrapped up in finding the rebel and Rema, that he actually jeopardized his friend's safety.

Neco sat, eating some beef jerky. "Thanks for saving me yesterday," he said. "I really thought that was it for me."

"No problem," Darmik replied. Staring out into the sky, it felt as if they were suspended in air. "I suspect we won't get very far in this weather."

"A storm is definitely brewing."

Darmik knew Neco was waiting for him to determine their next move.

"Just say it, Neco."

"What?" his friend innocently asked, masking a smile.

"That this is crazy," Darmik said.

"Apparently, I don't need to tell you it is, since you already know it." Neco ate the last bite of his jerky.

"I have to find these rebels."

After a few silent moments, Neco responded, "I'd like to know why."

"What do you mean?" Darmik asked. On the surface, he was the commander, and it was his duty. Neco knew this, so why was he asking?

"You have an entire army at your disposal," Neco said. "Why not use them to find the rebels? Why do *you* have to find them? Is it because of Rema?"

Neco rarely asked personal questions. Especially questions involving women. They often joked around, but when it came to things like love, Neco knew better than to ask. Ever since Jarcy was killed, the subject wasn't discussed.

Darmik looked at his friend, who patiently waited for him to answer.

"You want honesty?" Darmik asked. Neco nodded. "I don't know." Neco remained silent, waiting for him to continue. "If I let the army find her, then Lennek will know about it. He'll have her killed."

"But she was already sentenced to be executed. You didn't intervene then."

"I had my suspicions that there would be a rescue attempt. I figured she'd be saved. Then I could decide what to do."

"I thought something was going on between you two. But then, well, at her sentencing, I wasn't so sure." Neco grabbed his sack and packed his blanket and supplies inside.

"Neither was I," Darmik mumbled. "I brought you with me because I don't know what I'm doing," Darmik admitted. "I don't think Rema should be murdered. I made a promise to Trell not to kill any more people in the kingdom just because the king demands it. I want to be a fair leader, a good one." Darmik couldn't reveal Rema's true identity. At least, not yet. "When I figure it out, you'll be the first to know."

"Very well," Neco smiled. "Sure makes it a lot easier to be out here in the middle of nowhere if it's for a good reason, don't ya think?"

Darmik laughed.

❦

They decided to climb further down the mountain until they could walk on foot again. Just when the solid rocks started to thin and the ground became visible, Darmik slipped and lost his footing. The terrain was still fairly steep, and he tumbled down about fifteen feet until he was able to dig his heels in and stop himself.

Standing, he brushed himself off, lucky to have escaped the fall without any injuries. Crunching ground sounded as Neco ran to catch up. "Are you okay?"

"Fine." Darmik stood and readjusted his sack. He looked back up toward where he slipped. "A stone was loose, and I lost my footing."

Neco took the opportunity to take a drink of water. While Darmik waited for Neco to finish, he studied the area. Several of the rocks had slid down with him. Looking back to where he slipped, there seemed to be an odd arrangement of stones. Darmik hiked up to the area in question. In general, the boulders were set into the ground and spread apart. However, at the spot where he fell, there was an odd, almost unnatural cluster of rocks.

Getting down on his knees, he examined several of them. They were all loose. Darmik moved the stones off to the side, Neco eventually joining him. After several moments, a black hole was revealed.

"There's something here," Darmik said. The pair continued removing the rocks until the hole widened, and they discovered a small tunnel. Darmik easily passed through the three-foot-long section and entered a large cave.

"Neco," he called back to his friend. "Get our supplies and get in here."

There was enough light coming through the opening for Darmik to see a ring of small stones surrounding several logs.

"Ah, you built me a fire," Neco joked as he entered the cave and glanced around.

Darmik pulled out some lint and began the process of lighting it.

"What do you think?" Darmik asked. "This cave is situated similarly to the other one I found."

Neco looked at him with raised eyebrows. Darmik quickly explained how, after Rema's rescue, he'd tracked the rebel to a cave that had provisions.

"So we're in rebel territory," Neco mused. "Fun."

The fire finally caught, and Darmik stood. The light danced off the stone walls, and something off to the side caught his attention.

"Bloody hell," Darmik said with wide eyes.

Scattered over the walls of the cave were three distinct scenes. Each one contained pictures of trees, rocks, and dots in a configuration, perhaps stars.

"Interesting that there are no words," Neco thought aloud. "Just pictures."

Darmik studied the black markings in more detail. They didn't appear to tell a story. He turned around to the entrance of the cave. Starting to the right of the opening, Darmik walked around the perimeter, observing the three scenes.

"It's a map," he declared.

"How do you figure?" Neco sat on the ground next to the fire.

"Each picture reveals the entrance to a cave—like this one," Darmik said. "I'm assuming the previous cave, this cave, and the next one."

Neco stared at the strange pictographs, scratched his head, and grabbed his bag of supplies. He took out a small pan and suspended it over the fire, adding some vegetables while he spoke. "I'm not sure I follow your logic."

Darmik took a seat next to his friend.

"Why would there be a map of this cave *in* this cave? It doesn't make any sense." The vegetables sizzled, and Neco stirred them with a spoon.

"It's actually a great idea," Darmik mumbled. He leaned back, admiring the pictures. "The map reveals the next cave, and I bet that cave has a similar map revealing the one after that. This is how the rebels get to their base camp."

Neco set down the spoon. "Why not have just the one picture then? Why three?"

"In case anyone finds the cave. There are three possible locations. The only way to know where the next one is located is to know where you've been."

"So the map doesn't reveal the order of the locations?"

"No. The caves are out of order."

"Fantastic. This keeps getting better and better. Any ideas on how to crack the code?" Neco asked.

Darmik shook his head. They could attempt trial and error; however, if he chose wrong, they might be unable to find their way back to their current location in order to try another option.

Nine

Rema

Rema stepped into the hallway, closing the door behind her. The dimly lit corridor was void of people. Bright light came from the right wing, so she went in that direction. The floor was made of well-worn gray tile, the walls of similarly colored stone. Several arched doors lined the hallway, all of them closed.

Wearing thick, wool socks and no shoes, Rema was able to quietly move down the corridor. After passing a dozen doors, she came upon a single torch hanging on the wall, revealing an intersection. The wing to the left was tinged with the gray light of dawn. Heading in that direction, it became colder with each step and the hallway gradually lightened.

A voice shouted in the distance, and Rema froze. There was some sort of pounding noise. Rema carefully moved forward, curious to see what lie ahead. She came to a gallery—the wall on her left lowered to her waist, stone columns extending from the ledge to the ceiling—giving her a view of the outside courtyard below. Moving next to one of the columns, Rema leaned against the low wall, looking down below.

Her heart froze.

Hundreds of soldiers stood in perfectly formed lines. There were easily twenty rows with twenty men each. Everyone wore black, long-sleeved tunics and pants. With their backs to her, Rema was unsure if any embroidery or crest covered the front of their uniforms. Everyone held a single sword, moving in perfect synchronization with each other. Every time they changed from one position to another, they yelled in unison. One man stood at the front of them all, his hands clasped behind his back.

These were not the king's men, and Rema had no idea what she stumbled upon. This was something she should not be witnessing. Her hands shook, and her throat became dry. The feeling of danger overwhelmed her, and she took a step back, bumping into someone. Too afraid to scream, she spun around and found Mako's brown eyes staring intently upon her.

"You're out of your room," he said in a quiet voice, blocking her path. He wore a black tunic and pants, similar to what the soldiers in the courtyard donned. Mako's black boots were covered with mud, his face bore a few days' worth of stubble, and the skin below his eyes had a hint of reddish blue, indicating he hadn't slept in days.

Rema reached for her necklace, not sure what to say or do. The secret message inside the key told her to trust in Mako. Her aunt and uncle were here in this fortress, and they seemed to know and trust him. Rema had to assume she was safe, but she couldn't shake the uneasy feeling inside.

"I, um, am trying to find my Uncle Kar and Aunt Maya," Rema said. Mako remained perfectly still, looking at her with an unreadable expression. "Do you know where I might find them?" she asked.

Mako stepped around her and stood before the railing, staring down at the soldiers below. "Are you well enough to be moving about?" he asked.

Was he threatening her? Implying she should be in her room, not here witnessing the sword-bearing people? Or was he genuinely concerned for her? Rema didn't know him well enough to determine what he was getting at, and his body and facial expression gave no clue.

She raised her chin, feigning confidence. "I want to know where I am. And I want to know what's going on."

The courtyard fell silent. The man standing in front of the soldiers glanced up and nodded to Mako. Mako raised his hand, giving the man some sort of signal or command. The man nodded once again, called everyone to order, and dismissed them.

"Let's go to my office, where I will explain everything to your satisfaction," Mako said, turning to face Rema, his eyes not quite meeting hers.

Hundreds of men wielding weapons in the courtyard seemed like an army to her. How did the rebels manage to amass such a large army? Rema had wanted answers; now, she feared what they would be.

With the initial shock of the soldiers in the courtyard passing, Rema had time to survey her surroundings. The square-shaped castle contained six levels, with a lookout tower at each of the four corners. It was difficult to breathe the air in her room, and here, with exposure to fresh air, breathing was still laborious. Rema found herself constantly light-headed. She was also dizzy and tired, but that could be from the injury to her head.

Clouds brushed the tops of the lookout towers. The temperature felt as cold as winter, but it was only the fall season. The fortress had to be high up in the mountains.

Rema's parents must have somehow known about this fortress, and that's why they left the necklace for Rema telling her to trust Mako. She'd have to ask her aunt and uncle how her parents not only knew about this place, but how they came to know this man.

"Lead the way," Rema said, realizing Mako was patiently waiting for her to answer.

He paused for a moment and took Rema's arm, leading her down the hallway.

They descended three flights of stairs, not passing a single person along the way. Walking down a brightly lit hallway, torches hung on the walls every twenty feet on either side. It was much warmer there than on the previous levels, and the pleasant sound of voices filled the air.

The corridor contained several open doors, light glowing from inside. People went in and out of the rooms, others hurrying along the hallway. Everyone nodded to Mako with respect. Some looked at Rema with curiosity, but no one spoke to her. All the people wore heavy, black wool pants and tunics with a small, embroidered crest over the left breast. It was a white horse with wings and two red swords crisscrossed in front of the animal. It was the symbol of the previous royal family—Rema was sure of it. Aunt Maya showed it to her once.

Rema peered into a room as they passed by. It was an office with a desk and chairs where men sat talking and laughing. Maps and weapons covered the walls. Glancing back at the people in the hallway, almost every person had a sword strapped to his waist.

Mako stopped before a closed door. Unlocking it with a key, he pushed it open, holding the door for Rema. She entered an office similar to the other ones she'd just seen. A plain, wooden desk sat in the center of the room. Maps of the seven regions hung on one of the walls, while books and swords covered the remaining three. There was one single window fitted with glass facing outside the castle. Rema saw swaying treetops and fast-moving clouds similar to the view from her room. At various heights, several lit candles littered the desk, as well as the small shelves around the room. Beneath the desk, a large rug lay on the floor, which was so worn that she couldn't determine any pattern.

Mako offered Rema his brown, cushioned chair with a soft pillow for the back. She sat down, still dizzy and light-headed. This was the most activity she'd had in days. Mako went to the window, staring outside.

After several silent moments, Mako finally said, "I'm glad you're almost fully recovered from the incident." He continued staring outside.

Rema didn't feel like her almost execution was an *incident*. It was more of a traumatic experience that she was trying to forget, and she didn't want to sit there and talk about it. "I want to know where I am and what's going on."

Pulling the necklace out from under her dress, Rema unclasped it. "Have you seen this before?" she asked, holding the key on her palm for Mako to examine. He turned around and looked at it. "Do you know what it is?" The chain dangled from her hand.

Mako remained silent. Rema kept her hand extended, waiting for Mako to respond.

"No, I've never seen it before."

Rema noticed he didn't answer her other question. "Do you know what it is?" she asked again. At the castle, Ellie informed Rema the necklace was expensive. And Ellie was told to keep an eye out for the key. There were too many coincidences for this necklace to be some random family heirloom. It meant something, and if Rema's parents knew and trusted Mako, then he probably knew its significance.

"Yes," he said, "it was your mother's, and her mother's before her."

"But how did my mother come to own such an expensive piece of jewelry?" Maya and Kar never talked about Rema's parents, so she had no idea what their professions were. However, they couldn't have been anything of consequence; otherwise, her aunt and uncle would be of a higher rank than simply merchants.

"It's probably been in the family for generations, passed down because of its value." He bit his bottom lip and glanced to the door.

Rema did not appreciate Mako's elusive answers.

"Then tell me why your name is engraved on the inside."

Mako's brows bent inward, confusion filling his face. Rema snapped the key open and read the inscription aloud.

REMA
remember to always look
back
and you'll be
OK
but not at night, only in the
AM
Trust in him,
Your family

Mako shook his head. "My name is not there."

"It is," Rema insisted. "The OK and the AM. When you combine them, you get OKAM. Then the inscription says to look back, and when you do, you get MAKO. I don't believe this is a coincidence." This was in fact, the only reason Rema remained there at the fortress.

"I...I don't know," Mako said, his voice hoarse. "Your father and I, we were friends. We fought side by side when the Emperion army invaded. I swore to your mother I would protect you. But how could they have known?" He shook his head, appearing lost in thought.

"You knew my parents?" Rema was stunned. No one had ever spoken about them before.

Mako nodded. "But I don't know any details about the message in the necklace."

Perhaps Maya or Kar would have an explanation. "So," Rema said as she put the necklace back on, "where are we?"

"Make sure you keep that hidden." He pointed to the key. "It is valuable, and I'd hate for you to lose it."

Rema slid it under the neckline of her dress. Leaning back in the chair, she folded her hands, patiently waiting for Mako to answer her question. She had no intention of leaving until he told her their location.

"I've already explained that we are in a fortress." Rema nodded for him to continue. "This place is located in the Middle Mountains."

The Middle Mountains? A chill ran through her body. Rema was stunned. She assumed they were on one of the mountain ranges, but not the Middle Mountains. No one lived there—it was too cold, and impossible to navigate. This place was not built quickly; it would have taken years to construct. Supplies would have had to have been transported, along with animals and plants.

"Who does the fortress belong to?" Rema asked.

Mako hesitated. "The previous royal family." Rema wondered if her parents used to work in the castle. "The survivors came here." Rema knew her parents were killed during the takeover. Were they trying to escape to this fortress when they were attacked and murdered?

That was seventeen years ago. Vesha said she was stuck in this place; that she never left. But Mako knew the politics of the kingdom. Clearly, he didn't remain here in this fortress. "I saw you purchase horses from my aunt and uncle," Rema said, inviting him to share more information.

"Yes. We need additional horses on occasion. Kar is the best breeder." Mako glanced to the door.

Rema waited for him to continue, but Mako

rested against the window ledge, his hands folded in front of him. She suspected there was more to the story. They were in the Middle Mountains, in a fortress, harboring an army, and King Barjon was unaware of its existence. It didn't make sense.

In a previous conversation with Darmik, he revealed he was worried about the kingdom and the possibility of going to war.

After several minutes of silence, Rema stared into Mako's deep brown eyes and pointedly asked, "Are you rebelling against the throne?"

Mako held her stare. Tempted to look away, Rema forced herself to remain locked onto Mako's eyes until he finally spoke, "We are opposed to Barjon and his cruelty. But we will get into that later." His face was blank, not revealing any emotions. He reminded her of Darmik.

"Well, what about me?" Rema asked. "Why did you save me? Was it because you knew my parents?" Even though he had promised her parents he would protect her, it didn't make any sense. Why didn't he reveal his identity when he visited the horse farm? Why all the secrecy?

"Partly," Mako answered. "To fully understand, you must consider the situation from my point of view."

Her eyes widened. Was Mako going to use her as a hostage? Did he intend to ransom her off in order to make Barjon look foolish? Would Mako give her to the king in exchange for a list of demands? Rema glanced to the door, wondering if she could find her way out of the fortress if need be.

Mako sighed. "You're safe. You are not a hostage."

She hated that he could read her face and body language so easily.

Rema didn't quite believe him. She'd been confined to her room, everyone was being secretive, and Kar and Maya were even avoiding her questions.

Mako rubbed his eyes and yawned. "I promised your mother I would watch out for you. Also, I chose to save you, not to ransom you to Barjon, but to have access to what you know." He crossed his arms and walked toward the center of the room.

He saved her for her information? She had lived in the king's castle for weeks, engaged to Lennek, friends with Darmik, yet she didn't possess knowledge of any value.

"Like I said," Mako continued, "the people here stand in opposition to Barjon. You've been living at the castle, attending events. You had access to what our spies have not."

Spies…like the mysterious person who told Ellie *the key* was coming? How far did Mako's influence reach? And was Mako the one in charge of the rebels? Or was it someone else?

"What happens to me once I tell you what I know?" Rema said, pretending she knew something in order to ensure her safety.

"Well, I personally hope you will join our cause. From purely a tactical point of view, you should remain here. The King's Army is searching the seven regions looking for you. But I won't force you to do anything you don't want to."

Rema shuddered, imagining Lennek's rage. She

remembered the time on the cliff overlooking the ocean when he threatened her and pinched her arm, half-holding, half-hanging her over the edge, and when Lennek found her and Darmik alone in her bedchamber, landing Rema in the dungeon to be executed for treason. "I assume Darmik is leading the army?" she asked, trying to keep her voice level. With Lennek, she knew what to expect. However, with Darmik, she had no idea what she was dealing with.

"Yes, he's been searching the villages near Greenwood Forest. Anyone suspected of harboring or helping you is killed."

"But Darmik let you take me?" Perhaps merely a strategic move on his part?

Mako nodded, pacing the room. "He is desperate to find this location. I believe he's using you as bait. He's been attempting to track us since he let you go."

The door opened, and a young man entered. He also wore the uniform everyone else did, but with an additional element—on the crest above his left breast, the horse's head had a gold crown.

"Yes, Commander?" he asked, never looking Rema's way.

"Close the door," Mako ordered.

The young man did as instructed. He appeared to be a little older than she was. Although he was rather plain looking, his quick, easy movements were graceful, and he exuded an air of confidence.

"I want to introduce you to…Rema," Mako said a bit awkwardly, like he had forgotten her name and was trying to recover without notice.

Rema stood and nodded.

"Rema, this is my first in charge. I've just bestowed the rank of captain upon him."

The young man's eyes quickly scanned her body, finding nothing of interest. "This is the girl from the castle?" he asked Mako, ignoring her.

The captain stood, holding his chin high. He seemed to lack manners and social skills. Rema couldn't tell if he was simply arrogant or if he thought himself too important. Perhaps he was someone of consequence since his uniform had the additional mark on it. Still, there was no reason to be unfriendly.

"Yes," Mako replied, "this is her."

"Shall we begin the interrogation?" he asked.

Rema sat down, her blood running cold. She glanced to the closed door. There were three swords on the wall next to it, but she was still weak and had no training with a deadly weapon. These men were obviously skilled.

Clearing her throat, Rema faked confidence and said, "If you expect me to cooperate and answer any of your questions, I suggest you start behaving and be cordial. Otherwise, you'll get nothing from me."

The captain turned and stared at her with an incredulous look across his face. "Excuse me?" he exclaimed. "We rescued you!"

"We?" Rema said, while standing to face the young man. "I was unaware of your involvement in the matter."

"Well, I wasn't there, but I helped plan the escape." He took a step toward her.

"You mean, you weren't deemed necessary for

the mission?" Rema said. "Still learning how to wield a sword?" Rema wanted to put the arrogant bastard in his place. She'd dealt with enough threats from Lennek and King Barjon to last a lifetime. She didn't need this man irritating her too.

His eyes widened, and he took another step toward her, his hands clenching into fists at his side.

Mako's hand flew to the young man's shoulder, his knuckles whitening as he squeezed the captain. "There will *not* be an interrogation," Mako said. "Rema is still recovering. If she has any information of value, I'm sure she will share it when she feels better."

"*If?* What do you mean, *if?*" the young man yelled. "We just planned a near impossible rescue mission, it worked, and we have her here in our possession. She better have information, and she better share it."

Rema raised her hands to her hips, about to say something nasty right back to him.

"And what's with her blonde hair and blue eyes? Is she from Emperion?"

"Savenek," Mako said, "that is enough. Go to your office. That's an order. I will be there shortly."

Savenek's eyes narrowed at Rema with a look of hatred. For Rema, the feeling was quite mutual. He turned and stormed out of the room.

Wait—what did Mako call him? Savenek? The young man Vesha was in love with? How could she have feelings for such an arrogant person? Savenek wasn't even that attractive, but he was definitely mean and hateful. Why did Mako bestow the rank of captain upon him? It didn't matter. She would have nothing to do with the insufferable man.

"Well, that didn't go as I hoped," Mako mumbled.

"It's doesn't matter," Rema replied.

"Actually, it does. Now that you're up and about, you're going to start training with him."

Rema's legs buckled, and she fell onto the chair once again.

TEN

Darmik

Using a burnt stick from the dead fire, Darmik sketched the three pictures on the back of one of his maps before they vacated the cave. Outside, he and Neco replaced the rocks, covering the entrance as best they could. Once done, Darmik stood and observed the area. There were two trees to the left, another one slightly to the right and back. Only one of the pictures had trees situated in such a manner.

Having eliminated one of the options, Darmik studied the remaining two. Since they were traveling up, away from the dense forest, he chose the cave with only one tree. This particular picture had only a few stars and, to the untrained eye, meant nothing. But to Darmik, the stars revealed a particular constellation southwest of their current location. The pair set off in that direction. It was daytime, and Darmik had to rely on his memory to keep them on the right course. Shortly after they started hiking, dark clouds rolled in and it started raining. Cold and wet, the friends traveled over the rugged terrain in silence.

When evening came, the rain lightened to a soft mist. Just when it became too dark to continue, they stumbled across three oddly shaped boulders. Looking back at the picture, Darmik realized that these rocks were at the edge of the scene he'd copied. He turned slightly north. After ten yards, they came to a cluster of stones just like the picture. Neco and Darmik moved the rocks aside and discovered another cave with three new scenes.

The proceeding days followed the same course of events. They woke up early, ate, hiked all day through treacherous weather, and stopped at a rebel camp once it became too dark to travel any further. Three days later, they entered a cave only to discover it void of the firewood and maps they had come to rely on and expect. With the temperature dropping, they decided to spend the night in the cave anyway.

Darmik ducked and entered, tossing the firewood he just collected in the center of the darkened cave. Neco pulled out some flint.

"Maybe we're in the wrong place," Neco mumbled as he tried to start a fire.

"Not likely," Darmik said, taking a seat next to his friend. "We're just missing something. We're high enough that we're at the forest edge. If we go any higher, we're back to climbing like before. I just can't imagine the rebels doing that with supplies." Or with Rema.

"We should spend some time hunting tomorrow," Neco said. "We need to replenish our food."

Neco was right; their supplies were dangerously low. Darmik leaned back against his sack. Perhaps they were close to the rebel's base camp. If that was the case, they could use this cave as their own mini base while searching for them.

The fire fully caught, and warmth filled the cave. Staring at the ceiling, Darmik rubbed his eyes. He had to be seeing things. It appeared there were black marks everywhere. After blinking several times, he looked again. The black lines transformed into a detailed map. He'd seen lines like this once before—when he took a course on maps in Emperion.

"Neco," Darmik said, pointing toward the ceiling. "A map. Clear as day."

"Well, I'll give you it's a map," Neco responded. "But it most certainly isn't as clear as day." He scratched his chin, waiting for Darmik to explain.

"I bet that's it! Their base camp."

ৡৢ

They spent the morning replenishing their supplies. Neco gathered nuts and berries. Darmik hunted and managed to kill two rabbits. After cooking the meat, they packed their sacks. The friends debated about leaving everything inside the cave; however, if their supplies were discovered by someone passing through, their cover was sure to be blown. Instead, they took their bags with them.

Darmik had the map from the cave's ceiling memorized. The pair spent most of the day traveling directly south, not ascending into the mountains any higher. When Darmik estimated they were fairly close to the rebel base camp, they went into stealth mode and quietly swung around in order to enter from the west side undetected. As Darmik neared the area, the vegetation lessened and stones littered the ground. Large boulders began to emerge, and traveling became difficult.

"This doesn't look like a place one could easily survive in," Neco whispered, attempting to blow his warm breath into his gloved hands.

Darmik thought the same thing. According to the map, the camp should be straight ahead. Darmik didn't see anything; however, it was difficult to focus on small details because it was unbelievably cold. Crouching low, he neared a large boulder, his legs stiff.

"It should be right here," Darmik said. He was certain he had the correct location. Where was the camp?

"Maybe it's another cave," Neco said. "I don't think there's anyone here." He stood and searched the area in more detail.

Frustrated, Darmik stood and did the same.

"Over there," Neco pointed toward two boulders that stood side by side. It appeared that there was something at their base.

Darmik went over to investigate. Nearing the large rocks, he discovered a black hole the size of a man.

"Wonder why this cave's entrance isn't camouflaged like the others?" Neco mused. He removed his dagger and slid against the rock, Darmik following suit.

They stood listening. No voices or any noise came from within. Neco signaled for Darmik to hold his position. He left and returned a few minutes later carrying a piece of wood and some pines twisted around the top. He lit it, and shoved the makeshift torch into the hole. The ground was six feet below.

"Well?" Neco asked with a smile. "Shall we?" He pushed away from the boulder and slowly entered the black hole.

Darmik lowered his feet and jumped onto hard ground that gently sloped downward. He braced for an attack. Darmik remembered the last time he fought his way through a dark space while chasing Rema. He feared another ambush was about to happen, but nothing did. All was quiet.

"Where are we?" Neco wondered, waving the torch around to light the space.

The hole transformed into a narrow tube-shaped tunnel. Black, jagged rock surrounded them. "Let's go," Darmik said, pointing forward.

Even though it was tall enough for them to stand upright, there was barely enough room to pass through, making Darmik feel somewhat claustrophobic. The stale air inside was cold and difficult to breathe.

In the forbidden archive room at the king's castle, Darmik remembered reading a book once about a great fire that fell from the Middle Mountains like water. It lasted for several days, and then vanished. The book claimed the liquid fire created underground tunnels; however, Darmik had never believed it. Until now.

The pair traveled for several miles and still, the tube seemed endless. The torch was nearly burned down.

"I suggest we stop here for some sleep," Neco said. "It must be well into the night."

Darmik agreed. Their torch was gone, and darkness surrounded them. Sitting on the chilly ground, they ate a quick meal and then slept for a few hours.

When Darmik awoke, he had no idea what time of day, or night, it was. They were still in the solid black tunnel without any means to light their way. Nudging Neco awake, they ate a small meal in the dark, and continued. Neither spoke, afraid their voices would carry and alert someone to their presence.

The tunnel suddenly narrowed and sloped upward. Darmik forced himself not to think about where he was, and what he was actually doing, for fear he'd go mad.

The temperature continued to drop, and the air thinned. Their pace slowed.

"So," Neco breathed heavily, "are we just going to keep on walking indefinitely?"

"Until we find the rebels," Darmik heaved back. And Rema. He would not stop until he found her.

"Or until you step over the edge of a cliff and fall to your death."

"Thanks," Darmik muttered. "Now with each step, I have to pray it isn't my last. Nice and comforting."

Neco chuckled. "I keep sticking my hand out to feel the rock walls surrounding us just to make sure we're still in the tunnel."

Darmik knew Neco wanted to say more on the matter. Like how crazy this was. And Darmik had to admit, it was insane. They were probably in the belly of the mountain, and who knew how long until they would find a way out. They had better start rationing their food and water just in case. But Darmik knew, without a doubt, they were going the right way. The map led them here, and this had to be the way to the rebel's camp. It just had to be. He held onto that hope as they continued into the unknown.

ᘒᕉᕲ

All sense of time was lost. Darmik figured they had traveled for about three days, but he couldn't be sure. Almost all of their food and water was gone. Everything was still solid black, the air frigid, and breathing strenuous. The gradual incline increased, and Darmik's legs burned from the continued rise and non-stop walking. He couldn't think about his surroundings; he was starting to go mad.

He was ready to be out of this tunnel.

After what seemed like forever, the slope gradually declined, and they walked on an almost level surface. As least, that was what they thought. Perhaps they were going a little crazy from the continual darkness. Suddenly, Darmik smacked against something hard and fell backwards. "Bloody hell," he cursed. Neco didn't stop in time and tripped over Darmik.

"You okay?" Darmik asked, getting back onto his feet. Luckily, his foot had hit the stone first, followed by his leg, so his head was uninjured.

"What happened?" Neco asked. "Did you get turned around?"

Darmik had been walking with his arms slightly out, allowing his hands to lightly drift against the sides of the tunnel so he wouldn't get turned sideways and smack into a surface.

"I don't know." Darmik stood. There was solid

rock on all sides. The only open area was the one they had just traveled from.

"You have got to be kidding me!" Neco screamed, the sound echoing in the tunnel. "A dead end!"

"It can't be," Darmik mumbled, feeling around again. He was so sure this would take them right to the rebel's camp. How could they reach a dead end? Did they miss something along the way? Frustrated, Darmik kicked the wall in front of him. A small stone tumbled down.

"Did you hear that?" Darmik asked. "It sounded like a rock fell."

"Where did you kick?"

"Right here," Darmik said, taking hold of Neco's hand and placing it on the wall where he had struck.

Darmik felt along the surface. "It feels like there are several large stones, smoother than the walls."

"All right," Neco said, "let's pick one and push. We'll see what happens."

One of the rocks jutted out further than the others did. They each took ahold and shoved. It began to give way, and suddenly it came crashing down, light pouring in from the outside world.

Darmik squinted and moved away from the sunlight. "I thought I'd be happy to see the light of day."

Neco laughed. "Me too. Guess we'll have to wait a bit for our eyes to adjust to the light.

"At least the fresh air smells better."

◎⌒◈

Anxious to exit the tunnel, Neco and Darmik removed a few more rocks in order to make enough room to crawl out.

Darmik's eyes were still sensitive to the light, but he didn't care. It felt refreshing to be free from the dark tunnel. He scanned the area, getting his bearings. The air was difficult to breathe, and it was bone-chilling cold.

Neco stood next to him. "I could've sworn we would be surrounded by gray rocks. This looks just like a regular forest. Although, there's some snow on the ground. Strange."

Darmik agreed. "Let's cover the tunnel back up so no one knows we're here."

"I hate to be the bearer of bad news, but have you considered how we're getting back?"

"Same way we got here," Darmik said, looking Neco in the eyes. He had no desire to go back into the tunnel, but his gut instinct told him that was the only way.

"Where do you think we are?" Neco asked, while picking up a rock and closing up the hole they had just exited from.

"Based on the snow and thin air, I'm guessing we're high up in the Middle Mountains." Darmik placed another rock over the hole. "And look," he nodded to his right, "we're level with the clouds." Other, larger mountains loomed to the south some distance away. But from where Darmik stood, it appeared they were on the highest range in the immediate vicinity.

With the tunnel concealed, the two stood side by side scanning the area.

"We're going to need to find shelter and a water source," Neco said. "Especially before sunset."

The sun was above them in the sky. Most likely, they had four hours until they needed to be shielded from the harsh weather and dropping temperatures of the night.

The map from the previous cave offered no further instructions beyond the tunnel. The rebel camp had to be near.

"They probably have some sort of watch," Darmik said. "Let's keep our voices low and remain hidden among the trees. Eyes alert for traces of the rebel camp or shelter."

Neco nodded, and the pair began walking over the damp dirt dotted with patches of snow. The air blew hard around them. Darmik wrapped a scarf about his face, only leaving his eyes exposed. They headed north, Darmik careful not to lose his bearings for the return trip. A large boulder the size of three carriages loomed ahead.

"Give me a hand up," Darmik said, throwing his sack on the ground.

Neco clutched his gloved hands together and squatted, allowing Darmik to step onto his hold. He hoisted him up. Darmik grabbed onto a notch on the rock and pulled himself further up. It felt like someone was sucking the air away from him because the wind was so strong. After waiting a minute to regain his breath, Darmik scaled the boulder until he was on top. Crawling on his belly to the middle, he looked around. About thirty yards ahead, the ground dropped, revealing several mountaintops eye level with Darmik. Large pine trees covered the landscape, snow on some of them. Clouds quickly rolled by, caressing the peaks. Darmik was about to lower himself when something caught his eye.

As the cloud passed, a large, gray structure emerged on the mountaintop level with Darmik. Another cloud drifted by, once again concealing the building. When the cloud was gone, the stone castle was visible again. It was far enough away that Darmik couldn't make out small details, but he was able to see armed soldiers patrolling the perimeter on top of the structure. Was this the rebel camp? It couldn't possibly be. This castle was easily as large as King Barjon's.

Darmik slid down the boulder.

"Well?" Neco asked, jumping up and down, trying to maintain some sense of warmth. "Did you see the rebel camp?"

"I did," Darmik replied, looking his friend straight in the eyes. "And it's not a camp, it's a fortress. There's more going on here than either of us imagined."

ELEVEN

Rema

After making the bed, Rema sat down to wait for Vesha to arrive. The wind howled against the shutters. Hopefully, her new room would be fitted with a glass window like Mako's office was. At least then, she'd be able to see outside. Rema couldn't handle feeling like she was locked in a dungeon, soft bed or not.

It was strange not having any personal belongings to take with her. Even the clothes she had on weren't hers. When Rema had first arrived there, Nulea removed Rema's torn and bloodied dress and replaced it with this one. The wool fabric was thicker than anything Rema had ever worn, even in the winter. Glancing down at her feet, Rema wondered if Maya or Kar brought any of her possessions with them. She really would like a pair of shoes right about now. The socks were thick, and for the most part warm, but they weren't the same as her leather boots.

There was a knock on the door.

"Ready?" Vesha asked, sticking her head in the room.

Rema stood and took one last look around. "I am. I still can't believe your mother is allowing me to leave the infirmary."

"It feels like you've been here a long time, but it's only been a little over a week."

Vesha led the way down the hall. It surprised Rema that neither her aunt, nor her uncle, was there to help her to her room. Actually, now that she thought on the matter, Rema hadn't seen Maya or Kar in two days. They had diligently been coming every day to visit. Perhaps they were simply busy getting her room ready.

Rema hoped that staying in the fortress was the right thing to do. Even though the necklace told her to trust Mako, Rema still felt uneasy. Perhaps it was the fact that she was embedded with a rebel army. It would probably be safer for Rema to be on her own. If the need arose, she would leave the fortress. But for now, she would stay.

"Why are you dressed like a man?" Rema asked as she eyed Vesha's tunic and trousers.

The girl smiled. "Why should men be the only ones comfortable? I have a right to wear what I want. Don't you agree? Besides, it's practical. The trousers are warm and easy to move in."

Rema liked Vesha. She was glad they became friends.

Turning down another corridor, Vesha pointed to the wing they were just in. "That section is devoted to the infirmary. I live down the corridor over there with my mother. The rest of level six consists entirely of residences."

They went down a flight of stairs. On the fifth

floor, dozens of people were around, including several children. Unused to seeing kids, Rema smiled at the sight of two boys chasing one another in some sort of game.

"This level is devoted to residences. Same with level four," Vesha said.

"How many people live here?" Rema asked. There had to have been at least four hundred soldiers in the courtyard yesterday.

"A lot."

"Yes, I know, but how many?" They passed dozens of people all dressed in black tunics and trousers. A few women wore dresses, but most of the girls and women Rema saw were dressed similarly to Vesha.

Vesha stopped and turned to Rema. "There are almost fifteen hundred people living here, including the children. We have bases throughout the kingdom, but they only house numbers in the dozens. This is the heart of everything."

How could so many people live in one place? "And there's enough food and water for so many?"

"This is a self-sustaining town. But families have to live together. There are no extra rooms." Vesha continued walking, turning down another hallway. Rema lost all sense of where they were inside the castle.

"And people are happy here?" Rema asked. She hated never being allowed to venture far from home, never having the opportunity to go into town, and never being allowed to travel. It was stifling to be so limited. Wouldn't living here be the same?

"They are," Vesha said.

This fortress had an entirely different feel from

the king's castle, which consisted of light-colored stones and windows almost everywhere one looked. Here, however, windows were few and far between, and the only light came from torches hanging on the walls. Vesha stepped around a group of people dressed identically. They laughed with one another, although they appeared tired and were sweaty and dirty. At court, all Rema ever witnessed were impeccably dressed courtiers and stuffy servants. People rarely smiled or showed emotion.

They came to the end of a hallway that was dimly lit and cold. Vesha cleared her throat, shifting from one foot to the other while staring at the ground.

"Like I mentioned before," Vesha said, "there aren't any empty rooms. I offered to have you stay with me and my mother, but Mako insisted you stay here." Vesha glanced at Rema, and then knocked on the door.

Rema assumed she was staying with her aunt and uncle, but why hadn't they come to the infirmary to escort her here to their room? She felt uneasy, as if something wasn't right.

The door opened. "Come in," Mako said with a warm smile.

Rema entered a small sitting room, expecting to see Kar and Maya inside; however, the sofa and two chairs were empty.

"Where are my aunt and uncle?"

"They are busy," Mako answered. "These are my rooms." He moved behind the sofa, giving Rema space to sit down if she chose to do so.

"Why am I here?" Rema asked.

Vesha stood against the closed door, her eyes on

the floor.

Mako cleared his throat. "I'm sorry, but you won't be able to have your own room. Space is rather limited here."

She was staying with Mako and his family?

There were three additional doors besides the one Vesha leaned against. Candles lit the room. Books were scattered on the low table by the sofa, while others stood piled in corners. A large rug covered the stone floor. Tapestries and several swords hung on the walls. Overall, the place felt cozy, but it lacked a feminine touch.

"You can stay in my room," Mako continued. He went to the door on the left side of the small sitting room.

"Have my aunt and uncle been staying with you?"

"No," Mako replied. "They are staying with another family."

"Wouldn't it be easier if I just stayed with that family?" It didn't make any sense to stay here.

"There isn't any room. You are going to stay here for the duration of your visit. This will be your bedchamber." Mako pushed the door open and moved aside.

"I can sleep out here," Rema said. "I don't want to take your room from you. It's not necessary, nor is it fair to you and your wife."

Mako pinched his eyes shut. "My wife...and daughter...were killed during the takeover," he whispered, his voice laced with pain.

Rema knew his sadness. She, too, had lost her parents. Although she was too young to remember them, she still was forced to grow up without their love. Rema also knew pain from Bren's death. She couldn't fathom the hurt from losing a spouse and child. "I'm sorry for your loss."

He stared at her, the corners of his mouth rising. "You remind me of your mother."

No one had ever said such a thing to her before. Tears filled her eyes.

"Your room." Mako extended his arm. Rema hesitated. She didn't see the necessity of him giving up his room for her. "Please," Mako said, "I would be honored, and there is another bedchamber that I can use." He pointed to the door across the way.

"It's not necessary."

"It is. You're a young female, new to the castle. You'll be safest in my room."

Rema glanced to Vesha, whose forehead wrinkled in confusion.

"Please," Mako said, reclaiming Rema's attention. She turned and entered the bedchamber. "I've already removed my personal possessions."

A large bed covered with a tan fur stood in the center of the room. There was also a plain, brown armoire and a small fireplace.

"You said you knew my parents," Rema whispered.

"Yes."

"Is that why you're being so kind to me?"

"Partly," Mako chuckled. "I promised your parents I would watch out for you."

"Thank you."

"I must be going. I have duties to attend to. Vesha will make sure you get some clothes and personal items, and then she'll show you around the compound."

They reentered the sitting room. Vesha sat in one of the chairs, biting her lip and fidgeting with her hands, her eyes darting to one of the doors.

"Take her to the training hall last," Mako instructed Vesha. "I will meet the two of you there." Vesha nodded. "There is one more thing," Mako said, turning to face Rema. "Although my family is dead, I did rescue a child after the takeover. I found him half dead on the street. I've raised him as my own, and he lives here with me. If this is a problem, I can have him sleep elsewhere. But space is limited."

Rescuing a child required a good heart. Rema felt better about Mako knowing this kindness. "I have no problem with your son living here."

"He uses that room." Mako pointed to the door Vesha kept glancing at. "I will stay in his room with him. The last door is the washroom and privy. Let me know if I can be of service. I am glad you are here with us."

Rema was warmed by his sincerity. Mako left, closing the door behind him.

"Well," Vesha said as she stood, "Mother ordered a few dresses for you. They're in your armoire already."

"What about clothes for training, like the ones you're wearing?" Rema asked.

"We have to order those. The seamstress insists on measuring you so the pants and tunic fit properly."

Rema had a dozen questions for Vesha about training. Rema wanted to know how often she trained, how long she had been training, and if she intended to actually fight with the rebels or if it was simply a form of exercise or activity to pass the time. And did Vesha support the rebel's cause? Rema didn't have her feelings sorted out on the matter yet, but she knew she didn't agree with King Barjon and his treatment of his subjects. The thought of removing the king never occurred to her. She assumed that if they rebelled, King Barjon would change his ways. That thinking was naïve. The only way to rid the kingdom of its oppression was to remove the king. A plan needed to be in place regarding who would rule the kingdom and what would happen afterwards in order to ensure one tyrannical monarch wasn't replaced by another. Another question nagging Rema was the leader of the rebels. Was it Mako? If so, what were his plans? However, Rema kept all of her questions locked inside for now.

The main door to the residence flew open, banging against the wall. Rema jumped and looked up, expecting Mako. Savenek stomped inside the sitting room, glaring at Rema. What in the kingdom was he doing here? He went inside the bedchamber that Mako said his son used. Several loud sounds came from the room, like books were being thrown against the stone floor. Savenek exited a few moments later, holding a black leather satchel.

Rema turned to Vesha to ask what was going on when she noticed Vesha transfixed on Savenek.

Savenek glared at Rema, and then turned to Vesha. "This is who you were tending to in the infirmary? *Her*?" He pointed at Rema.

Vesha said, "Yes, this is—"

"Rema, I know," Savenek said, his face distorted with rage.

"Oh, right," Vesha mumbled. "Mako would've

told you about her."

"No," Rema said sarcastically, "we've already had the immense pleasure of meeting."

Vesha's eyebrows bent inward, confused.

"I'll see you later today, Vesha," Savenek said, ignoring Rema. Vesha smiled as he retreated from the sitting room, slamming the door behind him.

"I can see why your mother wouldn't approve," Rema said, crossing her arms.

"What do you mean?"

"Savenek," Rema said. "That's the boy you fancy. I can tell."

Vesha's face reddened. "Well, I um...."

"How can you like him?" Rema exclaimed. "He's rude and has absolutely no manners."

"You have to understand, he's a captain. Mako not only raised him, but he has been training Savenek his entire life. That's just who he is."

What did being a captain and training to fight have to do with being disrespectful? Seeing that she upset her friend, Rema said, "I'm sorry. I didn't mean to offend you in any way. Savenek and I just got off on the wrong foot. I'm sure he's nice once you get to know him." Rema didn't think so, and she had no intention of finding out.

"Please don't say anything to anyone about my feelings for him," Vesha pleaded.

"Of course," Rema said. "Your secret is safe with me. But, is Savenek aware of your feelings toward him?"

"No. No one is. And I don't plan to reveal anything. It's just a fling, and it will pass."

"He seemed rather friendly toward you." Vesha's face turned bright red, and Rema wondered if Vesha's feeling for Savenek were like what Bren's had been for her.

"We should get going in order to make it to training on time." They exited Mako's suite and descended the stairs. Vesha explained that the third level consisted solely of offices. They stopped at the second level where Vesha showed Rema the school, which simply amazed her. She had never seen so many children in one place and found the energy exhilarating. The kids all eagerly listened to the teacher, raising their hands to answer questions and prove their knowledge on the matter. Rema also thought the miniature desks the students sat at to be quite inventive. As a child, she would have loved to attend school with other children her own age.

Afterwards, Vesha took Rema to the library, which wasn't nearly as large as the one at the king's castle. The wooden shelves bowed and were cracked in several places. Hundreds of books were packed in the small room, not enough shelving for all of them. In some places, the books were simply stacked from floor to ceiling, leaning precariously to one side or another. A musty smell permeated the air. Vesha explained that the library was open to everyone, at any time.

Then they passed by an enormous room where games were played. There were several long tables on one side of the room, while the other contained sofas. A massive fireplace was situated in the center of the far wall. Finally, they visited the seamstress, who fitted Rema for clothes. There were some extra uniforms lying around, and the seamstress found one that was her size. Rema changed into the black trousers and tunic, and pulled the soft boots lined with fur over her feet. The seamstress said that she would make more uniforms and have them delivered to Rema's room once they were ready. Rema liked the feel of the rough fabric; it was the first time all day that she was warm.

Leaving the seamstress, they went down to the first floor, where Vesha showed Rema the kitchen. There was an odd sort of organized chaos going on inside the large room. People were kneading dough, while others chopped vegetables. There were stacks and stacks of pewter plates and cups. Rema couldn't imagine how they all got clean. Leaving the kitchen, Vesha led Rema to the mess hall where everyone ate their meals. Afterwards, they stopped by the blacksmith who was busy making a long sword before seeing the armory filled with weapons.

Once Vesha had shown Rema the main features of the castle, she led Rema to the training room located on the ground level.

TWELVE

Darmik

Darmik and Neco spent the rest of the day searching the area, careful to remain a safe distance from the fortress. Just before nightfall, they managed to find a small underground cave that would serve as shelter from the elements.

The following morning, they ate a quick breakfast before heading out. Darmik wanted to get a closer look at the castle to see what was going on. Soldiers patrolling the perimeter hinted at more than just a few dozen ill trained rebels, which in all actuality made sense. There had to be a lot, and they had to be trained. Otherwise, they wouldn't have been so successful in their endeavors.

Darmik and Neco used leaves and mud to cover their clothing and skin. Crouching among the vegetation, the pair moved closer to the rebel camp. When the compound was in sight, Darmik paused to examine the area. The wall surrounding the entire castle was tall, probably twenty-feet high. The men patrolling it wore matching tunics and were armed with weapons. Approximately a hundred yards beyond the wall, the top portion of the castle could be seen. Darmik needed to find the front entrance or climb a tree for a better view.

Looking to Neco, Darmik raised his eyebrows in question. Neco responded by pointing west, indicating they should find the front of the castle first. While carefully moving around the perimeter, keeping a safe buffer, Darmik looked at the stonework in greater detail. This castle had been here for quite some time. Bright green fungus clung to the wall, and the stones looked worn from many years of hard rain. But when was it built and by whom?

Up ahead, a solid wooden gate was fitted into the wall. Sliding behind a tree, Darmik knelt down. Neco positioned himself beside Darmik.

"We won't be able to see a thing," Neco whispered.

Darmik pointed up, and Neco nodded. Slipping a rope out of his sack, Darmik threw it around a low branch. He pulled the rope, making sure the branch was strong enough to support his weight. Then he hoisted himself up the tree, trying not to move any branches and alert the soldiers to his presence. Once Darmik reached the first branch, he released the rope and continued climbing on his own. When he was high enough, he slid on the backside of the tree and peered around the trunk in order to see on the other side the wall and get a better view of the castle beyond it.

Darmik almost lost his footing. Inside the walled area, there had to be several hundred soldiers dressed in uniform, wielding swords, practicing a series of moves. Unless Darmik warned his father, the kingdom would soon be under attack. No wonder these people had managed to spread the rumors and free Rema. But where were they from, and how did they get here? What kingdom would have interest in overthrowing King Barjon? It didn't make any sense. Darmik thought the rebels were citizens rebelling, but there were too many of them here, and they were far too organized to be regular people. This had to be an army from another kingdom.

Descending the tree, Darmik had an intense desire to get inside the fortress and spy. However, he'd never be able to get in, let alone remain unnoticed. And Rema—was she all right? Did she make it there safely? When his feet landed on the ground, Neco cocked his head, waiting for information.

"There's a bloody army inside," Darmik whispered, white mist from his breath puffing out when he spoke. "I don't know if they're rebels, or soldiers from another kingdom. Regardless, there's too many, and we won't stand a chance."

"What do you want to do?" Neco asked. "We could observe them for a few days. See if we catch a supply run and sneak in?"

"No," Darmik answered. "We won't survive in this weather. We need to return to King's City and get reinforcements and more supplies."

"We haven't even been here a day, and you're ready to leave?" Neco's face was rosy red from the frigid air.

"Yes. Now that we know the way, it won't take nearly as long. I bet we can get down in seven days." Darmik started back toward the cave. They needed to hunt, gather food, and collect enough water to make it through the tunnel.

"But when we return with the army, it'll take us forever. And the prospect of that tunnel ain't looking so enticing right now."

Darmik spun around to face his friend. "You're not going to tell anyone what you saw here. Is that clear?"

"You're not going to inform your father about an enemy army on our soil?"

"I will, after I know more about those so-called rebels." Darmik continued walking, ice crunching under his boots. "And after I've figured out what's going on with Rema," he mumbled to himself.

❧

Traveling back through the tunnel and down the mountain took a week. It was astonishing that it had taken them so long to find the rebels in the first place.

Overlooking the town Darmik was supposedly in, smoke and screams filled the air. "I can't tell what's going on down there," Darmik mumbled to Neco. They hid among the vegetation on a low hill just outside the village.

"Let's focus on finding your tent first," Neco said. "Then you can figure out what's going on. Who did you put in your place?"

"Yelek. He's the only one I trust who is remotely my height and build." They slunk away from the bushes and trekked down the hill. At its base, they headed to the northern end of the town, where the army had set up camp. Darmik had left instructions with Yelek to stay here and use this village as a home base, while sending squads to search the nearby towns for the rebels.

Darmik took out a wool hat from his sack and placed it over his head, trying to remain anonymous. The perimeter of the army's camp was surrounded by crude wood fencing with soldiers patrolling it.

"We could wait until it's dark," Neco suggested. "I bet we could slip in then."

"I've never had to assign a guard like this," Darmik said. "Things must be tense if Yelek felt these precautions necessary."

Darmik searched the faces for someone he recognized. There was a young man clutching the hilt of his sword, his body tense, eyes roaming the land. Nudging Neco, the pair approached the soldier.

"Kerek," Darmik said in a low voice. The young man stood up straighter, recognition flickering in his eyes. "I've been on a mission," Darmik continued, "and I don't want anyone to know I'm back yet. I need to be granted entrance."

"Of course, Commander," Kerek quietly replied. "Follow my lead."

Several other soldiers nearby took notice of Darmik and Neco, but they mistook them for commoners from the village. The soldiers gave them looks of either hatred or fear. Darmik kept his head down, careful to avoid eye contact with anyone.

"Corporal," Kerek said, "I have two men who have information for Sergeant Wilek. I've checked them—they pass."

"Papers?" the corporal asked.

"Yes," Kerek replied.

The corporal opened the gate, granting them entrance. "Don't leave their side, Kerek."

"Yes, sir."

The three entered the camp. The ground was muddy from heavy rainfall and thousands of boots tramping over the ground. Kerek led them through dozens and dozens of tents until they came to a large one flying the commander's flag. Darmik opened the flap and stepped inside, motioning Neco and Kerek to follow.

The room was alight with several half-used candles. Four men stood around a table, arguing with one another.

"Commander!" Yelek said. Silence fell throughout the tent. All men turned toward Darmik and saluted in respect.

"Everyone except Lieutenant Yelek out," Darmik ordered. The soldiers, all lieutenants of the company, exited the tent. "Kerek, back to your post. Thank you for your assistance. It won't be forgotten." Kerek nodded before leaving. "Neco, go eat. I'll bring you up to speed once you've rested." Darmik raised his right shoulder, the signal for Neco to do some spying.

Neco half smiled. "Yes, Commander."

Darmik turned his attention back to Yelek. "Thank you for filling in while I was gone. I want a complete update."

Looking relieved, Yelek slid onto a chair next to the table. "It's good you're back, Commander. The situation here is hostile."

"Explain."

Yelek told Darmik that from the moment the

army arrived, the people refused to speak to any of the soldiers. Squads were sent to the nearby towns and villages, and they met with the same hostility there. Anyone suspected of harboring or aiding the rebels was killed, and their body used as an example to ward others away from similar behavior.

"Any traces of Rema?" Darmik asked.

"Nothing," Yelek replied. "Even though no one is talking, we haven't found any proof that the rebels even exist."

"Is that what you believe?"

Yelek's eyes sliced over to Darmik's. "Why do you ask, Sir?"

"You've been here for over two weeks. You must have an opinion as to what's going on. And I want to hear it."

"As far as proof is concerned, Sir, there is none. However, someone probably organized the citizens and told them not to speak to the army."

Darmik agreed. Did that mean the rebels had infiltrated the people of the kingdom? Or had they simply passed through, giving hope and some sort of plan? With any luck, Neco would find out something while snooping around the town.

❦

Sitting atop his horse, Darmik rode through the village, surveying the atmosphere for himself, a squad of soldiers accompanying him. The people he passed carefully kept their heads down, eyes averted. Like everywhere else in the kingdom, these people were gangly and malnourished from a lack of food.

Neco managed to learn that a group of men rode through the area several weeks ago, telling everyone to avoid the army and that the kingdom was about to fall out of unfit hands and back to the rightful heir. And something about a key—people spoke of the key arriving to restore peace and prosperity.

At this point, Rema could practically walk into the castle, and it would be handed over to her. That is, if the people had their say. But they didn't, and that's where Darmik came into the equation. Commanding an army of ten thousand men gave him the power to suppress the rebels and Rema.

King Barjon had the support from the Kingdom of Emperion. It was Emperor Hamen after all, who had sent Barjon to Greenwood Island with a small army to overthrow the king and queen. Emperor Hamen controlled the largest and deadliest army known to man. He promised protection over Greenwood Island on the condition King Barjon open trade with Emperion and consult the emperor on all matters.

The alliance proved most beneficial for the king and emperor. However, the people of Greenwood Island suffered, starving to death. And seventeen years of cruelty had taken its toll. Revolution was brewing in the air, and it was Darmik's job to stifle it. It was his duty to protect his father and his brother. Exactly how Rema fit into all of this, Darmik still couldn't be sure. He knew he couldn't bring any harm to her, yet it was his job to protect his father.

"Murderer!" a young woman screamed at Darmik. Two soldiers grabbed her arms, restraining her from coming at their commander.

"You gonna chop off my head?"

The two soldiers forced her to her knees. "Kneel before your prince," one of them demanded, sliding his sword from its scabbard.

The woman struggled against their strong hands, her eyes locked on Darmik. She spat at him, wrinkling her nose in disgust. Darmik's thoughts drifted back to the town in Telan where he ordered a half dozen men be killed for treason. They had spread the word that a blood heir survived the attack seventeen years ago and would be restored to the throne.

Darmik swung off his horse, standing before the irate woman. Her bloodshot eyes never left his.

"Release her," Darmik ordered.

"But sir, she's out of control!" one of his soldiers said.

Darmik looked to the men, waiting for his order to be obeyed. Each soldier let go. She remained kneeling on the ground.

Lowering himself to her level, Darmik whispered, "Let's talk."

"I have nothing to say to you!" The woman laughed, exposing yellow, decaying teeth. "Your time is done!" She swiftly stood and reached for Darmik's sword. Darmik grabbed her wrist, stopping her.

Her eyes widened and she fell to the side, a sword sticking out from her back.

Darmik looked to his soldier, who had jammed

the sword into her. "I had the situation under control," Darmik said, seething with rage. "There was no need to kill her."

"She threatened your safety," he responded. "Standard protocol, Sir."

Looking around, Darmik saw several people watching from behind closed windows and down dark alleys. He quickly removed his cape and covered the woman, concealing her identity.

"Let's get her back to camp," Darmik said, standing. Thunder boomed in the distance. A storm was coming. It seemed everyone except Darmik and his squad had suddenly disappeared. "Quickly now," Darmik ordered. "And keep your eyes open for retaliation."

The squad of soldiers formed a circle around their commander as they rode back toward the camp. The woman who was murdered had been someone's wife. She was probably a mother too. And Darmik's soldier took her life without a second thought because Darmik was threatened. Was his life more precious than hers? Did she deserve to die in his place?

A scream, wild and untamed, shattered the silence. A man ran toward them, sword in hand. All of Darmik's men unsheathed their weapons and turned toward the assailant, ready for the lone attack. When the man was twenty feet away, several other screams rang through the air. Darmik glanced behind him. Dozens of people came running from the alleyways and buildings, wielding stones and small swords.

"Behind you!" Darmik yelled to his men.

As they turned to face the new attackers, more

men and woman came running, joining the original attackers. They were now surrounded on all sides by a hundred people, wild with anger.

Darmik grabbed one of his men. "Get out of your tunic and head back to camp. Get archers. Now! Go!" He hoped his soldier would be able to slip through the crowd unnoticed in the fray.

Swords sliced through the air, followed by the sound of piercing flesh. Rocks flew around them. Several of his men were hit in the head, toppling off their mounts. Darmik had no desire to kill these people, who were desperate and starving to death. He wanted the opportunity to talk to them and make things right. But that was not going to happen right now.

Darmik's men surrounded him, using their bodies as shields. He wanted to push them away, so he could fight and defend himself, but it was no use. The horses went crazy in the chaos.

Arrows sailed around them. People yelled "retreat," while additional squads from the King's Army arrived. Bodies lay littered on the ground. Dozens of them. Blood flowed in the street like water.

THiRTEEN

Rema

Entering the large indoor training facility, Rema was astonished by the number of people practicing inside. There were roughly six groups of twenty running through various drills, one person leading each group. Wooden practice swords and weapons lined the walls.

"Is this the training you mentioned?" Rema asked, remembering Vesha alluding to it.

"Partly. In addition to hand-to-hand combat," Vesha said, indicating the soldiers practicing, "we have conditioning, combat skills, and additional practice as needed or assigned."

"How often?" Rema asked.

"Daily. Conditioning is held outside. Skills class is here in the morning. We rotate. There isn't enough room for everyone all at once. Training is mixed with school and duties."

These people were more dedicated than Rema first thought. It took a lot of discipline to devote oneself to training on a daily basis. Not only that, but the room contained both men and women. The King's Army didn't allow women to join. Paying particular attention to the women, they appeared just as capable as the men did. Where the women lacked in strength, they made up for in speed. Still, it was rather unconventional to allow men and women to fight alongside instead of separating them.

Rema spotted Mako walking around to each of the groups, offering advice and giving individuals pointers. When Mako glanced Rema's way, she smiled at him, and he immediately came over to her. He thanked Vesha for showing Rema around, and instructed her to join her assigned training group.

Silently, Rema and Mako stood side by side watching Vesha throw a series of punches as she melted alongside twenty men and women, all of similar age. Her group's leader had his back to Rema, so she couldn't see his face to determine if he, too, was young like Vesha. The other leaders looked to be in their twenties or thirties, and it seemed that all of the soldiers were clustered according to age.

Focusing on Vesha's group, they all moved with the grace and skill from doing these drills repeatedly. The leader must not have liked something he saw because he raised his hand and everyone stopped—all attention on him. He demonstrated the drill much faster than they had been doing it. His quick, elegant, and lethal movements mesmerized her, his muscles flexing and tensing, revealing years of training.

"How did you feel when Lennek took you from your home?" Mako asked, pulling her attention away from the man.

Rema blinked several times, forcing herself to focus on Mako instead of the group leader. She hated Lennek, and just hearing his name turned her stomach. Thinking back to that day, Rema shuddered. "I felt completely helpless. Angry. I had no choice but to go along in order to protect Aunt Maya and Uncle Kar."

"Exactly," Mako nodded. "I want to make it so you never feel helpless again. I want you to be able to protect and save yourself."

"I'd like that very much," Rema said.

"Training here begins at age five. We incorporate it into a child's schooling."

"Do you educate all the children here, regardless of status?" The king didn't allow everyone to be educated. You had to be from the noble class in order to attend school.

"We educate and train everyone. It goes hand in hand. We have no class division here."

The idea of not dividing people based upon job, money, and family was both foreign and intriguing to Rema. But training children to be soldiers was something she did not agree with. They should be playing, not learning to kill. "You mean to tell me that from age five, you train children as soldiers, capable of murdering?"

"Yes," Mako says shamelessly, "and saving lives. If we only trained, then we'd have killing machines. That is why we educate. We want individuals capable of thinking for themselves and making decisions based upon morality."

Rema stared into Mako's clear, brown eyes. He was serious. "You want an army that thinks for themselves instead of following orders?"

"I want soldiers that won't blindly follow someone into battle and kill simply because someone ordered them to."

He was referring to the king and Darmik. Rema knew Darmik followed the king's orders, even though he struggled with them sometimes. However, she never thought about Darmik being immoral for obeying the king. Not following would be treason. He didn't really have a choice, did he?

Setting thoughts of Darmik aside, she returned her attention back to the idea of children training as soldiers. "The issue I have is that you don't give them a choice. They're born here, so they are automatically in your army. What if they don't want to fight?" And how was that any better than the current monarchy?

"If someone chooses to leave the compound, they may," Mako responded.

Rema found that hard to believe since Mako insisted this place remain hidden.

Mako continued, "No one has ever left, though. A couple of people have considered it, they even went on a mission to see the kingdom, but eventually came back with a renewed purpose to defeat Barjon. Others not suited to fighting have chosen jobs—like teaching, being a blacksmith, or a cook—instead of fighting. But everyone here has the same goal…to overthrow the king and his sons."

Rema looked at Vesha's group. They all moved in unison, with ease and grace. "But these people do not know of King Barjon's cruelty firsthand because they live here, in essence sheltered."

Mako smiled at Rema. "We can discourse on the matter further. For now, I'd like you to join a group your own age so you can get to know some of the people. I think you'll learn a lot just by being around those who live here."

"You want me to join Vesha's group? There is no way I can do that." She pointed to Vesha, kicking higher than her head, spinning around, ducking, and then throwing several punches.

Mako chuckled. "You'll be doing it sooner than you think."

A horn sounded, and Mako explained that the sound indicated the end of the training session. The groups dissolved. "There is a brief period of an activity of your choice before the midday meal. Most use it to go over techniques or to receive extra help. Some run additional laps around the fortress."

Vesha went over a series of moves with her instructor and another boy, while small groups worked together and others left.

"When will I begin training?" Rema asked, relieved that she didn't have to join Vesha's group right then. Perhaps she could get Vesha to help her, so she would have some basics down before practicing with her peers.

"Now," he answered. "Savenek," Mako raised his voice. Vesha's instructor turned around and for the first time, Rema had a clear view of his face. Sure enough, it was Savenek. Her stomach felt hollow. She'd had enough of that arrogant man to last a lifetime.

Mako waved Savenek over. Vesha and the other boy continued drilling together.

Savenek swiftly walked toward Mako, never looking at or acknowledging Rema. His damp tunic clung to his shoulders. Using his sleeve, he wiped the sweat from his brow. Savenek was nowhere near as handsome as Lennek, but he had an air of confidence and grace that came from years of training. Rema refused to find him appealing.

"Savenek," Mako said when he stopped before them. "I have an assignment for you." Savenek nodded for Mako to continue. "I need you to teach Rema how to fight. I want her brought up to speed in sword fighting and hand-to-hand combat as soon as possible."

Savenek stilled, not uttering a single word or looking her way.

"I would personally train her," Mako continued, "but I don't have the time to devote. So, I want you to."

Savenek's brows rose. His eyes darted to her and away. "Sir, I understand you wanting to get her trained, but my day is also full." He clasped his hands behind his back, holding his chin high.

For once, Rema agreed with Savenek and hoped he would win the argument. There had to be someone else capable of training her.

"This assignment is your priority," Mako answered. "You can appoint someone else to your other duties."

Savenek's gaze finally fell upon Rema. She tried not to cower under his intense scrutiny and kept her eyes locked onto his. She was obviously an inconvenience to him—someone he couldn't be bothered with.

Mako patted Savenek's back. "You have some time now. I suggest you two get started."

"Yes, sir," Savenek answered. "I'll find someone suited to the task."

"No," Mako softly said. "You may appoint someone to your other duties. But *you* will train Rema."

Savenek turned his attention back to Mako. He opened his mouth to say something, but Mako silenced him with a glare. "We can privately discuss the matter later, in my office. For now, get started. That's an order." Mako turned and walked away, two of his advisors standing at the door waiting to speak with him.

Savenek faced Rema, his skin slightly flushed—whether from physical activity or embarrassment, Rema couldn't be sure.

"Trust me," Rema said, "I'd rather have someone else instructing me as well. I don't particularly want to work with you either."

"Do you even know anything?" Savenek practically growled.

"Plenty," Rema seethed. "Probably more than you." Maybe not with regards to fighting, but she was well educated.

Savenek raised his eyebrows in disbelief, the corners of his mouth turning up. "I sincerely doubt that."

Rema's hands went on her hips. "Are you always so arrogant and conceited? Because I've had enough with Prince Lennek, and I don't need it from you too."

"I'm nothing like *him!*" he yelled.

"Oh? And you've spent time with him like I have?" she yelled right back.

Savenek was at a loss for words. Well, that certainly was something. Glancing around, Rema noticed several individuals staring at the two of them.

Lowering her voice, Rema asked, "I assume you have horses here?" Caught off guard by the change in topics, Savenek nodded. "Is there an area where you can ride them?"

"We have an exercise pen and a course we practice on," Savenek answered.

"Can you race on the course?" Rema's heart quickened.

"Yes."

Didn't he know her uncle was Kar? And she was raised on a horse farm? She desperately wanted to put him in his place and was eager for the opportunity to do so.

"Why? Do you ride?" Savenek snidely asked.

"Do you?" she countered with a smile.

"Care to find out?" Confidence oozed from him.

"Let's make a wager. That is, if you're up for it?" Rema taunted. Her horse wasn't here, but she'd never been beaten, and she had no intention of letting this smug man be the first.

Savenek turned toward Vesha and the young guy she was practicing with. "Vesha, Audek," Savenek called out to the pair. "We need witnesses." He waved them over.

Audek rubbed his hands together, smiling. "This should be good." Standing next to Savenek, Audek was almost as tall as him, but skinnier and all lean muscle. Both men towered over Vesha, who was at least a foot shorter.

"I thought Mako told you boys to stop betting, especially after what happened last time," Vesha said, shaking her head.

Audek laughed aloud, the sound echoing in the room. "Yeah, that was some fun!"

"It wasn't my idea—it was hers," Savenek pointed to Rema. "And the bet is between the two of us. Audek has nothing to do with it."

Audek raised his hand to his heart. "Ah, you wound me. How could you make a bet with another?"

Savenek looked annoyed. "Cut it out, Audek."

"Will you boys focus?" Rema asked, exasperated. "We haven't even set the terms."

"Why are the two of you betting?" Vesha asked, fidgeting with the bottom of her tunic.

"Savenek here has been *ordered* to train me," Rema said. "Neither of us particularly like the arrangement, but I need to learn to defend myself." It was only a matter of time until Darmik found her and tried to drag her back to King's City for execution.

Savenek snorted. "You actually think Prince Lennek would waste his time coming after you? It's not like he actually loved you, like you were special. You were simply a tool. He was done with you—or hadn't you gotten the message with your execution order?"

Rema took a step toward Savenek, wanting to tear him apart. She had to force herself to take deep breaths in order to calm down. Lennek wouldn't be the one coming after her; that would require too much work. It was Darmik who would hunt her down. And he certainly had the capability to find her—hidden or not. The only hope she had was being able to defend herself, so she could get away when he came.

Audek whooped and slapped Savenek on the back. "Finally someone that isn't afraid to challenge you. And it's a girl! I love it!"

Rema turned to glare at Audek. "Do you want in on the bet?" she asked.

"No," he laughed. "I'm just here for the entertainment." Suddenly serious, Audek said, "But I suspect there's more to you than meets the eye."

"I suggest you keep your mouth shut," Rema said. Audek stared at her with an intense gaze, as if he was trying to figure her out.

Vesha spoke up, "So what are you betting?"

"The terms of the bet will be as follows," Rema said. Savenek attempted to interrupt, but she continued. "If I win, Savenek will train me with respect. No wise comments, nothing. I need to learn, and Mako seems to think he's the best."

"I know I am," Savenek answered. "But when I win, Audek here will train you, so I don't have to be bothered wasting my time. And no one will tell Mako otherwise."

"Deal," Rema said, sticking out her hand. Savenek's calloused hand slid into her hers. They shook. Rema pulled her hand free, surprised by the warmth she hadn't expected to feel from Savenek.

"Now that we have the terms," Audek said, "what is the actual thing you two are betting on?"

"We're racing one another," Rema said.

Audek scratched his head, looking from Savenek to Rema. "Hate to break it to you, darlin, but you won't be able to keep up. Savenek here is one of our fastest runners."

"Don't be a fool," Rema said. "We're racing on horseback."

Audek fell to his knees. "I'm in love!" He took Rema's hands in his own.

Savenek mumbled, "Cut it out, Audek."

"A girl that's challenging you to a horse race? You know how I feel about a girl that can ride!" Audek laughed as he stood up.

Vesha grabbed Rema's arm and whispered. "Do you ride? Savenek's never lost a race before."

"Of course. Don't you remember where I was raised? And by whom?" Rema smiled deviously.

"That's right!" Vesha exclaimed. "I forgot. Still, Savenek is very good."

"So am I," Rema whispered, touched by Vesha's concern.

"Let's get going!" Audek said. "Vesha and I will pick your horses. You'll do one circuit. Vesha and I determine the winner. Agreed?"

"Agreed," Rema and Savenek answered in unison.

They left the training room and headed outside across the courtyard, where, to Rema's utter shock, the temperature dropped lower than she thought possible. Frost covered the ground. The four reentered the castle, and then exited through one of the side entrances. The landscape was barren. Trees surrounded the castle; however, most were stripped of their beauty for winter.

At King Barjon's castle, everything was vibrant and colors filled every corner. Here, gray coated the landscape like a blanket.

The barn was situated in front of the castle. Audek and Vesha insisted Rema and Savenek wait outside while they chose appropriate mounts. After several silent minutes passed, Audek and Vesha exited, each leading a horse of similar build, saddled and ready to ride. The group quietly walked around the barn to the course located behind it. The track wasn't an open field like Rema assumed it would be. Instead, it was a simple dirt road, which had been cleared between the dense trees. The path looked uneven and dangerous. It vaguely reminded Rema of racing through the forest back home.

"Since I am unfamiliar with the course," Rema said, "I'd like to take a lap."

Vesha handed Rema the lead rope.

Savenek mumbled, "It won't help."

"Nevertheless, I'd like a lap."

Savenek shrugged, and Rema motioned for the horse to move forward while she commanded the animal to walk. She didn't want to mount in front of Savenek and give away her ability to ride. After rounding a corner out of sight, Rema said, "Whoa," bringing the horse to a halt.

Rema stroked the horse's nose. "I remember you," she said in a soothing voice. "It's been a while though. Do you remember me, River?"

She named the beautiful mare River because its coat was an odd, grayish black like a river and the animal was fast like rushing water.

After getting reacquainted, she mounted, getting a feeling for the worn saddle. Nudging the horse forward, she explored the track, while making sure River responded to her commands. There were several areas of concern on the course—a rut here, a sharp turn there. There were also a couple of places where two riders couldn't ride side by side because the road was too narrow. Rounding the last bend, the stretch leading to the finish line widened, allowing more than one rider. Rema could make up ground here if needed. But so could Savenek. She remembered Vesha saying Savenek never lost a race either. Well, there was a first for everything, and she did not intend to lose today.

Rema trotted River to where Savenek sat mounted, waiting for her.

"Let's get this race over with," he said, steering his horse onto the track. "I'd like to eat."

The two horses stood side by side on the dirt road. Audek waited off to the side next to Vesha. "On my count," he yelled, "Three, two, one, go!"

Rema squeezed her legs while making kissing noises. River took off, flying over the ground. She laid low in the saddle, urging the horse onward. At the first bend, Savenek was right at her side. His leg brushed hers as she kept the inside position of the bend, taking a slight lead. The horses remained neck and neck. Rema wanted to glance at Savenek, but didn't want to lose focus. During all of her races, Bren never managed to maintain such a fast pace. The freezing wind beat against her face, making her eyes water. Her hands were bare, the fingers numb with cold.

Savenek pulled ahead and took the inside position for the third turn. She refused to lose this race, and she refused to lose to him. Now a foot behind, Rema slowed her horse ever so slightly, hoping Savenek would let his guard down. Going into the fourth and final turn, Rema was completely behind Savenek's horse. As the track straightened, Rema lifted her body in the saddle, her legs squeezing River. The horse responded with a burst of energy. She came neck and neck with Savenek. Rema felt him look over at her. It was all she needed. Leaning further forward, she took the lead and flew across the finish line, finishing first by a couple of inches.

Slowing River to a trot, she smiled, glancing back at Savenek. His face was distorted with rage. He jumped off his horse, throwing the reins at Audek. She watched him storm away without saying a single word to anyone.

FOURTEEN

Darmik

Nearing King's City, Darmik gave the signal to the lookout tower, requesting the city's wall gate be opened and the army granted entrance. Darmik, one of only a dozen men mounted on horseback, rode in the middle of the First Company, the ensign carrying the prince and commander's flags, riding alongside him. The soldiers were on foot, boots and trousers muddy from the recent rain.

As the gates opened, the soldiers shifted formations, now marching three people wide in order to fit through the wall and narrow streets. When Darmik passed the gatehouse inside the wall, his sentries saluted. Once inside the city, the army turned toward the military compound. Usually citizens watched the army pass, children running out to see the soldiers dressed in uniform. Today, however, the streets were almost empty. Glancing down alleys, Darmik saw people going about, doing their business. Had the rebels managed to infiltrate King's City, turning the people against the army?

A group of children up ahead stood watching.

When Darmik neared them, a woman ran out and grabbed the kids, yelling at them to get inside. She quickly glanced up at Darmik, fear in her eyes—like Darmik would swoop down from his horse and murder them. This woman had no way of knowing he wouldn't harm her or her children. After all, his reputation said otherwise.

Killing had never bothered Darmik before. He'd always been able to detach himself from the actual act of it. But for some reason, the unnecessary death in the village town disturbed him. Yet, it wasn't the king's fault the woman died—it was Darmik's. The army was under his control, and his own soldier had pierced her body with a sword. It was how they always operated. No mercy. So why did it feel so wrong now?

While training in Emperion, Darmik was taught to instill fear in order to maintain control. However, Darmik no longer felt that fear was necessary. He no longer wanted control that way. There was value in listening to the citizens, in treating others with respect and compassion…as Rema had done.

Since meeting Rema and witnessing her kindness to strangers, Darmik rethought the necessity of killing and the harshness of his army. Was there another way to rule? And again, that nagging question in the back of his mind—would Rema be a better ruler?

Darmik shook his head, forcing his thoughts to remain hidden. He had to focus on the task at hand. The army entered the compound, and he dismissed his soldiers to the barracks.

RED

෨ඏ

Sitting at the desk in his office, Darmik rubbed his face with his hands.

"Are you sure?" he mumbled. This was one headache he wasn't prepared for.

"Yes," Neco replied. "They haven't returned."

It was only a half-day's journey to Trell's home in Werden. Darmik's elite squad should have been there and back already.

"I can go," Neco offered.

"No." Darmik leaned back in his chair. "We'll both go tomorrow. Tell no one."

Neco laughed. "I wouldn't have it any other way."

A knock sounded on Darmik's door. "Your Highness," a mousy voice crooned. "May I please be granted entrance into your office, so I may deliver a message from His Majesty?"

Darmik growled. What was Arnek doing here, delivering messages for the king? He hated Arnek, who was, after all, Lennek's personal steward, not the king's.

Neco raised his eyebrows. "Is he for real?"

"I wish he wasn't," Darmik seethed. "Enter!" he yelled loud enough for Arnek to hear.

The short, mousy man came in carrying a sealed letter. "From the king, Your Highness." He held the letter out.

Darmik plucked it from Arnek's hand. "You're dismissed." Breaking the seal, Darmik quickly read the hastily written letter. "I've been summoned," he said to Neco. The king was hosting a dinner tonight and requested his son's presence.

Neco stood. "Does that mean you'll be busy this evening?"

"Unfortunately."

"May I have the night off?" Neco softly asked.

There was only one other time Neco asked for time away from his duties. "Same girl?" Darmik asked with disbelief. Neco was not known for relationships. He took the occasional woman to his bed, but never the same girl.

The corner of his mouth rose. "Don't get the wrong idea," Neco said, "but yes, the same girl."

It never occurred to Darmik that Neco would eventually marry. Neco cleared his throat, waiting for Darmik's answer.

"Of course," Darmik said. "Just be packed and ready to go tomorrow morning before the sun rises."

⚬⚬

After quickly bathing and changing into his silk tunic bearing the royal family's crest, Darmik headed to the Dining Hall. He had no desire to be around his father and brother this evening, but there would be other people there, helping to relieve the tension he felt around his family.

Turning a corner, he heard someone crying. He stopped to listen so he could locate the person and offer assistance.

"Please," the young woman pleaded, "don't do this

to me."

A man laughed. "Don't do this to you?" he chided, the voice familiar. "I didn't do anything. You're the one that can't keep your legs closed. If you think I'll share you, you're wrong," Lennek said.

The girl was crying. "Please," she begged. "I love you."

Darmik slid against the wall and walked toward the voices, wanting to remain unseen.

Lennek laughed, the sound echoing down the corridor. Darmik was almost to an intersection.

"You take plenty of women into your bed," the girl said.

"What I do, and whom I do it with, is none of your business," Lennek seethed. "I will *not* share a bed with you any longer. Get out of my sight."

Footsteps echoed from the hallway to the right. Darmik quickly turned so his back was to the intersection, and he walked down the corridor, away from the voices. Lennek must have walked in the opposite direction. Once Darmik no longer heard footsteps, he spun around and headed back to where his brother had been. Sitting in the corridor was a servant girl. Darmik went to her and knelt down.

"Are you okay?" he asked. It was unheard of for royalty to aid anyone, especially a servant. But Darmik wanted to know what his brother was up to.

"I'm fine," the girl sobbed. She looked up at Darmik, recognition flashing in her eyes. She abruptly stood. "Can I assist you with something, Your Highness?"

"Where are you stationed?" Darmik asked.

"I'm a chambermaid, Your Highness." Her dress indicated so, but she wore an apron over the dress, which chambermaids did not do.

"And your business with Prince Lennek?"

She glanced down to the ground, her cheeks turning a brighter shade of red. The girl folded her hands together in a nervous gesture, pulling her apron tight, revealing a small, bulging belly. She was with child.

"Nothing," she whispered.

"I'm demanding you tell me."

"He took me to bed. That is all." She wouldn't meet Darmik's eyes.

"And the child you carry?" If it was Lennek's, Lennek was sure to kill the baby shortly after birth. He would never allow a servant to father one of his children.

The girl's eyes flew to Darmik's, blinking several times. "Not his," she said, her voice cracking.

Darmik stared at her a moment. She was lying. He was sure of it. "I have healers at the military compound. If you need anything, please come see me. I will make sure you get the care you need." He stood and walked away, leaving the girl shocked and alone in the corridor. He would have to address this matter in greater detail, to ensure Lennek did not discover the child was his.

❧

Arriving at the entrance to the Dining Hall, Darmik nodded to the sentries, and the doors swung open. The sentries' staffs hit the ground, causing a boom to echo through the room. Silence fell, and hundreds of eyes turned to stare.

"His Royal Highness, Prince Darmik," the sentry on his left announced.

Everyone bowed, and Darmik entered the room. He headed toward his father, who was sitting in a chair on the dais, watching over his subjects as they mingled about the room, socializing. Walking through the dining hall, the sounds and smells assaulted Darmik. After weeks in the mountains and surviving on very little, the opulence astounded him. Perfumed bodies clad in silk, bulging hemlines and chests, and people laughing without a care in the world encompassed the room.

The king stood. "Now that both of my sons are here, let's eat."

Everyone moved to the tables and chairs situated throughout the room. When Darmik reached the dais, he saw Lennek off to the side, his head bent toward a wealthy landowner's daughter, her face flushed.

"Darmik," the king said. "Nice of you to join us. I sincerely hope you have some good news."

Lennek was instantly at his side. "Yes, brother, do tell."

The brothers took their seats on either side of the king. Servants brought in plates with steaming food towering on them: chicken, potatoes, and carrots. Wine was poured. After the royal table was taken care of, the servants served everyone else in the room.

Darmik chugged his wine. "Progress has been made," was all he said.

"Have you found her?" Lennek asked, hatred radiating from his eyes.

"I can hardly discuss such matters here, in public, before these people," Darmik responded.

"These people," the king said, "are responsible for financing the army. They aren't the enemy."

Lennek chuckled. "Brother, you really need to be around more. Then perhaps you'd have an idea of things."

Darmik tensed. "And if you left the comfort of the castle a little more, perhaps you'd see how the people of this kingdom are starving and running to join ranks with the rebels."

"Enough," the king said. "The two of you are ruining my dinner. We will discuss this matter later. For now, let's enjoy ourselves."

Darmik had no appetite to eat. Faces filled with hatred plagued him. Sunken-in faces, people starving and dying for no reason. And here Darmik sat, his plate piled high with food—food from the very people who were starving. No wonder they hated him. He hated himself right now.

When the king finished, he stood, and everyone stood along with him. They exited the Dining Hall and entered the adjacent room. Musicians played, and people paired up, dancing and laughing. They had no idea that citizens were withering in pain, starving, while food sat in the other room, discarded like trash.

The king took the hand of a wealthy landowner's wife, and led her to the dance floor. Lennek was also dancing. Of course he was. He always did. No lack of partners awaited him. The prince's head fell back, laughing. The young girl he was with twirled around him, her hand tracing a line across his back and chest. Lennek pulled her to him, whispering in her ear. The girl's face reddened.

Darmik slid into the shadows of the room, leaning against a wall, hoping to be left alone. He pulled the collar of his shirt, taking a deep breath, trying to steady his nerves. The song ended, and another one began. Lennek released his partner, and turned to another young girl, pulling her into his arms. He was shameless.

Now that Rema was out of the picture, would Lennek choose another to marry? Would he align himself with a wealthy landowner's daughter, or pluck a poor merchant girl and use her to further the king's political agenda?

The king was no longer dancing, and instead stood off to the side, talking to several people. One in particular caught Darmik's attention. He was a wealthy landowner from Lumen named Barek. The gentleman was far way from home and rarely visited court. The king and Barek moved away from the group and stood alone, talking. Darmik decided to join them.

"Father, Barek," Darmik said, erring on the side of familiarity rather than formality, hoping to gain Barek's confidence.

"It's good to see you, Commander," Barek said. He was a tall man with sharp features, giving him a shrewd look.

"We were just discussing a little business," the king said. "It's good you *decided* to join us."

"How can I be of service, Barek?" Darmik asked. He knew the use of his title as commander was no accident.

The king said, "Barek is going to be paying a little extra in taxes to ensure the safety of his land. Isn't that correct?"

Barek laughed. "Yes, to guarantee the safety of my family and land." He focused his attention on Darmik. "Can you do this? I hear stories of the rebels running wild like animals. Are you capable of handling them?"

Darmik treaded carefully. "The situation is under control." He wouldn't guarantee the safety of anyone right now.

"And you'll send extra soldiers home with Barek," King Barjon said. "They will be stationed on his land. At least, for as long as the extra payments are made." The king laughed, grabbing a glass of wine from a serving tray.

"As always," Barek said, "it's a pleasure doing business with you, Your Majesty." He bowed and left.

King Barjon put his arm around Darmik's shoulders. He never showed affection toward his son, and Darmik stiffened by the contact. "See how much better things are when you're working with us?"

Darmik remained silent.

"These rebels may prove to be of use to us," the king chuckled. "Still, I want Rema's head on a silver platter. Are we clear?"

Looking into the king's black, cold eyes, Darmik nodded.

Lennek joined them, a girl draped on each of his arms. "Darmik, you must join us." He passed one of the girls over to Darmik, and then returned to the dance floor.

"You Highness," the girl said, curtseying. "I'd be honored."

Having no choice in the matter, Darmik led her out among the dancers.

"What's your name?" Darmik inquired.

"Silvena, Your Highness." Her arms slid around Darmik's neck, and she pulled her body against his. Silvena appeared to be about twenty years old. Her black hair was pulled back, away from her plump, round face. Darmik couldn't wait for the dance to be over.

"Thank you for dancing with me," she whispered in Darmik's ear, her breath smelling of fermented grapes. "I'm glad for the change of partners." Silvena tilted her head back, looking up into Darmik's face.

There was a clarity to her eyes Darmik hadn't noticed before. They stepped away from one another, twirling, and then rejoining as the dance required.

Silvena pulled herself closer to Darmik, as if she was trying to hug him. "There is someone out in the corridor who wishes to speak to you," she whispered. Then her body went slack, and she spun around him, appearing tipsy from alcohol.

When her eyes locked on Darmik's, he gave a curt nod. Her cheeks slightly rose as if she were trying not to smile.

"Where are you from?" Darmik asked.

She smiled now, shaking her head.

Glancing over to Lennek, Darmik recognized the girl his brother danced with as the governor of Adder's daughter.

"My cousin," Silvena said, following his line of sight. "And now you know more than you should." Her voice was clear, articulate. Obviously, she wasn't drunk.

"Or you're a good actress."

She rested her head against his shoulder, laughing softly. "You'd be surprised how many are acting. A lot are joining the rebels. Tread carefully." The music ended, and Silvena slipped away.

Darmik slowly made his way to the corridor outside the Dining Hall. A few people stood about, sentries still posted at the doors. He moved down the hallway, trying not to look over his shoulder. Rounding a corner, a hand shot out and grabbed him, pulling him into a dark archway.

"Is she okay?" a female voice urgently demanded.

"Who?" Darmik asked, his hand sliding into his pocket to find the dagger strapped to his thigh.

"Rema," the girl whispered. "Did she get out unharmed? There was so much blood. We didn't think she'd hit the platform."

Darmik grabbed the girl's upper arms, pinning her to the wall. "What do you know about Rema?" he demanded.

"I was her chambermaid," she answered.

Darmik pulled the girl forward, toward the hallway, trying to see her face in the light. "Ellie?" he asked.

She nodded. "I just want to know if she's okay." Darmik didn't answer. "And I have a message for you," she continued. "You're wanted back at the compound. Neco said a package has arrived that you've been waiting for."

Trell? Darmik wondered. "Why did Neco send you?"

"I volunteered," Ellie answered, trying to wiggle free.

Darmik released her, and she slipped into the hallway, hurrying away.

☙❧

Entering his office, Darmik found Evek and Chrotek from his personal guard. "You've returned," he said, taking a seat at his desk.

Neco entered, closing the door behind him.

"What's going on?" Darmik asked.

"Branek and Traco are guarding him now. We've hid him in the interrogation room."

They must have slipped in through the tunnels. "And no one knows he's here?" Darmik asked.

"No one, and Trell wants to keep it that way. He's been waiting for you to return before he let your squad bring him in. He wants to see you."

"He has surprising strength for one so old." Evek chuckled. "We had to leave behind the rest of your guard. He wanted to ensure his house was protected."

"I suggest a few more soldiers be sent as reinforcements," Chrotek added.

Under Trell's house was a vault with priceless and irreplaceable artifacts. "See to it," Darmik said. "Send a unit from the First Company."

"Yes sir," Everk and Chrotek replied. They took their leave.

Darmik was alone with Neco. "How do you know Ellie?" Darmik asked.

Neco looked at his friend. "Care to tell me what's going on with Rema?"

The friends sat there staring at one another for a minute. "Is Ellie the girl you wished to see this evening?"

Neco didn't respond.

And Darmik had no intention of revealing his feelings for Rema. Yet.

Fifteen

Rema

Rema sat at one of the long tables in the mess hall, Vesha and Audek on either side of her. She hadn't seen Savenek since the race. The room was packed with people eating their midday meal, which consisted of a vegetable soup and bread.

Audek chuckled.

"What?" Rema asked.

"Just remembering the look on Savenek's face when you crossed the finish line first," he answered.

Vesha tried suppressing her smile. "I've never seen him lose," she said. "Not a race or a fight. He's always been the best at everything."

At first, Rema was worried Vesha might be mad at her for beating Savenek, but so far, Vesha seemed fine with it.

"I hope he's not too upset," Rema said. After all, she still needed Savenek to train her. "Will he make good on the bet?"

"Yes," Vesha said. "No matter what you may think of him, he's an honorable man."

Good, because Rema wanted to begin training as soon as possible. She could almost feel Darmik closing in on her.

"Ah," Audek smiled, "he's here."

Rema glanced at the main entrance. Savenek stalked into the mess hall. After grabbing food, he headed to their table. Instead of sitting in the empty spot on the bench next to Audek, Savenek sat at the other end of the long wooden table near a group of young men.

"Wow, he's more upset than I thought he'd be," Audek mumbled.

"His ego took a beating," Vesha whispered. "I'm sure he'll be fine once he cools off."

"Or finds a way to get back at our dear Rema," Audek laughed.

Would he attempt to seek revenge upon her? If he was honorable, as Vesha claimed, then he should take the loss with grace and move on. Rema peered down at the other end of the table. Savenek talked and laughed with the group of young men around him. He seemed just fine to her.

"What will he do?" Rema asked, curious about this man.

"Nothing," Audek answered. "He values structure and our cause above all else. He would never risk losing his position."

"Your cause...you mean overthrowing King Barjon?"

"You bet," Audek said. "It's all Savenek cares about." He patted Vesha on the back, giving her a sympathetic look.

Wanting to change the topic, Rema asked, "What happens after lunch?"

Vesha pushed her empty bowl away and answered, "Depends. All of us are on different schedules. But I have class followed by archery, and then skills."

"Skills?" Rema asked. "What does that involve?"

"Specialized instructors work with students on things like knife throwing, setting traps, and making poisons. You can attend whatever interests you or what you're particularly good at."

"We should be going," Audek said, standing with his now-empty bowl.

"What class do you have?" Rema asked him.

"I'm going to history. I'm studying the major battles on the mainland and their outcomes," Audek said.

"And I teach basic medical skills," Vesha answered.

"Does Mako want me to stay with you?" Rema asked her.

Vesha's attention was on something directly behind Rema. "Um, I don't think so," she answered.

Rema twisted around and found Savenek's cold eyes staring down at her. "Ready?" he asked. Audek and Vesha quickly left, leaving Rema alone with Savenek. Rema nodded her head. "Your *training* begins now." He turned around and walked away, not looking back to see if she followed.

Scrambling to her feet, Rema grabbed her empty bowl, putting it with everyone else's on the table near the kitchen door, and then hurried after Savenek. She jogged in order to not lose sight of him. All the hallways they traveled through were dark with a musty smell to them.

Savenek rounded a corner. Rema hurried to catch up. When she turned down the corridor, she found Savenek off to the side, talking to Mako.

Mako glanced up, his eyes meeting hers. "Rema, I was just about to come looking for you." His usual smile was gone.

"Is everything all right?" she asked. The lines around Mako's eyes were creased.

"Of course," he answered. "I just have a message to deliver." Mako shifted his weight from foot to foot, and Rema wondered if he was nervous.

"Has Darmik found...?" Rema began to ask, thinking that Darmik might be close to finding her. Maybe she should leave in order to lead him away from this place.

Savenek made an odd sound like he was close to laughing. He stood there, shaking his head at her. Perhaps she should have referred to Darmik as Prince Darmik, or Commander, instead of so informally, or maybe he still thought the idea of Rema remaining any of Darmik's concern, laughable. Her face warmed.

"No," Mako answered.

"Then what's—?"

"What's going on around here is none of your business," Savenek snapped at her. "Leave the running of the army and the military details to those of us who actually know what we're doing."

Rema straightened her back and glared at Savenek.

"Savenek," Mako chided, "you will not address Rema in such a manner. Is that understood?"

Savenek's eyes widened in surprise. It looked like

he'd been slapped across the face. "But—"

"Is that understood?" Mako repeated, louder this time, the expectation of being obeyed clear.

"Yes, sir," Savenek answered in disbelief.

"I have a message from Maya and Kar," Mako gently said to Rema, his face softening. "They wanted me to tell you they've left the compound for a bit, but will return shortly."

"What?" Rema practically yelled. How could they leave her?

"They went home, but won't be gone for long."

Rema went cold all over. Lennek probably had soldiers watching the place. "It's not safe there for them." She grabbed Mako's arm, pleading with him.

"I know, but Kar insisted they leave against my request that they remain here."

"I don't understand." Tears filled Rema's eyes.

Mako placed his arm around her shoulders, half-hugging Rema. "I'm sorry," he whispered. "Kar was afraid that staying here would jeopardize your safety. He felt that if they were seen elsewhere, like near their farm, then word would reach the king. Kar's hope is that the king sends Commander Darmik after them, with the intention of thereby finding you."

"If anything happens to them, it'll be my fault. I should go help. Maybe if I'm seen. . . ."

"No," Mako firmly said. "You'll be killed."

"But Maya and Kar!"

"If caught, they will be used as leverage to get to you, not killed. Then there's the chance to save them."

Tears slid down her cheeks. If anything happened

to them, she would never forgive herself.

"Kar, the horse breeder?" Savenek asked in a deadly voice. He stood perfectly still with his hands clasped behind his back. Rema nodded. "Kar is your uncle?" he confirmed.

"Yes," Rema answered, wiping the tears from her eyes.

Savenek's face hardened. "Perhaps that bit of information should have been revealed before our race."

"What race?" Mako asked.

"Nothing," Rema answered, not wanting Mako to be mad at her for challenging Savenek. She moved away from Mako. "Please let me know if you hear anything about them."

"Of course," Mako answered, bowing slightly.

Rema walked away, assuming Savenek followed. At the end of the corridor, she stopped, not sure which way to go, or even where they were headed. She felt numb. Rema had just been reunited with her aunt and uncle; she couldn't lose them already.

Savenek stepped around her, going down the dark corridor to the left. He abruptly stopped and spun around to face her. The hallway was void of people. Rema took a step back, away from him. His eyes darkened as they stared at her.

"I don't know why Mako has taken such an interest in you, and I don't know why you think you're so special," Savenek said in a quiet voice.

"But I'm not—"

"Silence," he ordered. "I didn't ask you anything." He pointed his finger at her.

"I don't know what your problem is." Rema shoved his hand away. "But we had a bet. Do you plan to honor it?" She squared her shoulders, standing tall.

Savenek shook his head in disgust. "Yes," he finally spat. "I never go back on my word."

"Then let's get on with it. There's no need to stand around talking."

Savenek growled, running his hands through his brown hair, pulling it in frustration. "Fine." He continued down the hall, stopping before a door on the left. He shoved it open, revealing an empty room. The only light came from a single torch hanging next to the door.

"What's this?" Rema asked. She assumed they would be working in the training hall with other people.

"A private room. It's used for individualized instruction. Mako *ordered* me to use it." Savenek grabbed the torch, walking around the room, lighting a half dozen others. After he replaced the torch, Savenek stood in the middle of the room, staring at Rema.

Savenek cleared his throat, and motioned for Rema to come to him.

"What are we going to work on?" Rema asked, standing a good three feet away from him.

"I haven't decided," Savenek admitted.

They stood, staring at one another. Rema felt like he was trying to figure her out. Was she the first person to join their cause from the outside? Had he ever left the compound? Did Savenek have any idea what life was really like in the kingdom?

"So Kar is your uncle?" Savenek finally asked. Rema nodded. "Did you spend a lot of time on his horse farm? Is that how you learned to ride so well?"

Rema didn't want to talk about her family with Savenek. There was no need to pretend to be friends, for him to know the details of her life.

"Well?" he asked, waiting for her to answer.

"Yes, my Uncle Kar taught me to ride," Rema whispered.

"And what about your parents? What do they do?"

Rema looked up into his eyes. "Why do you want to know anything about me? Does it matter?"

Savenek sighed. "No, it doesn't." He crossed his arms and glanced at the ceiling. "I'm just trying to find out about your background in order to determine your strengths and weaknesses." He looked back to her.

Rema felt oddly exposed before him. Focusing on the ground, she said, "My parents died during the takeover. My aunt and uncle raised me." Rema didn't want Savenek to feel sorry for her. Peering up at him, she saw a look of sadness flutter across his face. His focus was on the wall behind her. Then she remembered Mako saying his adopted son had lost his parents too.

"So you have some basic combat training, then," he said.

"No," Rema answered, confused by the change in topics. "Why would I have any combat training? I was raised on a horse farm, not a battlefield."

Savenek stared at her like she was stupid. "You mean to tell me that you lived with one of the greatest military captains from King Revan's Army, and he didn't bother to teach you any basic skills?" Savenek raised his eyebrows in disbelief.

"Perhaps you have my uncle confused with someone else." Her aunt and uncle had never mentioned anything about Kar being in the military, let alone a captain. However, thinking back, Rema did remember seeing scars on his arms, and she'd wondered if he'd once been a soldier. But her aunt and uncle wouldn't keep something like that from her. Savenek must be thinking of another Kar.

"No," Savenek said, shaking his head. "Kar was a captain, right under Mako."

"Mako?"

"Don't you know anything?" Savenek asked, shaking his head in disbelief. "Mako was the commander for King Revan and Queen Kayln. That's how Kar and Mako know each other."

It didn't make any sense for Uncle Kar to have kept this from her.

Savenek tilted his head, his eyes boring into hers. "What about your parents? What did they do?" Rema shook her head; she had no idea. "What are their names?" Savenek asked. "Perhaps I know their professions since you don't seem to know anything."

Rema was embarrassed to admit she didn't know that information either. She suddenly felt ridiculous for not knowing. But her aunt and uncle always referred to her parents as *her parents* or called them Rema's mother and father. They never used their names.

"Speaking of not knowing much," Rema said, "are we going to stand around talking all day, or are you going to teach me something?"

"Very well," Savenek said, leaving the subject

unfinished. He raked his hands through his hair, clearly agitated with her. "So you know how to ride a horse like nobody I've ever met, but you don't know a thing about defending yourself?"

Rema gave a curt nod.

"First of all, you'll need to start conditioning. Otherwise, you'll never be able to keep up."

"Just tell me what to do, and I'll do it."

"Tomorrow morning, run five laps around the castle with everyone else. Then, every week thereafter, add an additional lap until you're able to run twenty."

"Got it."

Savenek smirked. Rema knew she'd have difficulty running a single lap, let alone five. But she wouldn't give Savenek the satisfaction of seeing her fail. She'd complete the task, no matter what.

"All right," Savenek said, stepping closer to her. "Let's start with the basics. Punch me."

Gladly, Rema thought. She raised her right arm and punched Savenek with all her strength.

Only, she completely missed.

Laughing, he said, "You punch like a girl."

She went for him again, and missed.

"Okay." Savenek laughed, raising his hands in surrender. His smile vanished, and he became serious. "If someone is coming at you without a weapon, the goal is to stop them before they can hit you. Since you don't know how to punch, and they'll most likely be bigger than you, focus on incapacitating them."

Rema had no idea what he was talking about.

"Watch me." Savenek came at her with his fists

raised as if to punch her. "When my hand comes at you, I want you to hit my forearm downward." When his right arm struck out toward her face, Rema did as instructed. Then his left arm came at her. "Good, now step next to my arm that's throwing the second punch." Rema turned sideways, moving to Savenek's left side. "Perfect, now hit the back of my head."

Rema hesitated, not sure how to hit his head without hurting him.

"The goal is to knock your attacker out. Here, let me show you." Savenek came up behind Rema. "You want to hit here." He touched the base of her skull near her neck. "Use your palm. If you can't, then just try to hit hard enough so your attacker falls to the ground. It will help buy you time to run away."

They practiced the drill several times until Rema was able to do it without thinking. Then he taught her how to accurately throw a punch without hurting her hand. It was surprising that Savenek had the patience necessary to teach without making fun of her. At the end of their first session, Rema's body ached. She suspected Savenek knew it, although he didn't make fun of her.

Sixteen

Darmik

"Glad you made it," Darmik said, closing the door behind him. "Can I get you anything?"

Trell regarded him with a cool indifference. "Bold move bringing me here, don't you think?"

"Calculated, not bold," Darmik replied.

Two men from Darmik's personal squad, Branek and Traco, had put a bed in the room and moved the table with the interrogation instruments off to the side. Several candles were lit, but the room was still cold and unwelcoming.

Darmik ordered his men to leave to get more blankets and some hot food for Trell.

Finally alone, Darmik sat on the bed next to the old man.

"Why didn't you tell me?" Darmik asked.

Trell raised his eyebrows. "Tell you what, exactly?"

"I'm not a fool," Darmik said. "I came to you for help about the tattoos. But you knew, the whole time, you knew. You were the one who told my father babies weren't marked until their first birthday."

Trell leaned back against the wall and sighed. "Get to the point, Commander."

"You've known since the takeover that Princess Amer escaped."

Trell's eyes found Darmik's. He held them, not responding to the accusation before him.

"Why?" Darmik demanded. "I don't understand."

Trell shook his head, a sad smile across his face. "You've been to Emperion," Trell finally said. "You know how things are there."

Emperion was ruled by a man more cruel than King Barjon. It was the largest kingdom on the mainland, and solely focused on war.

"Emperor Hamen sent me here to ensure the king and queen were overthrown and his brother-in-law Barjon crowned in their place. There was so much killing. Blood everywhere." His voice faded, lost in memories.

"When Queen Kaylen was murdered, the baby stabbed in her own arms, I knew I'd had enough. Killing in battle is very different from cold-blooded murder. What we did to the royal family—that was murder, plain and simple. I decided I would never take another order from the emperor. I made the deal with your father for the art, books, and relics, and then retired. I left the city, built my house in Werden, and have lived a secluded, peaceful life ever since."

"When did you discover the baby had been switched?" Darmik asked.

"Afterwards, Barjon ordered the bodies be brought to him as proof. He decapitated them and removed their tattoos. The baby didn't have one. I knew then and there that it had been switched. I saw no need for further killing. What if King Barjon ordered all babies of that age be slaughtered? I told him the lie, and ended it."

"Do you know where the child is now?" Darmik asked, curious if Trell knew about Rema.

"I have my suspicions. It isn't hard to figure out."

The door opened, and Darmik's men slipped quietly inside with steaming food and blankets.

Trell took Darmik's wrist. "Don't forget what you promised me," he whispered. Darmik nodded. He remembered—no unnecessary killing. "I plan to hold you to it," Trell said. "It's time to fix our wrongs and help this kingdom. You are the only hope we have."

⁂

Darmik entered the king's office, taking a seat across from his father. A man dressed in solid black with blond hair and blue eyes stood just outside the doorway—he had to be from Emperion.

"You want to see me," Darmik said, unnerved at the sight of someone from the brutal kingdom.

The king stood, leaning forward on his fists toward Darmik. "I want to know what's going on," King Barjon demanded, a note clutched in his hand bearing the emperor's seal.

"I've been telling you," Darmik seethed, "people are being overtaxed, they're starving. They are banning together to overthrow you." He did not intend to take the fall for his father's mistakes.

A flash of irritation shadowed the king's face.

"That's not what I was referring to," King Barjon spit. "I'm not worried about some *rebels*." He said it like the word was foul. "The army will get the situation under control. Of that I have no doubt." The king came within inches of Darmik. "What I am referring to is *Rema*."

King Barjon's eyes pierced Darmik's, like he was looking for something. The truth perhaps? Or lies?

Surely, his father couldn't have made the connection of who Rema really was. King Barjon crossed his arms, his eyes darting to the man standing outside the door. "I want you to tell me why the rebels saved Rema. Does she hold some importance among them? Family ties? Anything at all?" Darmik shrugged. "Emperor Hamen has heard about this. I don't want him questioning your lack of competence."

"I will use all of my resources to find out," Darmik replied.

"Isn't that what you've been doing?" King Barjon yelled, throwing his arms up in the air. "And what do you have to show for it?"

Nothing that Darmik could admit to. He knew where Rema was, who she was, and he had Trell. If Darmik admitted to any of this, the king would have Rema and Trell executed. Although Darmik felt obligated to protect his father and brother from harm, he felt the same compulsion toward Rema and Trell. No unnecessary killing.

Darmik needed to speak with Rema. He had to find out what she knew, how involved she was with the rebels, and what her plan was for the future. Darmik had to go back to the Middle Mountains.

"If you don't find Rema and end these rebels, Emperor Hamen will send his army here and slaughter us all!" The king's face reddened. "I won't be murdered like the king and queen before me. Use the army and fix this mess. Or else I'll take the army from you and do it myself." The king's arms were shaking, and there was fear in his eyes. Darmik had never seen his father afraid. It was unnerving.

Why would the emperor kill King Barjon? He was the emperor's brother-in-law. The emperor put him in power. Why would he take it away?

And as far as the king taking over the army, Darmik couldn't let that happen. His father would destroy it. Darmik had a responsibility to his men to take care of them, just like the ruler should take care of his subjects.

Watching the king pacing behind his desk, Darmik knew, without a doubt, that Rema would make a better ruler. His father only cared for himself. He didn't deserve to rule.

"Oh, and one last thing," King Barjon said. "Send a squad of men and bring that old, crazy man Trell here. I'm issuing a warrant for treason."

ෂ

Darmik entered the interrogation room. Trell lay sleeping on the rusty bed cot.

"Trell," Darmik said, "Wake up."

The old man opened his eyes. "What is it, boy?"

"You're no longer safe here. I need to get you to another location." Darmik helped Trell sit.

"Did Barjon put out a warrant?"

"Yes," Darmik said, "for treason. He ordered me to send a squad to retrieve you." Darmik pulled Trell to his feet. "And a man from Emperion is here."

Trell's face whitened. "The emperor knows," he mumbled. "He wants all evidence of her existence erased." The old man took hold of Darmik's arms. "You have to save her. He'll kill her just like her parents."

"My father has already tried," Darmik said, assuming they were talking about Rema.

Trell whacked Darmik. "Yes," he said, "you weren't very vigilant with that one. I hope you're quicker on your feet than that."

"I'm working on it," was all Darmik answered. "But why does my father care about arresting you for treason?" Darmik asked.

"Many reasons." Trell put on his cape and hat, preparing for the journey ahead. "You do understand her vast importance, yes?"

Darmik nodded. "She's the blood heir to the throne and thus has a legitimate claim to it. The rebels want her in power. She can change everything."

Darmik opened the trap door in the floor that led to the secret tunnel, then grabbed a torch and descended the stairs, Trell following close behind.

"It's so much more than that. Don't you understand?"

Yes, Darmik thought, *she is the only hope the kingdom has to bring peace, stability, and prosperity to the island—and the people will support her.*

"The emperor fears her," Trell said, his voice

bouncing off the walls in the narrow passageway as the men climbed down the stairs.

Branek and Traco waited for them at the bottom, so Darmik remained quiet. The group of four traveled through the tunnel and exited outside the city walls. A squad of men waited with Neco to take Trell to the first cave Darmik had discovered, on the day of Rema's rescue, near the bottom of the Middle Mountains. Neco would return as soon as Trell was safely deposited there with the squad. If anyone saw the soldiers, they were heading out under the pretense of going to Werden to find Trell.

"Remember," Trell whispered to Darmik, "her blood ties everything together. She is the weapon you need for peace." He bowed, and then climbed onto a waiting horse.

Darmik watched his men ride off before returning to the interrogation room to remove all evidence that Trell had ever been there.

❦

Darmik made his way to his bedchamber, located on the top floor of the castle. The posted sentries saluted him while he unlocked the door. Darmik entered the dark, unwelcoming room. He never allowed anyone, including servants, inside unless he was present.

After lighting a few candles, Darmik kicked off his boots and plopped down on the sofa. A soft knock came from the door. Who could it be? He hadn't ordered any food. All he wanted was a few hours of sleep. The plan was to leave with a squad in the morning for the

Middle Mountains. He needed to talk to Rema, so he could decide how to proceed.

Someone knocked again. Darmik opened the door and found a young chambermaid, holding logs, standing between the posted sentries.

"You ordered a fire, Your Highness," the girl said, taking a step forward.

Darmik recognized her voice. He nodded, opening the door wider, granting her admittance. This was the pregnant chambermaid Lennek had been fooling around with. Closing the door behind her, Darmik grabbed the logs from the girl and put them in the fireplace. He waited for her to speak.

"I need your help," she said, her hands clasped together before her.

"Explain," Darmik said, taking a seat.

"Ellie suggested I talk to you. Can you help?" She touched her slightly bulging stomach.

A hint of panic swelled in Darmik. Was this girl devoted to Lennek? Perhaps testing Darmik's loyalties? But Neco trusted Ellie.

"Your name?" Darmik demanded.

"Cassie."

"And you're friends with a chambermaid named Ellie?"

Cassie shifted her weight from foot to foot, unsure how to respond.

"I suggest you tell the truth," Darmik said, rubbing his face. His eyes were heavy, and he had a long journey ahead of him. He hoped to get a few hours of uninterrupted sleep.

"We work together," Cassie clarified. "Both of us were assigned to Rema."

She had Darmik's attention. "What is it you want from me? I offered you medical assistance at the military compound; that is all."

Cassie moved to the window, looking outside.

"Drop to the floor," Darmik demanded. Cassie did as instructed. He went to the windows, pulling the curtains closed. Then he reached down and helped Cassie to her feet. She was cold to the touch. Darmik moved to the hearth and lit a fire to warm the room.

"A little more discretion is called for," Darmik said. "I am not like my brother." Darmik never slept around. And if word got back to Lennek that a girl was in Darmik's bedchamber, especially one Lennek had bedded, it would raise suspicion, to say the least.

Cassie's face reddened, and she moved away from the curtained windows.

"There isn't much time," Darmik prompted. Cassie needed to leave soon, before anyone took notice.

"Can I fake the baby's death?" she whispered, tears springing in her eyes. "This isn't a life I want for my child." Any baby conceived and born at the castle was considered property of the king and in his service for life. "Ellie thought perhaps you could help. She said you weren't like *them*."

"Time to go," Darmik took Cassie's arm, leading her to the door. He wasn't sure she could be trusted.

"Please," she pleaded. "I don't know what to do!"

"Pull yourself together," Darmik whispered in her ear. "Be patient. I'll contact you. Do not attempt to get in touch with me again." He pushed her out into the hallway. He needed time to think on the matter.

SEVENTEEN

Rema

Rema was never one to back down from a challenge. Every day she ran, she constantly reminded herself that she couldn't let Savenek win. He had assigned her five laps, plus an additional one each week. She intended to complete all six laps today. Finishing the second one, she smiled—only four more to go.

It seemed a majority of the inhabitants of the castle were out running in the early hours of the day. They sprinted on a narrow, dirt track that surrounded the castle but was still inside the wall. Luckily, the dirt was wet from the evening frost. Otherwise, it would be hard to breathe with so many feet trampling upon it.

Rema focused on maintaining a slow pace, so she wouldn't tire too soon, although it was difficult to remain at that speed with so many people whizzing past her. Rema's toes were cold, but her body quickly warmed, despite the frigid air. Keeping her head facing forward, she continued jogging, concentrating on steadily breathing in and out, and not on the other runners.

A pair of men passed her. She thought she heard

one chuckle, but she wasn't sure. One of them glanced back at her and smiled before his running partner shook his head and gave him a shove, throwing him off balance. The two ran with steady strides, and finally as they rounded the corner, Rema caught a glimpse of their faces. The man who did the pushing was Savenek. They rounded the corner, and were gone.

Three laps down. Three to go.

Rema's legs burned, and her chest clamored for air. She forced her thoughts on something other than running, hoping the time would pass quickly. Although she had only been out of the infirmary for a week, Rema's days had fallen into a routine. She woke up and ran the torturous laps. When she finished, she slipped off among the trees, gagging and puking until her body calmed down. After breakfast, she worked with Savenek on basic hand-to-hand skills until the midday meal. Then Savenek taught her how to wield a sword. They always joined a group in the afternoon for skills training, allowing Rema the opportunity to be exposed to a variety of things without Savenek having to teach her.

Savenek was an excellent instructor, and Rema understood why Mako had insisted he work with her. Their sessions were always intense and focused. They never discussed anything personal. Savenek always ended the workout right when Rema was about to fall over, unable to continue. He pushed her a little further each day, always seeming to know exactly how far to go without pressing too hard.

Rema spent most of her free time with Vesha. Audek occasionally joined them for a meal or a game after supper. Rema never talked to Savenek outside of their practice sessions. Whenever she did see him, he either ignored or didn't notice her. He never mentioned their race or riding horses. She came to learn that Audek and Savenek were best friends and often together; however, when she was with Audek, Savenek never came around. Rema suspected he wasn't over her beating him in the race and, although he taught her, he was never going to be friends with her—which was just fine with Rema.

She rarely saw Mako even though she was staying in his rooms. Not once had she seen Savenek there. He was up and out before she awoke, and he didn't return until after she went to bed.

Four laps down. Two to go. Rema tried staying to the outside of the track, allowing people to pass her on the inside. Her legs shook. Most of the people running had completed their assigned laps and headed inside to eat.

Coming around a corner, Rema veered a little too far off the track and hit a patch of ice. Trying to keep her balance, she tensed and threw her arms out. She managed to stay upright, but her leg cramped, and she pulled a muscle. Biting her lip, she refused to scream. Forcing herself to jog, tears sprung in her eyes from the pain. She would finish the laps. Quitting wasn't an option.

∞

After breakfast, Rema's leg was so tight, she could barely walk. The last thing she felt like doing was drilling with Savenek. He'd probably make fun of her injury.

Rema intended to try to hide it from him, if that was possible.

Limping down the hallway, she ran into Vesha.

"Are you on your way to meet Savenek?" Vesha asked.

Rema pursed her lips. "Unfortunately. I really don't feel like working with him today. I could use a break."

"Yeah, he can be intense." Vesha laughed. "I'm heading up to the infirmary today. Several children are ill, and my mother needs my help. Want to join me?"

"Can I?" Rema asked, hope blooming in her chest. A day off from training was just what she needed.

"Of course. I'll send a message letting Savenek know."

The girls headed up to the top level. Rema hadn't been back to the infirmary since she was released. Although Nulea was strict, Rema missed the skilled healer.

Almost a dozen children were sick. Nulea was busy attending to several injured men who just returned to the fortress the day before. Nulea assigned Rema and Vesha to watch over the kids.

Rema spent the morning making sure the children had water to drink and a fire roaring in the hearth. She placed cool washcloths on their foreheads if they were running a fever. Sometimes, they simply needed a hand to hold. Rema gladly sat at many bedsides, offering comfort where she could.

After feeding the children their midday meal, Vesha said that the kids needed a nap. Two sisters, ages six and ten, shared a room. They missed their mother terribly, but she was too busy working in the kitchen to be with them. Understanding their loneliness, Rema asked them if she could tell them a story to help them go to sleep. Both girls eagerly agreed, so Rema told them all about her horse, Snow, and racing through the forest with her friend, Bren.

The girls listened until their eyelids drooped, and they both fell fast asleep. Rema was afraid to leave them in case either awoke. She didn't want them to be alone. Grabbing a blanket from the edge of the bed, Rema wrapped it around her shoulders, curled up in the chair, and fell asleep.

She awoke to voices yelling.

"What is she doing here?" Mako demanded.

Rema quickly sat up, her leg still stiff.

"She is helping with the sick children," Nulea answered. It sounded like they were just outside the door in the hallway arguing.

"Rema could get sick." Mako's voice was harsh. "She is supposed to be training with Savenek, not working here."

Nulea laughed. "I have several patients that need tended to. Rema offered. She's been invaluable today. She's excellent with the children, and should help more often. Perhaps she's found her profession here."

"You have no idea," Mako responded. "Rema will never step foot in the sick ward unless she is ill. Do you understand?"

There was a long pause.

Why couldn't Rema help at the infirmary? Was

Mako so desperate for warriors that he couldn't spare her? Rema glanced at the girls, still fast asleep. She stood and made her way to the door, slipping out into the hallway.

Mako and Nulea stood facing one another. Nulea's face seemed honestly confused, while Mako's was red with anger.

"What's going on?" Rema asked.

"Nothing," Mako answered. "But you've been assigned to train with Savenek. You are not authorized to work here. Let's go." Mako grabbed her elbow, steering her away from the infirmary.

Rema had difficulty walking, but Mako dragged her along without noticing her injury.

"Where are you taking me?" she asked.

"To my office," he said. "We need to talk."

She was tired of everyone dictating what she did. For once, Rema wanted some control over her own life. Pulling her arm free, she stopped walking. Mako spun around to face her, his eyebrows pulled together in confusion.

"Whatever it is, just tell me now. I'm going back to my bedchamber to rest."

Mako came closer, concern filling his face. "Are you feeling unwell?"

"I'm fine," Rema said. "I'm just tired from all of the physical activity."

His face immediately softened. "Of course. Why don't you rest for the remainder of the day? You can resume your training tomorrow."

"Thank you."

Heading down the corridor toward Mako's rooms,

she saw Savenek. He had just closed the door and was headed straight for her. She hesitated, not wanting him to see her injury. He was focused on something in his hands. When he was five feet away, Rema moved to the side and averted her eyes. Savenek passed by without so much as a nod. She wasn't sure he'd even seen her. Rema relaxed, leaning against the stone wall.

๑๑๑

"Rema," Vesha said. "It's your turn."

"Oh," Rema glanced down at the cards in her hand, then at the ones lying on the table. She completely missed the previous play.

"You aren't even paying attention." Vesha sighed.

"I'm sorry. I'm just really tired." Her leg still ached from the run earlier that day.

Vesha's focus shifted to the entrance of the game room. Her body went stiff, her cheeks turning red.

Rema knew who must've just walked in. She kept her eyes focused on the cards in her hands.

"Hi, Vesha," Savenek said, giving her a quick nod. He never looked Rema's way. Savenek went over to a group of guys gambling at a large table in the center of the room. He sat down and joined them.

Rema picked up another card from the pile, and laid down a pair. "Your turn."

"Oh." Vesha looked back to the cards in her hand.

"Do you get a chance to talk to Savenek very often?" Rema asked.

"Yes," Vesha said, putting down a pair. "But not

alone. He's always with people."

"He doesn't talk much during our training sessions. He's very focused."

Vesha nodded her head. "And he always seems so busy. I don't want to bother him."

"You could go talk to him now," Rema suggested, nodding her head toward the table.

Vesha's widened her eyes in horror. "I could never!"

"No, not in front of everyone. I mean, ask him to join you in a card game or go for a walk. Something so the two of you can be alone and get a chance to talk."

"I don't think so." Vesha shook her head and glanced in Savenek's direction. "Don't look now, but the guy next to Savenek keeps staring at you."

"Who is it?" Rema asked.

"Horek. He's in my tactical training group. Nice guy." Vesha laid down two pairs. "I won."

Rema tossed the rest of her cards in the pile. "I'm done. I think I'll turn in for the night."

Vesha collected the cards and put them in a small, wooden box. "Looks like you're about to have a visitor." Vesha grinned.

Glancing up, Rema saw Horek moving toward them.

"Vesha," Horek said with a smile on his face, "care to introduce me to your friend?"

"Sure," Vesha said. "Rema, I'd like to—"

"No," Savenek cut in. Rema didn't know how he got there so quickly. "Leave her alone," Savenek ordered.

Horek's shoulders slumped forward, but he nodded and followed Savenek. They left the game room, never looking back.

"What was that about?" Rema wondered. She was too tired to be upset with Savenek for his rude behavior.

Vesha stared at the boys with a confused look on her face. "Let's just go," she mumbled.

Rema stood and stretched. "I'll see you tomorrow."

"I'll walk you to your floor. I'm going that way."

It was difficult for Rema to hide her limp, and she didn't want Vesha to know the extent of her injury. "You don't have to," Rema said.

Vesha smiled and took Rema's arm, helping to steady her. "That's what friends are for." She knowingly looked down to Rema's leg.

"Thanks," Rema said. Vesha didn't question her or push the matter.

They slowly made their way to the fifth floor, where Vesha said good-bye before heading to the infirmary to help her mother. Rema made her way down the long hallway to Mako's rooms. She couldn't wait to put on her nightgown and crawl into bed.

After unlocking Mako's door, Rema pushed it open to find the sitting room lit with candles. Usually when she returned in the evening, it was dark.

"Hello?" she called out. No one answered. "Mako?" The room was silent. Perhaps he was already asleep.

Rema went to her bedchamber and changed. Her face was covered in sweat. One of the few luxuries she missed from the castle was having a washbasin in her room. Slipping on her wool socks, she padded across the sitting room to the privy. She brushed her teeth and washed off as best she could. Rema's leg screamed from having to support her weight. She just had to make it back to her bedchamber. A good night's sleep was all she needed. After exiting, Rema dragged her feet across the sitting room. When she reached the sofa, she reached out, using it for support.

A loud bang echoed in the room, making Rema jump. She spun around and saw Savenek standing outside his bedchamber, a dropped book at his feet. His eyes scanned her body from head to toe, and then his face turned a deep shade of red. He lowered his gaze as he knelt on the ground, retrieving his dropped item.

Rema felt her own face flush from embarrassment. She was wearing her nightdress without a robe, and her hair was down. Releasing her hold on the sofa, she crossed her arms in an attempt to conceal her body.

"I'm sorry," she stammered. "I didn't know you were here."

Savenek stood and carefully focused on Rema's face. "I didn't realize you had retired for the night," Savenek said. "Don't you usually do so much later?"

Rema was shocked he knew this bit of information about her. Perhaps noticing the comings and goings of others was ingrained in him from years of training.

"What are you reading?" she asked, pointing to the book clutched in his hand.

Savenek moved the book behind him, shielding it from sight. "Nothing," he said. "Just a novel for fun."

Rema couldn't imagine Savenek reading for fun. Military or war tactics, she could visualize, but not something for the sake of enjoyment. For some reason, this unnerved her. "I'll let you get back to reading then.

Goodnight."

Taking a step toward her room, Rema's leg cramped and gave out. She grabbed onto the back of the chair, preventing herself from falling. Gritting her teeth, she forced herself to stand up straight and take another step. She didn't want to show weakness in front of Savenek. He'd probably find a way to use it against her.

Savenek's hand encircled her upper arm. "Are you okay?" he asked, his eyes penetrating into hers, the concern clear.

"I'm fine," Rema said. "I just pulled a muscle while running. It'll be fine by tomorrow."

She tried tugging her arm free, very aware of the feel of Savenek's warm hand through the thin fabric of her nightdress.

"Have you seen Nulea?"

"No, I'll be fine." She didn't understand Savenek's sudden interest in her well-being.

He sighed and grabbed the knitted blanket draped over the chair. Wrapping it around her shoulders, he ordered her to sit. Too tired to argue, Rema did as instructed. "Which muscle is it?" he asked.

Rema pointed to the area on the back of her right leg, below the knee. "It keeps cramping when I walk." She relaxed back into the chair, the warm blanket wrapped around her body.

Savenek knelt on the ground in front of Rema.

"I'm fine," she said. "I'm sure it'll go away."

Savenek gazed into her eyes. Before she had a chance to protest, he took her right foot and removed her sock. Rema jerked and tried pulling her leg away from him. "What are you doing?" she demanded.

"Relax," Savenek said, not looking at her. "If you'd gone to the healer, she would have done the same thing. We're all trained in basic medical skills. I need you to relax so I can massage a salve onto your muscle. It will relieve the cramping." His head jerked up. "Don't you trust me?" he suddenly asked, his lips curling slightly, like he was trying not to laugh.

Rema had no idea if he was being serious or not, and she really didn't know how she felt on the issue of trust. She had trusted Darmik, and look where that landed her. However, Savenek was certainly not Darmik. Rema had spent hours training with Savenek, and he'd been nothing but respectful. He also proved to be quite skilled and knowledgeable. On the other hand, he also made it perfectly clear that he wanted nothing to do with Rema outside of their mandated training. So why was he helping her now?

He raised his eyebrows, waiting for an answer.

"Sure," she responded, "I trust you."

"Then lean back and relax." Savenek grinned. "I promise I won't hurt you." He found a small container in one of the drawers in the low table. Removing the lid, he used two fingers and scooped out the minty-smelling goo. "I use this all the time," he mumbled. "I wish you'd said something earlier today."

Still kneeling on the ground, Savenek rubbed the substance between his hands, and then gently took hold of Rema's foot, placing it on his thigh. His hands slid over her ankle and then slowly beneath the nightdress to her calf. She froze, unsure what to do. She'd never had a man touch her like this before, and she was pretty sure this is what Aunt Maya would constitute as inappropriate behavior. But it's not like Savenek had any interest in her. He was simply a mentor giving her aid.

"This might be uncomfortable, but I have to work it into the muscle."

He rubbed the mixture deep into her calf, her muscle tightening in protest. Rema bit her bottom lip, trying to focus on something other than her aching leg. Gradually, the cramping receded as the medicine began to relieve the pain. All thoughts of Savenek's motivations fell short when Rema experienced the wonderful effects of the catnip.

Savenek chuckled. "I assume it's working?"

"Yes," Rema sighed, "how can you tell?"

"You're smiling. You never smile around me, so I figure your leg must feel better." His hands continued working her muscle.

Of course she never smiled around him. Whenever they were together, he was training her in fighting techniques and pushing her body farther than she thought possible. "We never spend any of our free time together," Rema pointed out. She really wanted to say that he treated her like the plague and never came around; however, Rema didn't want to risk upsetting him while he was touching her. Although her leg felt immeasurably better, she didn't want him to stop his ministrations.

Rema peered down at him, wondering if he'd respond. His focus was on her leg. Several times Savenek opened his mouth to say something, only he ended up snapping it shut, bending his eyebrows in confusion.

A few minutes later, he lowered her foot to the ground. "I must be going," he said as he stood up. "Audek and I are running a mission tonight."

Audek never mentioned anything to her. Rema wondered how much was actually kept from her. "What about Vesha? Will she be joining you?"

"Vesha?" Savenek said, confused. "No, she never goes on missions with us. Her mother insists she remain here to tend the injured and sick."

Rema was about to push herself up off the chair when Savenek effortlessly lifted her in both his arms like a child.

"I can walk!" Rema exclaimed. Her face was mere inches from his; one of his arms wrapped around her legs, the other around her back. She carefully avoided looking directly into his eyes and instead, focused on where he was carrying her.

"You need to stay off your leg for the rest of the night."

She felt him breathing against her cheek. Her rapid heartbeat was so loud she was sure that Savenek heard it. Why was her body reacting this way to him? It couldn't be simply that he was a man—she'd never felt like this with Bren. The unwanted feelings Savenek stirred inside her reminded Rema of Darmik.

And she was attracted to and had fallen in love with Darmik.

Savenek was nowhere near as handsome as Darmik. She'd never looked at Savenek that way before. She didn't want to look at him that way now. Vesha was in love with Savenek after all.

He carried Rema into her room. Lowering her onto the bed, his arms gently released her. For a mere second, Rema wondered what it would feel like if he kissed her. Staring into his eyes, her breath caught as he leaned forward.

"Get some sleep," Savenek whispered, hovering above her. As if suddenly realizing what he was about to do, he jerked away from her.

"Goodnight," Rema said, her voice coming out a little huskier than usual. "Thank you for your help." Crawling under the covers, she attempted to ignore him. There was no way possible she could be interested in Savenek that way.

He blew out the single candle and left her room without another word.

She still hated him, right?

೫ಎ

Rema awoke to hushed whispers. Glancing toward her door, she saw that it was slightly ajar, allowing the voices to be heard. Savenek must not have closed it all the way last night.

"I did," Savenek said in a soft voice. "When we met at the rendezvous location, I asked and he said no one saw him up close. When his men infiltrated the town, they only caught glimpses of the commander from a distance." Rema's heart froze. She strained to listen.

"Then it's not him," Mako whispered.

"Why the ruse?" Savenek asked.

"I'm not sure," Mako answered. "But I fear Darmik is one step ahead of us. Make sure you attend the meeting after breakfast."

Rema went ridged. They were talking about Darmik. Was he getting close to finding her?

"What about my training with Rema?" Savenek asked.

There was a long pause.

"How is her training going?" Mako finally asked. There was an odd hitch to his voice.

"Good. She's picking up the techniques quickly. I'm surprised she had no training though, considering who her uncle is."

"I'm assuming you're getting to know her, then?"

Rema remembered the way Savenek gently touched her leg. She still wasn't sure how she felt on the matter. The man was utterly confusing. She thought he hated her, but the way he tended to her last night suggested otherwise. However, kindness and fondness were two separate things, and Rema didn't want to confuse herself with affection and feelings that weren't there. She shook her head and forced herself to focus on the conversation in the adjoining room.

"A little," Savenek said.

"I've been told you two don't talk outside of training."

"Why do you care?" Mako didn't respond. "Did you put us together on purpose?" Savenek asked. "Hoping there would be something between us?"

"What do you mean *something between us*?" Mako asked, alarm in his voice.

"Nothing," Savenek mumbled. "I just thought you might want me to settle down and marry. I thought this was your way of forcing me into it."

Mako sighed. "No, my dear boy. I simply wanted the best to train Rema. Nothing more. The thought of you two never even crossed my mind. And it shouldn't cross yours either. We have work to do."

Savenek chuckled. "Don't worry," he said, "she's not my type. Besides, I want to serve and be a great commander like you. It's what you've been preparing me for my entire life."

There was a shuffling sound from the sitting room.

"Have you made contact with the heir?" Savenek asked. "I'd like to know when we're going to finally meet our ruler."

"I have," Mako answered. "It's almost time."

"I want to devote my allegiance to the true king."

"I know," Mako whispered. "And you will."

It seemed to Rema that Savenek's life wasn't so far off from all the people in the kingdom suffering under King Barjon's rule. They, too, spent their lives preparing for one profession. Mako said everyone here had a choice, but did the people here truly understand what they were choosing?

EiGHTEEN

Darmik

Darmik sat at his desk, staring at his best friend and closest confidant, wondering how well he really knew Neco. Darmik had no idea what was going on between Neco and Ellie—but there was definitely something between them.

Neco looked tired. The lack of sleep from riding hard through the night made his cheeks flush and put dark circles under his eyes. Darmik had intended to leave before sunrise for the Middle Mountains, but Neco hadn't returned until just now, and he needed a few hours of rest before they set off.

"What did you find out yesterday about the person here from Emperion?" Darmik asked.

Yawning, Neco answered, "According to my spies, he arrived via a military ship."

Chills surged through Darmik. A boat from Emperion was here? The only other time a non-merchant ship came to Greenwood Island was when it arrived to take Darmik to Emperion for military training.

"According to the dock's records," Neco continued,

"the vessel is still in port. There is no scheduled departure date."

Darmik had the sudden urge to run to Rema and protect her. It didn't make any sense, but he was sure this had something to do with her. "What's the size of the ship?"

Neco leaned forward, his arms resting on his legs. "Small, meant for speed. If I had to guess, maybe two dozen soldiers on board."

The implications of Emperion sending soldiers to the island were too great for Darmik to wrap his brain around. It was time for Neco and Darmik to leave. "Keep a dozen men watching the boat. Have anyone that leaves it followed."

Neco nodded.

"I had a visitor last night," Darmik said, abruptly changing the subject. "Her name was Cassie. Recognize it?"

"I'll talk, if you talk," Neco said, smiling.

"Not here," Darmik said, just in case anyone was nearby. He didn't want to risk Rema's safety. "I just want to know if you trust her."

"Cassie?" Neco asked.

"No, the other one." Ellie, Darmik thought, not wanting to say her name aloud.

"Absolutely. She was instrumental in certain events."

The rescue? Did that make Ellie a rebel? "Where does that put you?" Darmik whispered. "And your loyalties?"

"To you," Neco responded without hesitation.

"She's not one of *them*," he continued. "But was asked to help, and did. Said it was the right thing to do." Respect shone on Neco's face.

That was enough for Darmik. "Very well." He nodded, believing Ellie could be trusted. "We'll talk later." He owed Neco an explanation. His friend had, after all, followed him through the Middle Mountains without question. Well, mostly without question—which left Neco dangling from a cliff. And Neco was about to follow Darmik for a second time.

The office door flew open. Darmik spun around to ream whoever had opened it without knocking when he saw what stood framed by the archway.

An emerald green tunic with an embroidered sun—an Emperion soldier.

"Commander Darmik," the man said with a thick accent. He had blond hair, blue eyes, and fair skin. It looked like he was in his late twenties, early thirties.

"Yes?" Darmik said, refusing to stand. He wanted to maintain his position of authority so he wouldn't rise to greet him. Neco tensed.

"I seek an audience with you," the Emperion soldier stated.

"Enter." Darmik gestured to an empty chair.

The soldier glanced to Neco. "I seek an audience with King Barjon and Prince Lennek as well. They would not come here to your office. I wish for you to join me in the Throne Room." The man chose his words carefully. This was no low-ranking soldier.

"Your name?" Darmik asked.

A slow smile spread across the man's face. "Call

me Captain," he answered.

"I'll join you shortly," Darmik said, dismissing him.

Captain stood his ground. "I will wait to escort you there."

Darmik clutched his hands into fists, forcing himself to remain calm. It would serve no purpose if he attacked *Captain*. Why wouldn't the man give a name? Did he think himself above Darmik? Darmik was the commander and wouldn't back down.

"Do I need to have you removed from the compound?" Darmik asked. He would not give this man power. After all, Darmik went to the same military school and received the same training as this soldier, and Darmik outranked him.

Captain smiled. "I'll wait for you outside the guardhouse."

A compromise then. Darmik gave a curt nod.

When the door closed, Darmik leaned down to Neco. "You're not going to get a chance to sleep. Go pack and be ready. Have one of my elite squads prepare for departure. No one is to know our destination." Darmik stood and straightened his tunic. "I suggest you tell *her* to get out while she can."

"And Cassie?" Neco whispered.

Darmik wanted to help. The child was Lennek's and technically Darmik's nephew. "I don't know," he mumbled. "Tell her to leave as well. I'll figure something out." Darmik supposed it was the right thing to do, even if it wasn't the easiest or most convenient.

ЯЄᎠ

Inside the Throne Room, King Barjon sat on his royal chair, Lennek slouched on the chair beside him.

Darmik and Captain strolled down the aisle to join them. No one else was present. Not even a single soldier, save the one walking next to Darmik. The man hadn't said a single word since leaving the military compound.

King Barjon tapped his finger, looking perturbed. Lennek appeared to be on the verge of falling asleep.

"Thank you all for meeting with me," Captain said, bowing before the king.

"What's this about?" King Barjon demanded. "You're a guest here and hold no authority to order me around."

Captain stood staring at the king, his cheek twitching. "Your Majesty, has Lord Trell been brought to the castle?"

King Barjon pointed to Darmik. "My son has sent a squad to fetch the old man."

Captain turned his focus to Darmik. "And have your men returned? I understand Werden isn't far from here."

"Trell was found dead," Darmik quickly lied.

"And the body?" Captain asked.

Darmik kept his eyes focused on Captain's, careful not to blink. "Burned, as is the custom for traitors."

Captain held his gaze. Darmik wasn't sure if he bought the lie. Captain turned his attention back to the dais. "It has been brought to Emperor Hamen's attention that a girl by the name of Rema was living at this castle, engaged to Prince Lennek?" He looked to Lennek for confirmation.

"I'd prefer not to discuss the whore," Lennek said, still slouched on his chair. "And why would the emperor care about some merchant girl?" His hand fluttered in the air before him, as if he couldn't even be bothered to discuss such matters.

Captain turned his attention to Darmik, a shrewd look on his face. The corners of his mouth twitched slightly. "What say you?" he asked.

Darmik had to assume Captain was sent here to Greenwood Island for a specific reason, and that reason appeared to be Rema and the rebels. But why?

Trell's voice echoed in Darmik's mind—something about Rema's blood tying everything together. Darmik knew she was the blood heir to Greenwood Island's throne. He recalled King Barjon's account of how the island was populated. About a hundred years ago, the emperor of Emperion arranged a truce with a neighboring kingdom. The result was a marriage treaty between their children. The emperor's son, Prince Nero, was in love with a girl from the lower class and refused to enter into the marriage treaty. Thus, Prince Nero doomed Emperion to imminent war. Prince Nero fled Emperion with the girl he loved, Atta, and three ships with approximately one hundred people. They came here, and Prince Nero declared himself king of Greenwood Island.

That meant that Rema was a direct descendent

of Nero—and thus had a claim to the Emperion throne, perhaps even a more legitimate claim than the current emperor did.

Her blood tied everything together.

The emperor must have figured out who Rema was, and he wanted her dead. Captain was most likely an assassin sent there to kill her.

Captain smiled. "You know, don't you?" he said to Darmik in a low voice, so the king and Lennek couldn't hear.

But how in the world did the emperor figure out Rema's true identity?

Captain turned toward King Barjon, "I came here to confirm the execution, but since that failed, now I'm here to ensure its success."

"Why does the emperor care?" the king asked, leaning back on his chair.

"He wants confirmation that you are capable of leading this kingdom. In order for this to be the case, we need to find Rema. Is Commander Darmik heading up the search?"

"Yes," Lennek seethed. "My brother is looking for her. It's been weeks and what does he have to show for it?" Lennek stood, coming before Darmik. "I want her found and brought before *me*. I want to kill her myself this time. Slowly. I want to see her life slip from her, to watch her beg for mercy." Lennek's eyes gleamed with anticipation.

"Prince Darmik," Captain said, "will you be able to find this girl?" His tone was mocking, almost as if he were talking to a child.

"Yes," Darmik replied.

"I'm wondering if you really are *capable,*" Captain said, his tone sharp. "You may have been trained by Emperion, but you haven't been in war like I have."

There was a lethalness to Captain. It reminded Darmik of a viper—quick to strike and very deadly.

"I said I'd find her, and I will." Darmik knew something was wrong. He felt like he was being pushed into a corner.

"But you haven't," Lennek said, moving back to his chair. "I, too, doubt whether you're capable."

"Enough," King Barjon interjected. "Work together. Find her and bring her to the castle."

Work together? Was his father referring to Darmik working with Captain or with Lennek? Both options were out of the question. "Father," Darmik said, "I said I'll find her, and I will. Send this *Captain* home and let me do my job."

Lennek laughed. "How hard can it be to find one person? You have the entire army at your disposal. Even I could do a better job than you. Why don't you just let Captain take over? I'm sure even he can locate her faster."

"Exactly," Captain said, smiling. "I have a proposal. Everyone up for a fun, friendly wager?" Captain looked too pleased with himself. Darmik knew he'd walked right into whatever trap Captain set.

The king looked weary. Darmik knew he would never hand the army over to an Emperion soldier. King Barjon may despise his son, but he trusted Darmik more than an outsider. "What do you have in mind?" the king asked.

"A contest of sorts," Captain said. "Darmik against

Lennek. First brother to find Rema wins."

The king brightened to this idea. "What are the stakes?" King Barjon asked.

"If Lennek wins, he can privately do whatever he wants with Rema before she's executed. And Darmik is removed as commander. You can send him to Emperion with me."

"And when I win?" Darmik asked, a hard edge to his voice.

Captain smiled. "If you deliver Rema to King Barjon first, you keep your position as commander, and a simple, public execution will be held with you as the hero for her capture."

King Barjon laughed.

"I don't know the land as well as Darmik," Lennek whined.

"It won't matter. You'll have half a company, two platoons of five hundred men total, at your disposal," King Barjon said, "including Captain here."

A wicked smile spread across Lennek's face. "Deal."

Nineteen

Rema

"No," Savenek yelled, "other side!"

Rema screamed in frustration. This particular series of moves was difficult. "I don't understand why I have to be able to disarm my opponent with my bare hands."

"Because," Savenek snapped, "your opponent most likely will be stronger and able to disarm you of your weapon in a matter of seconds. You need to be able to evade his own weapon, and if possible, disarm him."

"Fine." Rema understood his reasoning, even if the task seemed impossible. "Let's try it again."

"No, you need a break." Savenek went to the corner of the training room and grabbed two leather-skin water pouches. He handed one to Rema as he sat on the ground.

Plopping down across from Savenek, Rema took a drink and then lay down on the ground, trying to catch her breath before they began the exercise again.

"How's your leg?" he asked.

Rema peered over at Savenek. He never made

small talk with her, and she wondered what he was up to. "Much better, thank you."

"Mako mentioned to me that you know Darmik."

Just hearing Darmik's name aloud made Rema's heart skip a beat. She eyed Savenek with suspicion. Was he being nice in an attempt to get information from her? Mako didn't ask her anything about her stay at the castle since that day in his office. It was only a matter of time before they pushed her.

Savenek took a drink, waiting for her answer.

"He stayed at the castle during my brief time there," Rema carefully said.

"Did you have an opportunity to speak to him?"

Even though she vividly remembered the way Darmik look revolted by the mere sight of her that day Lennek caught them kissing, she couldn't betray him. All the time they spent together was fresh in her mind.

"Why do you ask?"

"Did you know he went to Emperion for his military training? Mako says he's the best of the best. In the short amount of time that he's been the commander, he's managed to restructure the army. People are lining up to join—and this is a time when everyone hates the king." There was a hint of respect in the way he spoke of Darmik.

Rema knew Savenek wanted to be the commander of this compound's army. Mako held the position right now, but Vesha said Mako was grooming him to take over once the new monarchy was in place.

"Yes," Rema finally answered, "Darmik told me."

"He told you?" Savenek's eyes lit up, and he leaned

forward. "What else did you two talk about?"

"Nothing," Rema said as she sat up. "Lennek and Darmik are scum, and I despise them both." She turned away from Savenek and took another drink.

"I'm sorry," Savenek said. "I forgot you spent time in the dungeon."

Rema didn't want to discuss her time in the castle. She didn't want to think about the evil way Lennek treated her or about her feelings for Darmik. "Let's get back to work." Rema stood, ready to put her hurt and anger into her fighting.

Savenek sat still, studying her for a moment. When he got up, he asked, "Did you ever figure out why Lennek chose to marry you?"

The way Savenek said it implied that no one in their right mind would choose to marry her. Rema knew she was only a merchant's niece, not of the noble class, so a prince shouldn't have even noticed her. But it wasn't like Lennek decided to marry her because he loved her; that was far from the case. Rema suspected she was some sort of pawn between the brothers, and that Lennek choose her because of something Darmik did. "I don't know," she said, unable to look Savenek in the eyes.

"I think you do," he whispered.

Rema forced herself to meet Savenek's gaze. "I have my suspicions, but none of that matters now."

"You're the niece of a once-great military captain, now horse farmer. I think there's more going on than some mere coincidence, don't you?"

"No," Rema answered, sure it had nothing to do with that. "I was simply in the wrong place at the wrong time. Now, let's get back to work."

Rema stood with her legs shoulder-width apart, arms at her sides, relaxed. Savenek picked up his sword and slowly moved toward her. When he raised the weapon, she stepped to the side, her back against his chest, coming in close, so he couldn't swing. Then she spun around and hit the back of his head.

"Perfect," Savenek said. "Again." They ran the drill several times, speeding it up a little with each run-through. "Last time," Savenek ordered.

As Rema did countless times, she stepped to the side as Savenek raised his sword. When her back touched his chest, she was about to step away, but his arm came up, encircling her. She froze.

"What are you going to do?" he asked, his breath brushing the hair by her ear.

Feeling his arm just above her breast, Rema blushed at the possibility that he could feel her. Thinking back over everything Savenek taught her, she took a step and slammed her foot onto his, then swung her right arm into his groin. Savenek released her with a loud "umph."

"Excellent," he said, hunching over. "But maybe next time, since we are practicing, you could hit with a little less force."

Rema smiled.

⁂

Savenek stood at the archway, waiting for her. "I'll walk you to the mess hall." Not once had he offered to walk Rema anywhere. After they finished their morning session, he usually took off to eat with his friends.

Since she was going that way, Rema joined him, not sure what to make of this turn of events. Perhaps he was finally getting over her beating him at the horse race, or maybe something changed between them the night he tended to her cramped muscle. Whatever the case, Rema was glad he now treated her with some measure of kindness.

When they entered the mess hall, Rema spotted Vesha sitting alongside Audek. Rema took a small loaf of bread and some cheese. "See you later," she called over her shoulder to Savenek as she moved toward her friends.

Savenek grabbed her arm. "Wait." He threw some food on his plate. "I'll eat with you." Stunned, Rema didn't know what to do, so she just nodded.

When they reached the table, Rema sat next to Vesha, assuming Savenek would sit on the other end by Audek. However, Savenek slid on the bench beside Rema. She felt Vesha staring at her with wide eyes. Rema had no idea what was going on, so she proceeded to eat her food like nothing was amiss.

"Savenek," Audek laughed, "finally decided to join us?" Savenek ignored his friend and continued eating his bread and cheese. "I knew our dear Rema would finally win you over. No one can resist her charm." Audek moved his eyebrows up and down, smiling.

Rema's face reddened. She longed to reach over and smack Audek on the back of his head.

"Oye," Audek yelled. Rema glanced up in time to see a bread roll hit him in the eye. "What did you do that for?"

"You deserved it," Savenek answered.

Vesha stood, picked up her plate, and left without saying a word. Rema shoved a piece of bread in her mouth and jumped up, taking off after Vesha. Rema caught up to her outside the mess hall in the corridor.

"You know how I feel about him," Vesha said, turning to face Rema.

"Yes, I do," Rema said. "You have nothing to be upset over." Vesha may be in love with Savenek, but Rema certainly wasn't.

"They why did he sit next to you?" Vesha asked, lowering her head in defeat.

"We've been training together. That's all. Him sitting next to me means nothing. You don't need to worry—I promise."

"I'm sorry," Vesha said, tears in her eyes. "It's just that I've been in love with him for as long as I can remember."

Vesha had told Rema that her feelings for Savenek were nothing more than a fling. Rema suspected it was more, and now she had confirmation. "Savenek and I work together," Rema assured her. "We're not even friends. You have nothing to worry about."

Vesha hugged Rema. "Thank you," she whispered in Rema's ear. "I have to help my mother in the infirmary. I'll see you later." She turned and quickly walked away.

Rema went back inside the mess hall. Sitting down between Audek and Savenek, she resumed her meal in silence. When Rema finished, Savenek stood and picked up her plate along with his own. Before she could say anything, Savenek nodded his head toward the door. Rema followed him.

"Where are we going?" she asked. All of their training sessions were held inside the same room.

"You'll see." They exited the castle, and Savenek led her into the forest and down a slope. They came to an area where the trees weren't as thick. There were targets placed about thirty yards away.

Savenek went over to a small storage shack. He pulled out two bows and quivers filled with arrows. "This is our archery range."

Rema froze. She knew how to shoot. Bren had been the one to teach her. She couldn't think of archery without thinking of Bren.

"What's wrong?" Savenek asked. "It's not that hard. I'll show you."

The image of Bren being struck with a sword was seared into her mind. Rema shuddered, trying to banish the image of her dead friend.

"What is it?" Savenek asked, coming to stand beside her.

"Nothing." Her voice came out hoarse.

"I don't believe you," he softly said. "You look like you're remembering something horrific."

The fact that Savenek could ascertain that much just by her facial expressions unnerved Rema. It reminded her of Darmik. She glanced up into his brown eyes, trying to figure him out. "Why do you care?" she asked. What had happened to the cold, aloof Savenek?

"Never mind." Savenek sighed.

Rema stepped back, trying to put some space between them. A friendly and sympathetic Savenek was something she was not prepared for. Rema didn't want to let anyone in her heart again because it was too painful when they died or betrayed her.

"Show me how you hold this thing," Rema demanded. Even though she knew how to shoot, she decided to pretend like she didn't. This bow was much larger than the one she was used to, and it had a very different feel.

After Savenek determined she was right eye dominant, he showed her how to hold the bow with her left arm.

"Good," he said, watching her. "Now you need to learn how to stand."

Savenek walked around Rema, surveying her body. She felt her cheeks warm, but she maintained her stance, waiting for Savenek to say something. He stopped before her and crossed his arms.

"What?" Rema asked.

"Turn to the side more."

"Like this?" Rema asked.

"No." He moved behind her to where she could no longer see him. Suddenly, his hands grabbed her hips, and he twisted her body to the correct angle. "Like this. Now spread your feet further apart, so they align with your shoulders."

Rema did as he instructed, adjusting to the correct position. With his hands still on her hips, she was nervous. When Bren taught her how to shoot, he never touched her. He simply modeled how it was done, and she imitated him. With Savenek's hands on her hips, she felt vulnerable and wondered if he was doing it on purpose.

"Is it necessary to touch me in order to teach me?" Rema asked, trying to sound confident, as if he didn't unnerve her. Why was her body responding this way to him? She didn't like Savenek that way and didn't want the confusion his presence brought.

Savenek released her, taking a step back. "Don't flatter yourself." He picked up his own bow, and then proceeded to show Rema how to nock the arrow.

He made her practice nocking the arrow and getting into position with one swift motion. It came naturally to Rema, since she was familiar with a smaller bow. The only difference was the draw weight was heavier with this one, requiring more muscle, but she welcomed the change—it kept her mind off Savenek.

"Very good," he said. "Now aim at the target." Rema did as instructed. "If you shoot like that," Savenek laughed, "you're going to completely miss." He came up behind her. "I'm need to touch you in order to show you the correct position, but this is in no way me coming on to you." His hands slid down the length of her arms, slightly rising them. "You want to angle just above your target, like this." His head was next to hers, his breath moving the hair near her ear. Rema shuddered. "Good."

She felt his body against her back, and she held still, trying not to focus on feeling him; instead, she kept her eyes on the target. Like he said, it wasn't as if he was doing it on purpose, he was simply trying to help her.

"Now focus on the target and release." His hand encircled hers, pulling the string back. Then he released the arrow, and it sailed through the sky, landing on the inner circle of the target. "Excellent," he whispered in her ear.

A shiver ran through her body. Rema knew Savenek was instructing her; however, his interactions felt strangely intimate. His behavior toward her lately was very different from when he first started training her. Why the change? Until recently, Rema was sure she hated Savenek and he her. Rema shook her head, trying to clear it.

"Care to make another bet?" she asked.

After staring at her for a moment, Savenek answered, "I've learned never to bet against you."

"Oh, come on. Let's do a simple wager this time. Person closest to the target gets to ask the other person anything they want. Loser has to answer honestly." She raised her eyebrows, waiting for his response.

Laughing, Savenek answered, "You're on."

After choosing a target about forty yards away, Savenek put on his bracer and lined up to take the first shot. He nocked an arrow and raised his bow, steading it. He released the arrow, and it soared through the air, hitting the inner ring, dead center.

Savenek smiled down at her, and then took a step back, allowing Rema to take her position. She had practiced enough with Bren to be a decent shot, but this bow was unfamiliar. Rema nocked her arrow and raised the bow. She took several deep breaths before releasing it. The arrow landed just outside the inner ring.

"I take it you already knew how to shoot," he said.

"Yes," Rema replied.

"I still beat you." He turned to face her. "Did Kar

teach you how to shoot?"

"No." Rema sighed and sat down on the leaf-covered ground. She'd never even seen Kar touch a bow, much less shoot one. Why Savenek insisted Kar was a soldier was beyond her.

Savenek plopped down next to her, waiting for her to continue.

"My friend, Bren. I was betrothed to him. When Lennek decided he wanted to marry me, he murdered Bren in order to end the contract. I saw Bren pierced in the stomach with a sword. I watched him die." Tears filled her eyes.

"I had no idea," Savenek whispered. "We can go."

"No." Rema shook her head. "I want to stay." Being outside the castle walls made her feel more at home.

"Good," Savenek said, clasping his hands together, "because you still have to answer my question."

"I just did!" Rema exclaimed. "You asked who taught me to shoot, and I told you!"

"I don't think so. That was friendly conversation, and you know it."

"Fine." Rema sighed. "What do you want to know?" When she made the bet, she assumed Savenek would win. She thought that maybe if they talked a bit, she wouldn't feel so awkward or confused around this rough man.

"Out of all the girls throughout the entire kingdom," Savenek said, "why did Lennek choose you?" His eyes bore into hers, as if waiting for some great revelation.

"I have no idea," Rema said, lying on the ground,

staring up at the sky.

"Why do you think? I suspect you have a decent guess."

She did, but she'd never shared her suspicions with anyone—not even her aunt and uncle. This question was simply too personal to answer.

"You're not reneging on a bet, are you?" Savenek chided.

Rema could lie, but she suspected Savenek would know if she was being truthful or not. "Let me ask you something before I answer."

"Quit stalling." Savenek threw a small rock at her arm.

"Why do you want to know?" Rema asked. If Savenek was simply seeking information to further his cause, then she had no intention of telling him.

"I'm curious," Savenek said. "If you like, I can promise not to tell anyone."

Rema turned her head in his direction, wondering how he knew the root of her hesitation. There was something about his eyes that made him look sincere.

Rema finally answered, "I ran into Prince Darmik in the forest one day. We were alone." Savenek's eyes widened. This was clearly something he hadn't expected. Rema continued, "We spoke briefly, then Prince Darmik warned me that Prince Lennek and his men were nearby. He suggested that I slip away unnoticed."

"Why?" Savenek asked. He shook his head in confusion.

"At the time, I thought he was protecting me from Prince Lennek."

"And now?"

"I'm not so sure. Shortly after, I saw Prince Darmik at the governor of Jarko's while I was delivering a horse with Uncle Kar. We spoke briefly. It was enough to garner my uncle and several stable hands' attention. Prince Lennek was staying with the governor at the time."

"What are you suggesting?"

"After my encounter with Prince Darmik, Prince Lennek demanded my acquaintance. I believe the brothers had some sort of bet, and I was simply at the wrong place at the wrong time."

Savenek sat silent for a long time. Then he said, "I believe there's a lot more to your story that you're not telling me."

"Perhaps." Rema smiled.

"Or maybe it's simply your blonde hair and blue eyes. I've never seen anyone with your coloring before." Savenek stood and pulled Rema to her feet. He declared that they were done for the day. Savenek collected the equipment and returned it to the storage shed.

"Are you going to the gathering room tomorrow night?" he asked.

Rema and Vesha usually went to the game room after supper. "No, why?"

"Once a month, we have a free day. That happens to be tomorrow. No training or classes. Mako insists we spend the day with family. Then at night, everyone gets together in the gathering room for a celebration." Savenek started walking back toward the castle.

Rema hurried to catch up. "Does everyone go?"

"Pretty much."

"And tomorrow, will you spend the day with Mako?"

His eyes sliced down to her. "Of course. I consider him my father."

Rema wished Aunt Maya and Uncle Kar were here. She would have loved spending the entire day with them.

"You haven't answered my question," Savenek said. "Are you going tomorrow night?"

"Oh . . ." Rema wasn't sure. She wanted to talk to Vesha about it. "If Vesha is going, then yes, I'll be there."

They climbed up the hill to the fortress. At the top, Savenek turned and looked out over the treetops below. "Vesha always goes. Same with Audek."

"Then I'll be there." The sight was breathtaking. The sun began to set, and the sky turned a bright shade of orange.

"Good," Savenek answered with an awkward look. "I'll see you there." He abruptly turned and went inside the castle, leaving Rema standing alone contemplating this new, and much nicer, Savenek.

☙❧

Mako and Savenek left the fortress before sunrise. Since Rema was alone, she spent the morning reading. In the afternoon, she decided to go to the barn. After a ride, she brushed down River, feeling centered and refreshed.

Upon returning to her bedchamber, Rema found Vesha waiting for her. Vesha wasn't wearing her training clothes; instead, she had on a plain, light gray dress.

"What's the occasion?" Rema asked as she took a seat in the chair opposite her friend.

"There's dancing in the gathering room tonight!"

Dancing? Savenek had only mentioned a celebration. No wonder Vesha was excited. She most likely got to dance with Savenek. Rema gave Vesha a knowing smile. "That explains why you're all dressed up."

"No." Vesha's grin faded. "Savenek sits with Mako and the other adults for the entire evening. He never dances. I think he's afraid to miss anything. He is so focused on overthrowing the king, that he doesn't take time to have any fun."

"What about everyone else?"

"Just the people our age dance. The children play games while the adults sit around, drinking."

Rema wondered why Savenek had asked her if she was going. He was probably just trying to be polite by making sure she knew about it. Rema chuckled; she never thought she would think of Savenek as polite.

"Do you dance?" Rema asked.

"Of course!" Vesha said. "It's a lot of fun."

"Why do you like Savenek?" Rema asked. She hadn't seen Vesha and Savenek together very often, and when they were, he didn't seem to pay any particular attention to her. Not that he was unkind, but he seemed rather indifferent toward her.

"I suppose it's his dedication," Vesha answered frankly. "He's so passionate about what he does—it's contagious. And I find him quite handsome." Vesha blushed.

Rema did not find Savenek even remotely

handsome. When she first met Lennek and Darmik, they stole her breath with their regal beauty. Savenek, on the other hand, was rather plain.

"I'm surprised that Savenek has never talked to me about the rebel's cause."

"Mako must have ordered him not to. He was probably afraid Savenek would scare you off. He can be a little intense."

"And you find that attractive?" Rema asked.

"Have you seen him wield a sword?" Vesha smiled. Rema nodded. Savenek was extremely graceful and skilled when it came to fighting. "I don't know anyone who doesn't find that attractive. Now, go change before we're late."

Rema found herself reluctantly agreeing with her friend.

TWENTY

Darmik

Darmik had sent a messenger late last night, calling up the Tenth Company of soldiers he kept on reserve. They hadn't been needed since Darmik became Commander of the King's Army. The person in charge of the company, Farnek, was a middle-aged man with a large family. Darmik appointed him as captain because not only was Farnek a skilled soldier, capable of organizing and leading several squads of men, but Farnek desired to be near his family. The position of captain for this particular company afforded him the opportunity of a prestigious job close to home.

Farnek entered Darmik's office. "Commander." He saluted Darmik and waited for instructions.

"Sorry to request your presence on such short notice," Darmik said, "but you and your company are needed."

"Of course, Commander," Farnek replied. "I am at your service."

Darmik closed the door, giving them the privacy needed for this conversation. Darmik pointed to the chair before his desk, indicating for Farnek to sit. Darmik took the seat opposite him.

"Half of your company is going to be temporarily assigned to Prince Lennek," Darmik said. Farnek's jaw twitched, but he didn't reply. Darmik continued, "We are having a...game, if you will. Who can find the fugitive first. You will aid Prince Lennek in his quest for victory."

"Is this truly a game? Or simply a training exercise?" Farnek asked.

Placing his elbows on the table, Darmik clutched his hands together and rested his head on top of them. "Neither. This is real. You will be hunting Rema."

Understanding dawned on Farnek's face. "Of course, Commander. We will aid in her capture."

Lowering his voice to a whisper, Darmik said, "If the half of your company should be victorious in capturing Rema before my men and me, I want you to see to her safety."

"I'm sorry, I don't understand." Farnek leaned forward, also lowering his voice to a whisper.

"I want you to personally make sure Rema is not harmed. The rules of the game state that she will be executed here, on the castle grounds. I want to bear witness to the event."

Farnek nodded. "Of course, Your Highness."

"I don't want her delivered here half-dead. If she is, I won't have the opportunity to interrogate her. I want her unharmed—or you'll be released of your position."

Farnek's eyes widened. Darmik had never made such a threat to any of his men before, but he needed to make sure Farnek understood the importance of these instructions.

"And there's one more matter," Darmik said, leaning back on his chair. "A man that goes simply by the name of Captain will be joining Prince Lennek on this venture. I want to be perfectly clear; you only accept orders from Prince Lennek, not Captain. Understood?"

"Yes, Commander."

"Good." Darmik looked directly into Farnek's eyes, holding his attention. "I'm counting on you. Don't disappoint me."

⁊⁊⁊

Standing at the front of the courtyard in the military compound, Darmik gazed out at his men from the Tenth Company, one thousand in all. Nervous energy radiated from them. He'd never called them up before. They'd never been needed—until now.

Captain stood to Darmik's right, Farnek to his left. Clearing his throat, Darmik said, "Thank you all for arriving on such short notice." His voice echoed against the stone walls. Clouds filled the sky, concealing the sun, casting a dull, gray haze to the courtyard.

All one thousand men stood dressed in full uniform at attention.

"I'd like to start off by informing you that this is not a drill," Darmik said. Captain's presence next to him grated on his nerves. Darmik took a step forward, away from Captain and Farnek, in order to distinguish himself and maintain authority. "As some of you may know, a small, rebel resistance is brewing in the villages. These insurgents have managed to capture Rema, a prisoner sentenced for execution. Our mission is to recapture her."

Darmik clasped his hands behind his back. He walked in front of his men, taking the focus away from Captain and Farnek. "You will be split in half. Two platoons will go with me, and two platoons will go with Prince Lennek."

There was a slight intake of breath. Lennek had never shown any interest in the army. "Captain Farnek will be assigned to Prince Lennek."

Darmik choose not to acknowledge the man from Emperion right then. Captain was currently dressed in nondescript clothes—probably so he could blend in with the soldiers.

"Brother." A voice rang through the courtyard, and all soldiers dropped to one knee.

Darmik spun around to find Lennek strolling toward him, a smile across his face. He was dressed in riding gear, his black cape billowing behind him.

Lennek clasped Darmik on the shoulder. "Ready to lose your position as Commander?" He chuckled. "I, for one, am dying to find the slut and see you humiliated."

Darmik was well aware Lennek's voice carried to most of the soldiers. As unprofessional as Lennek's behavior was, it worked to Darmik's advantage. His men needed to know what was at stake.

Darmik turned to face everyone. "Rise," he commanded. The soldiers stood, awaiting orders. "To make things a little more interesting," Darmik said, "the king has decided to turn this into a *game*." He annunciated the words carefully, making sure to convey his disgust for what was about to take place. He had no intention of losing, and certainly wouldn't hand his army over to Lennek permanently. Darmik would save Rema, and he would save his army.

Lennek smirked as he waved Captain over.

Before either man had the opportunity to step in, Darmik continued, "As I was saying, half of you are going to be following Prince Lennek's command, and half mine. The rules are simple—the first to find Rema wins. We depart in one hour. Dismissed."

Ignoring everyone, Darmik went directly to the weapons room for supplies.

"The Emperion freak is in the barracks, talking to your men," Neco said from the doorway.

Darmik took two additional daggers, strapping them to his arms. "I believe he's an assassin. If I were you, I'd be careful what you call him."

Neco stepped further into the weapons room. "Is he here to assassinate Rema?" he asked in a hushed voice.

"Are you packed and ready to go?" Darmik grabbed one last sword, knowing he'd need a backup for his backup, just in case.

Neco blocked the exit. "Where do I fit in to all of this?" he demanded.

He never spoke to Darmik this way before. Darmik stood there, staring at his friend, wondering why he was behaving in such a manner.

"You're coming with me," Darmik replied.

"And the rest of your personal squad?"

"They'll stay where they are." Darmik didn't want to say Trell's name aloud, especially since Darmik had told Captain that he was dead.

"I know you're not going to want to hear this," Neco said, "but I think you are going to be at a disadvantage not having your most trusted men with you."

"I understand your concerns." Darmik really did. He'd prefer to have his men watching his back. But Darmik had to get back up the Middle Mountains as soon as possible. An assassin, sent by the emperor for the sole purpose of hunting down and killing Rema in order to eliminate any threat to the Emperion throne, would have to be the best of the best of the emperor's killers. Darmik was out of his league. There was no way possible he could travel with his squad of twenty men and expect to eliminate all traces of where they traveled or what they were doing. Captain would hunt them far too easily. The only chance was for Darmik to travel alone—and he knew he couldn't enter the treacherous mountains by himself. He needed Neco.

"I can't risk it," Darmik said. "I need them protecting…the package…and watching the pass."

"You and I are going there alone?"

Darmik nodded. "While everyone else under my command is putting on a merry show of looking for her."

Neco smiled. "I can honestly say that the tunnel isn't looking so bad."

⊗ಾ

When Darmik went to the front of the military compound, he froze. Lennek sat on Nightsky, Darmik's black stallion. Captain was mounted on a horse next to

Lennek, and the five hundred men assigned to him were all on horses. How had Lennek managed to find so many animals? And where was Farnek?

"Brother," Lennek said, "you look like you've seen a ghost."

Captain laughed.

"Where did you acquire these horses?" Darmik asked.

"No idea," Lennek said, shrugging his shoulders. "Captain here rounded them up. He said it would help us cover more ground."

Darmik's eyes sliced over to Captain, who sat staring at Darmik. "Well?' Darmik asked. "Where did they come from?"

"They're yours," Farnek said, coming to stand next to Darmik. "All of your officers' horses. Once Captain confiscated all of them, he went into the city and commandeered more."

Darmik's hands balled into fists. Captain had stolen these horses from their own people. Lennek sat there, smug. He had no idea how upset the citizens would be with him.

"And I've been ordered to stand down," Farnek said.

Suddenly, Neco was beside Darmik, his hand restraining Darmik's wrists. "Careful now," Neco mumbled. "Don't do anything stupid."

Darmik attempted to contain his rage.

Captain smiled. "Now, if you don't mind, we have a game to win."

"Yes," Lennek mused. "And I have a brother to

destroy."

"Let's get moving," Captain said. "I don't care to waste any more time." His horse pranced, and Captain reined him in.

Lennek came closer to Darmik and leaned down. "I have someone to kill. And I swear I will get her. Even if it means I have to kill anyone—and everyone—who gets in my way." Lennek moved his horse forward, pointed his sword in the air, and yelled, "To Jarko!" Kicking his heels into his horse, he took off, the five hundred mounted soldiers rushing to keep up.

"Bloody hell," Darmik said, shaking. "He's going to kill everyone he comes into contact with until he finds Rema."

"He wouldn't," Neco said. "The kingdom would turn on him."

"He doesn't care," Darmik said, seething with rage. "He wants her dead, and he'll do anything to accomplish his goal."

"Sir," Farnek said. "How can I be of service?"

"Join us," Darmik said. "We leave now."

ஒ�->o

Darmik set out with Neco, Farnek, and his two platoons. Every single soldier was forced to walk, even those carrying the food and supplies. There wasn't a single horse left—no doubt part of Captain's plans.

Once outside King's City, Darmik sent one platoon of two hundred and fifty men north. He ordered them to split into units of fifty men once they reached

Werden. One unit was to go to Adder, one to Shano, two to Dresden, and one to Mullen. Darmik sent the other platoon south with Farnek. He instructed Farnek to send soldiers to Jarko, Telan, and Kaven. All men were told to look for Rema in the larger cities. They were to make their presence known, harm no one, and keep their eyes and ears open at all times.

Once Darmik sent all of his men away from the Middle Mountains, he and Neco began their trek up the mountain range, careful not to leave a trail. Darmik thought it prudent to backtrack several times to ensure they weren't being followed. Although Darmik didn't see any indication that Captain was pursing them, he did notice a scouting party of rebels. Darmik and Neco were forced to go out of their way on more than one occasion to avoid being seen. After traveling hard at a brisk pace for several days, they finally entered the tunnel.

Maintaining an extraordinary pace, they exited three days later. Darmik's first order of business was to locate some sort of shelter—one that was well concealed and would provide protection from the elements. Neco found a hole in the ground that connected to a short tunnel, which opened into a cave approximately thirty-feet-by-thirty-feet. There was also an additional tunnel that led to another exit. Since the cave was well suited to their needs, Darmik decided to use it as their shelter while in the Middle Mountains.

The sun was setting, night quickly approaching, and the temperatures plummeting. Darmik and Neco collapsed on their bedrolls. Tomorrow, Darmik would scout the fortress, looking for a way to slip inside unnoticed.

꧂

High in a towering greenwood tree, Darmik sat on a thick branch, watching the wall surrounding the rebel compound. Neco was perched in the same tree on a lower branch.

"There has to be a way in," Darmik mumbled.

Neco chuckled. "There's well over two dozen guards posted on that wall. I'm sure there's even more sentries on the interior. I know you have skill but this, my friend, may be beyond even your abilities."

It was hard to breathe in the Middle Mountains. The air was thin, making Darmik light-headed. Ignoring Neco, Darmik focused on the main entrance to the compound, about fifty yards away.

"How do supplies get in and out?" Darmik asked. "This is a fully functioning city. There has to be a pattern of people coming and going. Something we can use to get in."

As the hours passed, Darmik's hope dwindled. No one came or left the fortress. The main gate remained shut at all times, heavily guarded by soldiers patrolling the wall with bows slung over their shoulders.

"This might not be as easy as I had assumed," Darmik finally admitted. "Perhaps I could scale the wall?"

Neco didn't respond. He shifted in the tree, watching.

Darmik searched the surrounding land, looking for any sort of trails indicating another entrance.

"So," Neco said, breaking the silence. "I know you're not keen on…talking. But I'd really like to know what you plan to do if you get inside. Capture Rema? Warn her?" He climbed higher in the tree until he was on an adjacent branch, level with Darmik.

Darmik sighed, glancing sideways at his friend. "You have a right to know," he said. "But I want to ask you a few questions first."

Neco nodded.

"What do you think of the state of things in our kingdom?" he asked, leaning back against the tree trunk, trying to get more comfortable.

"Is this conversation private?" Neco asked.

"It is," Darmik confirmed. "Never to go beyond the two of us."

"My loyalty is to you, my commander and prince," Neco said. "I will do whatever you ask or demand of me."

Darmik was thankful to hear Neco's undying loyalty for him. It made what he was going to reveal a little easier.

"And the king?" Darmik asked.

Neco's eyes narrowed. "Like I said, my loyalty is to *you*."

"I understand," Darmik said. "My question is how you personally feel about the king and the direction he's taking this kingdom."

"Honestly?"

"Please."

"I don't like it. I hope you will one day have the strength and power to change things."

Darmik felt a mixture of emotions. Pride that his

friend had such faith in him—sad that he hadn't done more. Of course, Darmik was about to rectify that.

"And the rebels?" Darmik inquired.

"I hope their intentions are honorable, and they make positive changes to our kingdom."

It was time for one last question before Darmik revealed all. "How does Ellie fit into all of this?"

A ghost of a smile flitted across Neco's face. "We met a year ago. I've been secretly courting her ever since."

"Is she part of the rebel movement?"

"No," Neco said. "But she's crossed paths with them."

"Explain," Darmik demanded.

"Before Rema was brought to the castle, a rebel approached Ellie and said that a girl would arrive bearing the key."

"How do you know this?"

"Ellie confided in me, unsure of what to do. Then Rema arrived and showed Ellie her key necklace, with a secret message inside. I helped research and decode it, without Rema's knowledge."

How had Darmik not known the key necklace was a symbol? And the ruby—red—the color of the previous royal family. So many clues that he'd missed.

"The key mentions Commander Mako. Once we realized that, and heard the rumors of an heir being alive, the rest fell into place."

"Do you know who the heir is?" Darmik asked, holding his breath.

"I have my suspicions, although they haven't been confirmed. In the key necklace, Mako's name is spelled backwards—okam. So we took Rema's name and did the same. Her name backwards is Amer. That's the name of the previous princess, yes? I didn't know this, but some older people, who remember the time before, recognized the name. So I've had my suspicions."

Darmik felt like a huge weight was lifted from his chest. "Yes," he said. "Rema is Amer, the heir. Although, I believe she doesn't know her true identity."

"That's what Ellie thinks, too."

"Where is Ellie now?"

"I told Ellie and Cassie to leave the castle immediately. They're hiding in the city."

A gust of wind blew around the tree, causing the leaves to rustle and the branches to sway. Clouds rolled in, covering the sun, making the temperature drop even lower.

"The purpose of getting inside the compound and talking to Rema is to devise a plan. I want to reveal her identity to her and discuss how to proceed."

"What do you want her to do?" Neco asked.

"Take back the throne."

Neco's eyes widened in shock. "What about you?"

"I plan on helping."

Neco laughed. "I never expected you to turn your back on your family. Don't get me wrong, I believe it's the right thing to do, I just didn't think you'd ever do it."

"Neither did I," Darmik mused.

"I am proud to call you my prince, commander, and friend."

Darmik had never felt so honored. However, taking back the throne meant he would no longer be a prince or commander.

"Just one last question," Neco said. "How do you feel, personally, about Rema?" The corners of Neco's lips turned up, fighting a smile.

Darmik rolled his eyes and squatted on the branch. "It's time to go back to the cave."

"You like her, don't you?" Neco laughed.

"Let's go." Darmik took hold of the branch, lowering himself to the one beneath it.

"Oh, come on. I confided in you about Ellie."

"Fine," Darmik grunted, his feet landing on the branch. "I like her."

"Tell you what," Neco said as he shimmied down the tree trunk. "You do a perimeter run, and I'll cook dinner."

Twenty-One

Rema

Rema had only ever attended two dances. One was at the governor of Jarko's home, by force. The other was her engagement celebration at the castle, again by force. Neither experience was particularly appealing, so Rema had no idea what to expect from the festivities that night. Entering the gathering room, Rema was surprised by the sheer number of people in attendance. Everyone who lived in the fortress must have been there. The room was stifling hot, and the smell of sweat and food hung in the stale air.

Vesha laughed and grabbed Rema's arm, leading her toward the right side of the room where people their age were already dancing. The other end of the room contained tables where most of the adults sat eating, drinking, and talking to one another. Children ran around here and there, happily dodging the watchful eyes of their parents. A group of men played instruments. Two beat on tall drums, one strummed his gamba, while another blew on a zink. The remaining musicians used bows to play their rebecs. The music was lively and unlike anything Rema had ever heard before.

"This is utterly fantastic!" She stood on the perimeter, watching the dancers, allowing her the opportunity to learn the steps. Rema spotted Audek, red faced and sweating, merrily dancing alongside a few girls. When he noticed Vesha and Rema, he headed their way.

"Ladies." Audek bowed before them. "Care to dance?" It was difficult to hear him over the loud music.

Vesha laughed at his formality. "You want to dance with the both of us? At the same time?"

"Of course!" Audek said. "I can handle two beautiful women."

They each took hold of one of Audek's arms as he led them to the dancing area. The song ended, and everyone stopped to clap and cheer for the musicians. The volume was deafening. Audek swung Rema and Vesha in front of him and they lined up, waiting for the next tune to begin.

"You appear to be short a partner," a male voice said from behind Rema. She turned to find Savenek standing there.

"You're dancing?" Audek asked in disbelief.

"It appears that I am," Savenek said, his attention focused solely on Rema. "I can't allow you to be without a partner at your first celebration with us."

Glancing at Vesha, Rema saw her friend's smile vanish. "Perfect," Rema replied. "You can dance with Vesha while I dance with Audek." Rema took hold of Vesha's shoulders and placed her in front of Savenek, and then stood before Audek.

The music started up again. It was another fast-paced song. Audek grinned as he locked arms with Rema and they spun around, clapping and moving down the line. When they faced one another again, Audek raised his eyebrows and bent toward her. "Nice move back there."

Rema didn't respond. Instead, she focused on her feet, trying to keep up as they danced a quick, eight-step pattern.

Audek spoke again. "Vesha looks happy, but I'm not so sure about our dear friend Savenek."

Vesha smiled as she merrily danced. Savenek's face was closed, revealing no emotion.

"He likes you," Audek said.

"Why do you think that?" Rema asked. "He never acknowledges me outside of training." She spun around again, clapping her hands and moving back into the box step.

"He ate with you." Audek laughed, while moving around Rema. "And he just asked you to dance. Trust me, for Savenek, that's more than he's ever done for anyone."

"What about Vesha?"

"They're friends, that's all, no matter how much Vesha wants it to be more. He's just not interested in her in any other capacity than friendship."

The room was warm from so many people. Rema began to sweat. The song ended, and everyone applauded.

"So," Audek whispered, standing next to Rema, "what are you going to do about our mutual friend?"

"Nothing," Rema replied. "I'm not even interested in having him as a friend. Besides, my loyalty lies with Vesha."

The music started back up, and everyone started

dancing again.

"Care for another romp around the dance floor?" Audek smiled sardonically at Rema.

"No," she replied. "I'm hot, and I need to get something to drink."

"I was just heading over to grab something to eat," Savenek said, suddenly standing before Rema. "Care to join me?"

Audek grabbed Vesha by the hand, swinging her around him. They melted into the crowd of dancers, leaving Rema and Savenek alone.

Rema was starving. She hadn't eaten anything since her ride. She agreed, and Savenek led her to the other side of the room. They found an empty end at a table near the corner. Rema took a seat, while Savenek went and got two plates piled high with food.

"Here you go," Savenek said, sliding a plate in front of her. He took a seat directly across from her. "See, we are doing something outside of training."

"Yes," Rema mused, "but I'm wondering why." She bit into her chicken. This side of the room wasn't nearly as loud or stuffy.

Savenek grinned mischievously. "I want to recruit you."

"I was wondering when you'd start. In case you haven't noticed, I'm not fighting material."

"Are you kidding?" Savenek said with a mouthful of food. "You pick up the techniques fast. We could use you."

"Why? You seem to have enough people here."

"We need everyone we can get. Especially those

with some intelligence. Don't you want to see Barjon overthrown?" His excitement was contagious. Rema found herself wanting to agree with him, but she held herself back.

"It depends," she carefully said. "Mako mentioned that an heir from the previous royal family exists." Savenek nodded. "Have you met this person?"

"No. But what does it matter?"

"How can you remove one ruler and place someone else on the throne without knowing what that person stands for? What if this heir you so desperately believe in is worse than Barjon? After all, he's been in hiding for seventeen years. What does he know about the politics of our kingdom? Does he even know how to rule?"

Savenek sat very still, staring at Rema. After several moments, he said, "Mako believes in this heir. And I trust Mako."

"Still," Rema continued, "don't you think it a bit naïve to overthrow one king when you don't even know who the next one is going to be?"

Savenek's eyes slid past her. Rema glanced back and found Mako standing behind her with a warm smile. "Care if I join you two?" he asked.

"We would be honored," Rema said, sliding over to make room for him.

Mako sat down. "I see Savenek is trying to get you to join our cause."

Savenek's attention was on his food in front of him.

"He is," Rema said. "Before I can dedicate myself to something like this, I have questions."

"Of course you do," Mako said. "But now is not the time. Tonight is for celebrating our freedom and hard work. We can talk politics another day."

"Is there any word on my aunt and uncle?" Rema asked.

Mako glanced to Savenek. "Yes, they are well. No need to worry."

Rema wished he'd tell her more but was glad she at least knew they were well. Several large, burly men holding pewter mugs sat down next to Mako and Savenek.

One patted Mako on the back. "Making progress." He took a sip from his mug. "I just wish the king didn't have his army all over the place searching for us right now. It'll be harder to attack with them spread out."

"Can you believe the massacre down in Jarko?" another man asked.

Rema's head shot up. She hadn't heard anything about a massacre.

Savenek stood. "Rema, care to join me for a dance?" Rema didn't feel like dancing. She wanted to hear what these men had to say about Jarko.

"Good idea," Mako said to her. "Go have fun. You don't want to hear us old men talk all night."

Savenek came around and took Rema's arm, pulling her up and leading her away.

"I'm from Jarko," Rema said.

"I know. Trust me; you don't want to hear what they have to say."

"I do!" Rema said, trying to pull her arm free.

Savenek tightened his grip. "When you join our

cause, you can be privy to that sort of information."

Rema stood still, looking into Savenek's eyes. "So that's it? Join and you'll give me information? Or don't and you'll keep me in the dark? I have a right to know! Bren's family is in Jarko. My aunt and uncle are there right now!"

"You're a spoiled brat!" Savenek spit. "The world doesn't revolve around you. Would you put the lives of everyone here in jeopardy just so you can know what's going on? You're a stupid girl who doesn't know anything." He released her arm. His face was an angry shade of red as they stood still in the middle of the room, between the dancers and the tables, facing one another.

It felt as if everyone in the room faded away, and Rema only saw Savenek. At least now, she really knew what he thought about her.

She slapped him across the face so hard her hand stung.

He grabbed her wrist, restraining her.

"I know you have the misguided notion you're ready to command an army. Well, you're not." Rema was seething mad. "You've devoted your life to fighting a cause you don't truly understand. What do you know of the royal family? Nothing but what Mako tells you. You want to restore the throne to someone you've never even met. I'm not the naïve one, you are. Have you ever even been in battle? Have you watched someone you love die before your very eyes? You may know how to wield a sword and shoot an arrow, but you don't know the first thing about being a real leader."

Savenek's face was bright red where she'd hit him.

His eyes were glassy and it looked like he wanted to tear her to pieces. Rema pulled her arm free and stormed out of the gathering hall, the music floating into the corridor as she ran away.

The walls felt like they were closing in. She didn't ask to be here. All she wanted was to be home with her aunt and uncle. Mako said she wasn't a prisoner, but she felt like one. Her river—she needed her river. She longed for the freedom of running through the forest and jumping from her cliff into the cool water below.

Searching through hallway after hallway, Rema finally found the small, wooden door Savenek had led her through when he took her outside the castle walls. She slid the lock open and unlatched it. Frigid air slammed against her body as Rema stepped outside. She carefully shut the door behind her. The moon was bright, lighting the sky enough for Rema to see her way without tripping and falling.

It was stupid to be out in this weather. Rema knew she couldn't make it down the mountainside. She was high up in the Middle Mountains with no way back to Jarko, no way to find her aunt and uncle. But she couldn't be inside the confining walls right now. Otherwise, she'd suffocate. All Rema wanted was freedom.

Spreading her arms, the icy wind whipped around her body, giving her the allusion of flying. She just needed some time alone. Perhaps there was a water source nearby where she could sit and calm down. The archery range was down this hill, and she had no desire to go there. Walking to the other side of the fortress, Rema found a dirt path covered with frost, which disappeared between several trees. She followed the trail, wondering where it went. After about a hundred yards, she came to a stone wall four times her height. Following alongside it, Rema realized that it must surround the entire castle. Staying in the shadows cast by the wall, she glanced up and saw that there were soldiers on top, looking out away from the castle, each armed with a bow.

Rema walked along the wall until she came to a wooden door. There was a soldier directly above. Searching the ground, Rema found two rocks the size of her hand. She slowly slid the long bolt open, pulling the door toward her. After slipping to the other side, she wedged a rock between it and wall so she wouldn't be locked out. Rema threw the remaining rock inside the compound. The soldier above turned and looked back in the direction of the sound. Rema took the opportunity to run into the cover of the trees about twenty feet away.

She kept jogging, trying to stay in a straight line so she'd be able to find her way back. After heading downhill for several minutes, Rema slowed. There was a large boulder up ahead. It was taller than she was, but there were enough other rocks surrounding it that she had no trouble climbing it. The top of the boulder was dusted with snow. Pulling her legs to her chest, Rema sat and breathed in the chilly night air. Thousands of stars loomed overhead in the clear night sky. It seemed that if she reached her hand out, she could touch them.

Now that she wasn't moving, Rema's fingers turned numb, and her entire body shook. She'd been running on adrenaline, and now it was gone.

"And here I thought it was going to be difficult

getting you alone."

Rema jumped, twisting to face the direction the voice came from. "Who's there?" she asked, her breath coming out in a white puff, hanging in the air before her.

A cloaked figure detached from a tree, moving toward the rock. "You're going to freeze in a matter of minutes if we don't get you warm."

She knew that voice. But it couldn't be. How had he managed to find her? "Darmik?"

He pushed back his hood. "Shh," he said, "don't use my name."

Was he there to capture and return her to the castle?

"Come down from there. We need to talk." Darmik pushed the side of his cape back, revealing his sword. A dagger was in his left hand.

"So you can take me to Lennek to be executed? I don't think so." Rema glanced around, looking for something she could use as a weapon to defend herself.

"No," he whispered. "All I want to do is talk. I promise to see you safely returned behind the fortress wall." Darmik pointed toward the direction she'd just come from. "Hurry, we mustn't been seen, and we need to get you warm."

Rema slid down the rock. It was stupid of her to leave the protection of the castle. She could no longer feel her hands, and her legs were beginning to go numb. Her ears and nose were so painful that she feared they might fall off. Rema would either freeze to death, or Darmik would kill her.

In one swift move, Darmik removed his cape and

draped it around her body. "Follow me," he ordered, "and no talking. We don't want to alert anyone."

Rema contemplated running—but she wouldn't get far until she tripped and fell, froze, or Darmik got her. The only option was to follow him, hoping he stayed true to his word and safely returned her to the fortress. Rema wasn't sure she could actually move, but the warmth of the cloak and the familiar smell of horse gave her the strength to carry on. They wove between trees for about a quarter of a mile until they came to a large rock.

Darmik scanned the area, and then removed some branches, revealing a dark hole three feet wide. Before Rema had a chance to say anything, Darmik took hold of her arms and lowered her into the hole. It was pitch black inside.

"Bend your legs a bit," Darmik said. "I'm going to release you. There's a two-foot drop."

He let go. Rema felt herself falling, but only for a second. Her feet slammed into the ground, and she quickly regained her balance.

"Move out of the way," Darmik called down. She heard a rustling sound, and then a thump next to her.

Light appeared before her eyes. Darmik stood, holding a small torch. "This way." He turned and walked away from her. Rema looked back in time to see that the hole was again covered with branches.

Rema hurried after Darmik. Light bounced off the low ceiling and walls as they moved through some sort of tunnel. The only sound was the crunching noise from their feet walking on the dirt ground.

Where was Darmik taking her and why? If he

wasn't there to capture and return her to Lennek, then what did he want? Darmik moved through the tunnel with familiar ease. His hair was a little longer than the last time she'd seen him. The plain clothing he wore reminded her of when she met him by the Somer River. Rema's heart squeezed. She was supposed to hate this man—he betrayed her, right? She recalled Mako saying that Darmik let him escape with her. Yet Darmik had left her to rot in the dungeon and be executed. So why was she feeling drawn to him? Why did she want to hug him?

After ten yards, the tunnel opened into a small cavern. There was a fire in the center, along with a man. "Neco," Darmik said, "give us a moment alone." The man stood and exited through a different tunnel. "Sit." Darmik pointed to the fire. "You need to warm yourself."

Rema dropped to her knees before the fire, practically putting her hands in the flames trying to warm them. Darmik draped a heavy, wool blanket around her shoulders, on top of the cloak. She needed to be alert, and keep her head on straight. Rema avoided looking at Darmik, not wanting to get lost in the depth of his brown eyes.

Feeling gradually returned to Rema's fingers and toes. She sighed, knowing it was time to figure out what was going on. "Why are you here?" she asked.

Darmik sat down on the other side of the fire, across from her. His face gave no hint of his thoughts or emotions. He didn't respond.

Rema glanced around. Two bedrolls were off to the side, along with two sacks. Was it just Darmik and that one other man, Neco? Or were more soldiers there, hidden somewhere?

"What do you want to talk to me about?" Rema asked, returning her attention to Darmik.

His face was covered with whiskers, making him look older and slightly sinister, leaving no trace of the gentleman who once kissed her. "I want you to be completely honest with me. What is your real name?" he asked.

Although he looked a little different, this was still Darmik. He knew her. So why was he asking her such a silly question? "You know my name," she responded.

"I want to hear you say it. Your name."

"Rema."

"Really?"

"What do you want?" Rema dropped her hands into her lap and forced her eyes to meet Darmik's across the fire. Her heart skipped a beat. Although there was a hard edge to him, his eyes were tender.

"Rema isn't listed in the kingdom's birth records," Darmik said. He scooted around the fire until he was sitting to her left. "And do you know the names of your parents?"

"No," she admitted, wanting to put some space between them.

"But Kar and Maya are your aunt and uncle?"

It felt like he was interrogating her. Where was the Darmik she had known and loved? Had it all been an act? "What are you getting at?" Rema's eyes filled with tears. She didn't want to sit here with this man right now.

"Neither Kar nor Maya have any siblings," he

stated.

That didn't make any sense. There was probably just some error in the records then.

"Do you know who Mako is?"

Rema nodded, curious where he was going with this conversation.

"He was the commander of the army for the previous royal family," Darmik said. "The records state his baby daughter is alive." His eyes bore into hers, and she couldn't look away. "But we both know, records can be...incorrect."

"What are you getting at?" Rema asked.

"Seventeen years ago, Mako escaped the castle with a baby. You."

She shook her head. There was no way Mako was her father. What game was Darmik playing? What was he trying to do? Make her mistrust Mako? "I should go," she said, removing the blanket and cloak from her body. She wanted no part of this.

"Just one thing, and then I will escort you back to the fortress." Darmik put his hand on her arm, keeping her in place.

"What?" she whispered.

"Can you explain the tattoo on your shoulder?"

TWENTY-TWO

Darmik

onfusion filled Rema's face.

Darmik wanted to believe she was innocent of treachery, but he had to be sure.

"You're mistaken." Rema smiled as her shoulders relaxed. "That's just a mark from birth." She held her hands out to the fire again, her body shaking, the cloak and blanket lying on the ground beside her.

"It's not a birthmark," Darmik said. He reached for his bag, pulling out two small mirrors and a magnifying glass.

She ducked her head, embarrassed.

"I know my behavior toward you has been appalling since your arrest, but I'd like to explain things from my point of view." Her large, sapphire eyes bore into his. Darmik forced his hands to remain on the objects he held instead of reaching out to her.

Rema bit her bottom lip. Finally, she nodded, not saying a single word.

Relief filled Darmik. She was giving him a chance—that was all he wanted. Darmik pointed toward her left shoulder. "You'll need to remove your arm from your clothing in order to see what I'm talking about."

Rema's face reddened. "Turn away," she demanded.

He twisted his body to give her some privacy. His thoughts drifted to their kiss in her bedchamber. He'd been spellbound in her warm embrace when Lennek walked in and interrupted them. That was when Darmik had first seen her tattoo.

"Okay," she said. Turning back around, Darmik saw her exposed shoulder and arm. Goose bumps covered her flesh. Desire warred with common sense— he wanted to lean forward and caress her skin with kisses. Bloody hell, he needed to maintain control of himself. He couldn't let his want for her cloud his judgment.

Darmik handed Rema a mirror, while he held the magnifying glass up to her shoulder. "Look in the mirror," he instructed. When he saw her face reflected back to him, Darmik raised the second mirror, so she could see the enlarged tattoo.

The mark was pale, almost a soft gray, with delicate lines of red interwoven into a complex symbol— one that appeared near impossible to replicate. It looked like a unique piece of jewelry. The entire tattoo was one inch wide and circular.

Rema dropped the mirror, shattering it. Her entire body shook. "What is that?" she yelled, the color draining from her face. "I don't understand."

"Cover up," Darmik said. "I will explain everything." It felt like the huge chasm that had opened up between them was suddenly closing. His suspicions were confirmed. Rema had no idea she was Princess

Amer.

Darmik watched Rema slip her pale arm back in her sleeve, awkwardly lacing her shirt closed behind her neck.

"All right," Rema said, sitting down next to Darmik, careful to keep a safe distance between them. "Explain." She pulled his cape tight around her body, shivering.

Darmik cleared his throat and started at the beginning. He told her about the rumor he first heard in Telan, shortly after they had met. Darmik told her about the rebels, and everything he'd come to know and understand since his first encounter with them. He even told Rema about his father's proof—the head and tattoos. He told her about Trell and the secret royal tattoo, which led to his discovery that an heir existed. He explained everything in as much detail as he could, except her identity.

Now it was time to reveal that she was indeed the heir.

"As I mentioned before, Mako was Commander for King Revan. What you may not know is that he had a daughter named Tabitha."

Rema froze, reaching for her identification band that wasn't there. Darmik remembered it was marked with the name Tabitha. But the girl before him went by Rema—Amer spelled backwards.

Darmik continued, "I'm certain Mako switched his baby Tabitha with Princess Amer. They would've been about the same age. Mako smuggled Amer out of the castle. Then he placed her with Captain Kar. Now that the princess is of age, Mako and his rebels are ready to restore Princess Amer to the throne."

Darmik took a big breath, letting the air out slowly. "Amer...Rema."

Rema shook her head. "What are you saying?"

"That you are Princess Amer."

"No," Rema whispered. "That's impossible. You have to be mistaken."

"I'm not. I found a painting of you as a baby with the tattoo. You are the true heir."

Rema dropped her head onto her hands, mumbling to herself. He wanted to touch her, comfort her. Instead, he waited for her to understand what he'd just revealed.

"You left me in the dungeon," she said, suddenly looking into his eyes.

Darmik nodded. "I thought you knew your true identity. I didn't realize they'd kept it from you."

Rema inched backwards, away from Darmik. "Do you intend to finish the job now?" she demanded, her face harsh.

Darmik moved to his knees. "Please," he pleaded, "let me explain."

"I don't think so." In one swift motion, she jumped to her feet and grabbed a log from the pile of firewood off to the side. "I won't give you a chance to finish what you started." Rema swung the wood in a fluid gesture, indicating she had some basic combat knowledge.

Did she really think Darmik would hurt her? Of course she did. Looking over his actions, she could draw no other conclusion. He had allowed her to be thrown in the dungeon and be executed. She had no idea of the emotional journey he'd been on or how he felt—it took him long enough to even understand it himself.

Darmik raised his hands in surrender. "I know you have no reason to trust me, but please, let me finish explaining."

"Stay back!" She swung the log and moved further away from Darmik and the fire. She was almost to the tunnel that led outside.

"I thought you knew your identity and used me to gain access to the castle and the throne."

Her eyebrows narrowed, but she held her position.

"I thought you played me for the fool. I was hurt and angry. Despite all that, I realized I have feelings for you. I was about to rescue you myself when Mako beat me to it. I understood then that even if you knew your identity, I didn't want you dead. I realized…that…I love you." The words hung in the air.

Rema was utterly still. Darmik wished she'd respond. Did she feel the same way? Or had he managed to destroy what was between them? "Say something," he begged. Darmik moved to stand.

"Stay where you are," Rema said, waving the wood around. "I need a moment to think."

Darmik lowered himself back to his knees. Neco stepped from the shadows of the tunnel behind Rema. Darmik was about to ask his friend what he was doing when Neco wrapped one arm around Rema's neck, his other hand encircling her arm.

Rema yelped in surprise. Then the heel of her boot slammed on Neco's foot, her elbow jamming into his stomach. Neco's eyes bulged, and he released his grip on Rema. She swung the log. Neco ducked.

Darmik jumped up, grabbing the wood mid-swing. "Stop!" he yelled. Rema turned to him, about to strike. Darmik twisted around her body, hitting her arm. She dropped the log to the ground. He came up behind her, clasping his arms around her torso. "Calm down," he whispered in her ear. Her body heaved up and down, her breath coming fast. "No one will hurt you."

"Then what was that?" Her chin jerked toward Neco. "And why are you holding me?"

"Neco," Darmik said. "Explain yourself."

Neco clutched his stomach. "She was threatening you with a weapon," he said. "I meant to disarm her. Apparently, she had other ideas." He straightened up, nodding his head in her direction.

Darmik tried not to laugh. "I'm going to release you now," he said. "Does that meet with your approval?"

Rema nodded, still breathing hard.

"Neither of us will hurt you. Please refrain from attacking us. Agreed?"

"Yes."

Darmik slowly removed his arms. Rema remained standing there, staring at Neco.

"Rema, you know Neco from our ride to Greenwood Forest. He's my best friend and most trusted soldier. Neco, I'm sure you remember Rema, your future queen."

Neco smiled and bowed, while Rema's head jerked toward Darmik. "What did you say?" she asked.

Darmik knelt on the ground before her, bowing

his head as a subject to his royal ruler. He wanted her to understand the enormity of the situation—and that he was sorry about his actions and intended to pledge his loyalties to her.

"Stand up." She grabbed his arm, pulling him to his feet. "Don't do that."

Darmik chuckled. Rema's eyes were wide, and she shook her head, looking truly panicked.

Neco straightened up. "I'll leave you two alone. It's nice to officially meet you, Princess Amer." He turned and left.

Rema shook her head. "I am *not* Princess Amer."

"But you are," Darmik said.

Rema moved to the fire and sat down, staring into the flames. She was just as beautiful as he remembered. Yet, there was something different about her. Rema was thinner and more tone. He wondered what she had been through since the last time he saw her.

Darmik sat next to her. "What are you thinking?" She usually had an abundance of things to say. Her lack of talking started to worry him.

"What did you mean when you said *your future queen?*" she finally asked, still focused on the fire, lost in thought.

"Well," Darmik said, not entirely sure how to answer. "The rebels want to place you on the throne, making you Queen of Greenwood Island."

"But you're the reigning prince and commander. In order to place Princess Amer on the throne, they would have to overthrow your family."

"Yes," Darmik said. "And I agree with them."

Her eyes finally sought his. They sat, staring at one another. "I don't understand," she admitted.

"My father is cruel. He doesn't know how to rule a kingdom. Lennek is no better. I believe you'd make a great ruler. And you are the true heir. We never should have removed your family in the first place."

"You'd turn your back on your own father and brother?" she asked.

Darmik nodded. "Yes, I would, if it's the right thing to do."

"Don't you feel a sense of loyalty to them?"

"I do," Darmik admitted. Even after everything they had done to Darmik, he still loved them. "But I've seen enough of their injustice firsthand. I've also seen enough of your kindness."

Suddenly Darmik had a hard time breathing. He'd admitted to loving her, and she hadn't acknowledged his feelings yet. Rema was so close. He wanted to wrap his arms around her. His eyes drifted to her soft, red lips. He wanted to kiss her.

Darmik forced himself to look her in the eyes again. "There's something you need to know."

Rema shifted closer to him. "Yes?"

Darmik needed to tell her about Captain. She needed to be aware of the seriousness of the situation. "There is an assassin on Greenwood Island from Emperion. He's hunting you right now, even as we speak."

"Am I safe in the Middle Mountains?" she asked.

"This is by far the safest place for you right now. However, the assassin won't stop until he finds you."

"I need to get back inside the fortress."

Darmik agreed, but he wanted Rema to understand the entirety of his emotions before they parted. Darmik took hold of her hands. "I pledge my loyalty to you," he blurted out. He wished they had more time together, so he could explain himself better without blundering through it.

Her eyes widened, and she started shaking her head. "I don't want to be Princess Amer. I'm not her. I can't be."

Darmik squeezed her hands. "You are. Now it's up to you to decide if you will fulfill your destiny. Or if you will run and hide."

"I don't know how to be the leader of these rebels. I'm not strong enough."

"Yes, you are." Darmik thought of her perseverance in the dungeon and at the execution. And her fight with Neco. That was fun to witness. Rema was strong. She just didn't realize it yet.

Tears filled her eyes. "Maya and Kar aren't really my aunt and uncle? Everyone has been lying to me my entire life?"

"They had to in order to keep you safe," Darmik said.

A tear slid down her cheek. Darmik reached out, cupping her face. His thumb brushed the tear away, and he leaned forward. He wanted to feel her soft lips. He wanted to comfort her. He knew he shouldn't, that if she was indeed to be his queen and he her loyal subject, he shouldn't kiss her.

Rema closed her eyes and leaned forward. His lips brushed hers. All worry fell away, and all he could think about was this beautiful girl before him, so full of life.

To hell with position and formality. He was tired of things keeping the two of them apart. Darmik's hands slid around her waist, pulling her onto his lap. Rema's arms wrapped around Darmik's neck. "I love you," he murmured against her lips. Her tears mixed with their kiss, salty and precious.

Darmik wanted all of her. He kissed her chin, her soft neck. She gasped. The cape slid from Rema's shoulders, puddling on the dirt ground. Their bodies pressed against one another. Her blonde hair surrounded him, filling him with her sweet scent.

Their lips met again. Darmik deepened the kiss as his hands moved to undo the tie of her dress.

Neco cleared his throat. Rema pulled away, breathing hard.

"Yes, Neco?" Darmik asked. His friend had better have a good reason for interrupting.

"Sorry to disturb you," Neco said, avoiding eye contact. Rema grabbed the discarded cape, wrapping it around her shoulders. Her cheeks were a rosy red. "There's a great deal of activity at the rebel compound. I'm betting Princess Amer's absence has been noted."

Darmik stood, pulling Rema up. "We better get you back."

"Are you going inside the compound with me?" she asked.

"No," he replied. "I need to get back down and throw Captain off your trail." She nodded. "What do you plan to do with this newfound knowledge of your true identity?" Darmik asked.

"I don't know," Rema admitted. "But once I figure it out, I'll let you know."

Twenty-three

Rema

Darmik escorted Rema back to the boulder where he found her earlier in the evening. It already felt like a lifetime ago. So much had happened over the course of the past hour.

"The compound is right through there," Darmik said, pointing somewhere behind her. "Head straight, and you'll run right into the wall. From there, you should be able to find the door you exited through."

Rema knew she should be paying more attention to what Darmik was saying, but she couldn't focus. Her entire world had been turned upside down.

"Rema," Darmik said, placing his hands on her shoulders. "Are you listening to anything I'm saying?"

She looked up into his dark eyes. "I'm sorry, what?"

Darmik raised his eyebrows. "I need you to get behind that wall before they send out a search unit."

Of course, she couldn't let the rebels discover Darmik or Neco. Who knew what they'd do to them? Mako would never believe Darmik was loyal to Rema instead of King Barjon. She had a hard enough time believing it herself.

Darmik's hands slid down her arms, grasping her wrists. "Please be careful."

She nodded, understanding that the King's Army was searching for her, an Emperion assassin was hunting her, and she was embedded with rebel forces who believed her to be their savior. Yes, she would tread very carefully.

"I need my cape back."

"Of course." Rema unclasped the cloak, sliding it from her shoulders. The freezing night air swirled around her body.

She handed Darmik his cape and their hands brushed, sending unexpected warmth through her fingers, up her arm, and into her core.

"You better go," Darmik said, his voice gruff, "before you freeze out here." He threw the cape over his arm.

Rema nodded, clasping her arms around her torso. She didn't want to leave Darmik. Right now, he was the only one being honest with her. Once she returned to the rebel compound, she had no idea what she was going to do.

Darmik leaned down, kissing her cheek. She closed her eyes, reveling in the warmth of him.

"Stay safe," Darmik whispered. Then he was gone.

An animal howled in the distance. Rema turned and headed in the direction of the fortress.

She desperately wanted to sort through the events that had just transpired, but Rema needed to get inside—to safety. Her feet were going numb, and she couldn't feel her fingertips or nose. She decided to run.

Her boots crunched on the dirt ground as she dodged greenwood trees and large rocks.

Just up ahead, Rema caught a glimpse of the castle's stone wall. Her breath came out in white puffs. She slowed, scanning the wall for the door she had left propped open. Not seeing it, Rema decided to jog along the wall until she either found a way in, or someone spotted her. On top of the wall, there seemed to be twice as many armed men as usual.

Rema stumbled, falling forward on her hands and knees. A guard from above must have heard her because he called out, "Identify yourself!"

Glancing up, there was an archer with an arrow pointed at her.

"I'm," she stuttered. Who was she? Rema didn't even exist. She was Princess Amer. But that person was foreign to her.

"You have three seconds until I shoot."

"I'm Rema." She stood up, brushing the frozen dirt and ice from her numb hands.

"Over here!" the man shouted. Several torches appeared, lighting the night. "Commander! We found her outside the wall!" Shouts rang out. Rema remained where she was. After a few moments, a group of soldiers came running up.

Audek stepped forward. "Rema," he said. "You certainly gave everyone quite a scare!" He removed his cape and draped it around her. "We need to get you inside. You're freezing."

Audek wrapped his arm around her shoulders. They walked along the wall, toward the fortress's main entrance.

"So," Audek began, "you and Savenek have a lovers' quarrel? Had to throw a tantrum like a typical girl to get everyone's attention, did you?" Audek chuckled.

Although she was practically frozen, Rema pulled her right arm back and punched Audek in the stomach.

The punch didn't carry much weight—Audek barely made a noise.

"Is that what he told you?" Rema demanded. "That we had a lovers' quarrel?"

A few of the soldiers nearby glanced at Rema.

"Well, no," Audek admitted, lowering his voice so no one could overhear. "I just saw you two arguing and then you disappeared."

They passed through the entrance in the wall, the heavy, iron door grating along the ground as it closed behind them.

Rema's teeth chattered so loudly she could scarcely hear anything else. Now that she was safely inside, Rema stopped walking. "That's not why I ran off," she said.

Audek dropped his arm and turned to face her. "I was only toying with you."

"Well, don't," Rema said. "There was a massacre in Jarko—where I'm from. Savenek refused to tell me anything about it. I just wanted to know what towns were attacked to see if anyone I know was killed. He refused."

"Rema," Mako said as he approached, Savenek close behind him. "Let's get you inside."

She glanced around at all the soldiers who had been looking for her. If she truly were a commoner, Mako never would have assembled a search team such as this.

How had she been so blind?

Maya and Kar had kept her sheltered, rarely allowed to leave the property. She never went to market like other children. Her parents were killed during the takeover. Before today, she didn't even know her own parents' names. And her blonde hair and blue eyes were from her Emperion ancestry.

Rema felt the key necklace warm against her chest. The most incriminating evidence—her name. Amer spelled backwards.

Mako took hold of her arm, ushering her into the fortress. He barked out orders to everyone, but the words didn't register to her.

Rema's entire life was a lie.

Maya and Kar weren't even her aunt and uncle.

Rema was Princess Amer.

Her vision blurred, and her legs gave out.

***

Rema opened her eyes. She was in her bed, blankets piled on her body, a warm fire roaring in the hearth.

"You're awake," Vesha said, coming to stand next to her. "How do you feel?"

"Warm," Rema said. She wiggled her fingers and toes, able to feel all of them properly working. "What's around my feet and hands?"

"My mother put a salve on them, and wrapped them in hot towels." Vesha sat on the edge of the bed.

Rema lay there, staring at her friend. Did Vesha know Rema's true identity? Or was she in the dark, too? Given that Vesha was actually sitting on her bed, she doubted Vesha knew Rema was the true heir to the throne.

"What happened?" Vesha asked, scooting closer. "One minute you were dancing with Savenek, the next Mako announced you were missing. They found you outside the compound. How did you get out there?"

"I went on a walk," Rema said. "That is all." She didn't want to tell her about Darmik. Mako might see Darmik as a threat and order him killed. Besides, Mako kept plenty of secrets from Rema; she certainly could keep one from him as well.

Vesha glanced to the door. "But why?" she asked. "Savenek was making a big fuss. He kept telling everyone not to worry and to leave you alone. Mako's been beside himself."

Before Vesha could say anything else, Rema interrupted her. "Can you please explain how I got in bed?" she asked.

"You blacked out. Mako carried you here."

How embarrassing—she must have passed out in front of everyone. "Well, I'm fine now. I'd like to get out of bed." It was still dark outside, but Rema wasn't tired. She desperately wanted to speak to Mako and confront him.

Vesha pulled the covers back. "Are you certain?"

"Yes." Rema felt perfectly fine. If anything, she was a bit hot. Swinging her legs to the side of the bed, Rema looked at the bandages. "Can you please help me?"

Яℰ𝒟

Vesha quickly unwrapped Rema's hands and feet. "Mako is in the sitting room." Vesha nodded toward the door. "He was quite worried about you, which is unusual for him. I've never seen him like that before, not even with Savenek."

After thanking Vesha for her help, Vesha left. Rema slid her feet into fur slippers and grabbed her robe. Her stomach twisted from nerves, but there would never be a good time to confront Mako. Best to get it over with.

"Rema," Mako said as she entered the cozy sitting room.

She raised her hand, indicating for him to be silent. He obeyed. A chill ran through her body. "I want the truth," Rema said. "All of it."

He stood there, staring at her.

"Please. I deserve to know." If she was indeed Princess Amer, then Mako had to obey.

Mako ran his hands over his face as he took a seat on the chair. "First, may I please ask something of you?"

Rema hesitated. "You may ask, but I can't guarantee anything."

"Fair enough." Mako raised his head, looking at her straight in the eyes. "Please, I beg you, can you promise me that you will never leave the compound unaccompanied again?"

Rema's heart pounded. He would only ask if he believed her valuable. It was a simple request that she knew she should agree to, but she didn't want to. Rema would make no promises to anyone right now. Especially promises that would confine her. She'd been sheltered for far too long.

"I will think on the matter," Rema said, taking a seat. "Now, please tell me the truth."

Mako nodded. "Seventeen years ago, I was Commander for King Revan. The island was invaded by Barjon, and he killed King Revan and his sons, Prince Davan and Prince Jetan. Barjon's soldiers slaughtered my wife and baby, Tabitha."

Rema's hands started shaking. The room became stifling hot.

"I was trying to save Queen Kaylen and Princess Amer."

The room started spinning. She knew exactly where this story was going. Only, it wasn't a story, but her own past—one that was locked away from her all these years.

"The queen knew Barjon wouldn't stop until the royal family was exterminated. I offered to switch my dead baby with Princess Amer. The queen agreed. She took Tabitha and ran—leading the soldiers away from me and directly to her. I escaped through the tunnels with Princess Amer. I placed her in the protection of my most trusted Captain, Kar." His voice was gruff, eyes glossy from the memory.

"So what you're saying is that I am Princess Amer."

"Yes." Mako slid from the chair, kneeling on the ground before Rema. "I vowed to protect you and to make sure that you lived. I won't force you to do anything you don't want to, but you must understand what's at stake here. You are our only hope. I want to restore you to the throne, if you're willing. I believe you can turn Greenwood Island around to its former glory. I want you to know, Your Highness, that I am yours to command."

There was no doubt anymore. She was indeed Princess Amer.

"Although, technically, you're now Queen Amer. Of course, you'll need to be formally crowned."

Panic swelled inside of her. Having no idea what to say or do, she turned and left, going back to her bedchamber. She closed the door and sat before the fire.

Queen.

Such a huge responsibility.

Her thoughts turned to King Barjon. She always knew he was evil, cruel, and had murdered the previous royal family. The reality was that man had slaughtered her mother, father, and two brothers, ripping her entire life away from her.

Exhaustion overcame Rema, and she fell asleep.

Rema awoke. Vesha was standing next to the hearth, her back to Rema.

"What are you doing here?" Rema asked, stretching her arms above her head.

Vesha turned to face her. "I'm not sure," she admitted. "Mako ordered that I wait for you to awake. He told me to keep the fire going. I'm supposed to escort you to breakfast and to the meeting later this afternoon."

Rema slid from the bed, pulling on her wool clothes. "Meeting? About what?"

"I don't know," Vesha replied. "Mako called an emergency meeting stating that everyone is required to attend."

"Does he do that often?" Rema pulled on her boots, lacing them up.

"Never," Vesha said. "I suspect something huge is about to happen."

Rema froze. Was Mako going to tell everyone who she really was? She wasn't ready for everyone to know her true identity—after all, she was still coming to terms with it herself.

"Are you ready?" Vesha asked, startling Rema.

Rema glanced up at her friend. Would Vesha treat her differently once she knew?

After a quick meal, Vesha left to help her mother in the infirmary, and Rema headed to the training room. Rema wasn't ready to talk to Savenek yet. Even though they'd fought only last night, so much had happened, so much had changed.

When Rema entered the training room, Savenek wasn't there. There was, however, an arrow stuck to the far wall with a piece of paper dangling from it. Rema walked over and pulled the arrow out, tossing it to the ground. She took the paper and read it.

Stables. Now.

She presumed it was a note from Savenek, but she couldn't be sure—she'd never seen his handwriting. However, it made no difference. Going to the stables meant she most likely would be riding a horse.

Walking to the barn, her thoughts were of Savenek, his short temper and quick judgments. Vesha had told her Mako was training Savenek to take over as commander. That meant that Savenek would be the commander of *her* army if she chose to reclaim the throne.

She wasn't sure how she felt about that. Perhaps someone a little more controlled would make a better commander—someone more like Darmik. Her face warmed just thinking about him. The kiss they shared was intense, magical, and stirred feelings of desire and want inside of Rema. She could not think about him right now—not when she was about to face Savenek. She'd think about Darmik later—when she was alone—and she could digest all that had happened between them—and what he said.

Rema entered the stables. Savenek stood at the opposite end, his back to her, silhouetted in the open door.

Rema found River sticking his head out over the side of his stall. Ignoring Savenek, she rubbed River's nose. The horse snorted, and Rema laughed.

"We need to talk."

Rema spun around and found Savenek standing behind her. She didn't hear him approach.

"I prefer to ride," she said.

"Me too," Savenek mumbled. "But I have something to say to you, if you'll let me." He seemed nervous, fidgeting with his scabbard.

"Fine. What do you want to discuss?"

He cleared his throat. "Uh," he stammered, shifting his weight from one foot to the other. "I…um…I want…to…apologize."

She didn't expect that.

"I'm listening." She folded her arms.

Savenek rubbed his face. The gesture reminded

her of Mako. "Last night," he began, "I didn't mean to offend you."

"You know I'm from Jarko."

"Yes," Savenek said. "I didn't think." He turned away from her, kicking the ground with the tip of his boot. "It's just that," he wasn't looking at her, "that you throw me off kilter."

"So it's my fault!" Rema didn't have time for this. She had other things to do. Turning, she walked out of the stables.

"Wait!" Savenek called after her.

"I'm not training with you today," Rema said over her shoulder.

Savenek grabbed her arm, pulling her to a stop. "Wait," he said, again. "I'm not done."

"Well, I am," Rema said. "I'm not going to stand here listening to you insult me. I need to speak with Mako, and I want to find out exactly what happened in Jarko, since you deem me unworthy of such information."

"Will you close your mouth for a minute and let me speak?" Savenek said, exasperated.

Shocked, Rema snapped her mouth closed.

"Thank you," Savenek said, releasing her arm. "Like I was trying to say, I'm sorry for our quarrel last night. That wasn't my intention. It's just that, when I'm around you, you challenge me. No one else does that."

Rema had no idea what he was getting at. "I accept your apology." If you could even call it that. She turned to leave.

Snow started falling. Walking toward the castle, Rema closed her eyes, reveling in the feel of the soft flakes against her skin.

"I love you."

Rema froze. What did she just hear? She spun around to face Savenek. Yes, she'd heard him right. His face confirmed it. He looked like he was in pain.

"You love me?" Rema confirmed. He nodded. "But you don't want to."

Savenek looked down to the ground. "It's not really a convenient time for me right now." His eyes met hers. "Yet, I can't help the way I feel. I've tried to ignore it. But I can't any longer." He took a step toward her.

Rema had no idea what to say.

"I know you probably don't feel the same way, or at least not as strongly as I do. But given time, I think you could—I mean, you will."

Rema recalled the conversation she overheard between Mako and Savenek. Now she understood why Mako told Savenek not to harbor any feelings for her. Since Rema was really a princess, a relationship with a commander could never be.

"I take it you haven't spoken to Mako on the matter?"

"No," Savenek said. "I wanted to talk to you first, before I asked Mako to sanction the union."

This reminded her of Bren all over again. "We barely know each other," Rema said. She didn't want to turn him down outright—especially if he was to be the commander of her army. She couldn't make him an enemy right now. If she played this correctly, then Mako would prevent anything from happening without her having to hurt Savenek's feelings.

"Please," Savenek whispered, taking another step toward her. He reached out and grabbed her hands. "Please be my wife."

Rema was about to tell him that he needed to speak with Mako first when a twig snapped, and Rema glanced to her left.

Vesha stood there, shaking her head in disbelief. "How could you?" she yelled. Then she backed up and ran away.

"No, Vesha! Wait!" Rema turned to run after her friend. She needed to explain the situation to Vesha.

"Rema," Savenek said, squeezing her hands, not letting go. "You will not wander off again. Get inside. I will go after Vesha."

Rema hated how bossy he was. "Do you even know why she's upset?" Rema demanded.

"I think so. I've always suspected she had feelings for me," he said, "and that just confirmed it."

"Fine," Rema said. She watched Savenek chase after Vesha. Hopefully, Vesha would listen to him right now, because Rema wasn't sure she'd listen to her.

No matter what happened, Rema would not lose the one and only true friend she had.

❧

Inside the compound, Mako was nowhere to be found. Not sure what to do since she'd never had any free time, Rema made her way to the training room. Audek was wrestling with a young man, so Rema went over to watch.

Audek and his opponent were both covered with sweat. When Audek saw Rema, he smiled. The distraction was just enough for his wrestling partner to flip him over and claim victory.

"Bloody hell," Audek murmured. "A beautiful girl shows up, and I lose in less than a minute." He patted his opponent on the back, and then came over to Rema, all smiles.

"So," Rema said, unsure of what to say.

"So," Audek said, folding his arms with a wicked smile on his face. "Did Savenek talk to you?" He wiggled his eyebrows.

Rema felt her face flush.

"Ah!" Audek laughed. "He did!" He wrapped an arm around her shoulder, gliding her to an empty section of the training room. "Our man finally confessed his feelings! I knew it."

"First of all," Rema said, "get your sweaty, stinking arm off me." Audek pulled his arm away, still smiling. "Secondly, it is none of your business."

"He's my best friend. Of course it's my business. Unless...wait!" Audek turned to face her. "You don't feel the same way about him?"

"It's not that simple," Rema said, grabbing a wooden practice sword from the wall. "Vesha is in love with Savenek," she said.

"I know." Audek grabbed a wooden sword and stood opposite Rema. "What does that have to do with anything?"

"Vesha is my friend." Rema swung, and Audek automatically parried the blow.

"Savenek doesn't feel that way toward her, though." He counted, and hit Rema's side.

She acknowledged the hit. They reset, and started over. This time, Rema swung low and fast. Audek blocked, and quickly came in with a series of moves. She had no choice but to go on the defensive.

Rema couldn't tell Audek that her heart was already claimed by another. She dared not mention Darmik's name. She hoped he was halfway down the mountain, far away from this rebel army. She'd need time to decide how to tell Mako that Darmik was loyal to her. She'd have to wait until she was officially crowned, and her word was law.

Audek's sword rested at Rema's throat. "Either you're not focusing today, or Savenek hasn't taught you a thing."

Rema lowered her weapon, breathing hard.

"If you don't fancy Savenek," Audek said with a mischievous grin, "then perhaps there's someone else?" He wiggled his eyebrows again.

Rema rolled her eyes. "Oh, please. Like I'd confess my heart to you." She put the sword away.

Audek chuckled. "Rema, you could steal any man's heart. Easily." He put his sword away next to hers. "Don't look now, but our friends just arrived."

Rema glanced to the entrance of the training room. Savenek and Vesha stood there, staring directly at Rema. Neither one looked particularly happy.

The sound of a horn filled the room.

"Time for the meeting," Audek said.

Яᕪᗫ

⊙⌒⌐

Since everyone was required to attend the meeting, it was held outside in the central courtyard. Rema wore her fur-lined cape, boots, and hat. Still, her nose was red like an apple, and her eyes watered.

Standing next to Audek, Rema waited patiently for Mako to speak.

"You still haven't given me an answer," Savenek whispered in her ear, making her jump. He was standing right behind her, Vesha at his side.

"Now is not the time," Rema answered.

"Then when?"

"Bloody hell," Audek said, "I wish Mako would start."

"Vesha." Rema turned back to her friend. "I'm sorry for what you saw earlier."

Tears filled her friend's eyes. Vesha glanced to Savenek, and then away. "I know," she replied softly. "Savenek told me." She wiped her eyes.

"Can we please talk?" Rema asked. "In private? After the meeting?"

Vesha nodded.

"*We* still need to talk," Savenek said to Rema.

"Any day now!" Audek said, bouncing up and down, trying to stay warm.

"Thank you all for coming!" Mako bellowed. "Today is a day you will never forget!"

"Rema," Savenek whispered. "Please, you owe me an answer."

"You have no business asking me to marry you without consulting Mako first," she answered.

"Is that a *no*?" Savenek asked, his voice harsh.

"I am going to introduce you to the true heir to the throne!" Mako announced.

Total silence fell over the courtyard. Everyone had their eyes glued to Mako, transfixed on what he was saying.

"Savenek," Audek said, "do you know about this?"

"No, this is the first time I'm hearing of it."

"We have trained for years side by side," Mako continued. "We have planned, plotted, and looked forward to the day when we would reclaim the throne. Today, we are one step closer. Today, I introduce to you the sole surviving royal family member. Princess Amer, will you please join me?"

There was a collective gasp amongst the people. All eyes were front and center on the stage where Mako stood.

"I thought one of the princes survived," Savenek said. "Not a girl!"

Rema couldn't move. She couldn't stand up on that platform before all these people, claiming to be someone she did not fully know or understand.

Mako's eyes settled on her. "Rema, please come here."

Everyone turned to stare at her. People parted in front of her, giving her a clear path to Mako.

"Why?" Savenek said from behind her.

Putting one foot in front of the other, Rema slowly moved toward the platform. When she reached the bottom, Mako descended the stairs, took hold of her hand, and helped her up.

"I give you Princess Amer. Soon to be Queen Amer of Greenwood Island." Everyone dropped to their knees, bowing their heads.

Everyone that is, except Savenek.

Horror and revulsion filled his face. Rema didn't know what to say or do, so she just stood there.

Mako whispered, "You can tell everyone to rise."

"Oh, of course," Rema mumbled. Then in a loud, clear voice, she said, "Rise."

Everyone stood, staring at her, waiting. She turned to Mako for help.

"Princess Amer was smuggled out of the castle seventeen years ago, by me. She has been living with Captain Kar under a false name. Until yesterday, she did not even know her true identity."

Mako turned toward her. "I am honored to serve you." He took her hand, kissing her fingers in a pledge of eternal service to her.

"In one month's time, we overthrow Barjon and reclaim the throne!"

Cheering erupted. Rema turned to leave. She needed time to herself in order to think.

"Where are you going, Princess?"

She hadn't thought that far ahead.

"Now that your identity has been announced, you'll need an official royal guard."

Rema rolled her eyes.

"And some ladies in waiting."

Was Mako joking?

"Your safety is my number one concern."

Huh. And he didn't even know about the assassin.

ꙮ

Mako escorted Rema directly to his office amidst a great amount of chaos. It seemed like everyone wanted to talk to Rema—either with questions or words of support. Many wanted to officially declare their allegiance to her and the crown she had yet to lay claim to.

Mako just rushed her past everyone, telling them she'd be available later. If she was going to be queen—*if*—then she'd need to start taking charge and not allow Mako to have control of everything. For now, it was fine. But she would be no one's puppet.

Inside the office, Rema sat on one of the chairs. She had no idea where to start. She wanted to know exactly what was going on in Jarko, why Mako revealed her identity, and why he'd said they'd storm the castle in one month's time.

Rema felt like she was being forced into the matter—she really needed time to think. And she wanted to consult Darmik.

"I know I said I wouldn't force you into anything," Mako said, "but our timetable has just been moved up. Time is of the essence."

"What exactly do you mean?"

Mako took a seat on the chair near her, and pulled it closer so their knees almost touched. "Your Highness, word has just reached me that a ship from Emperion is here."

"You know about the assassin?"

Color drained from Mako's face. "What?"

The door flew open, and Savenek stormed in. "Why the hell didn't you tell me?" he yelled, directing his fury at Mako.

Mako jumped up and closed the door. "Savenek, calm down."

"You lied to me! You led me to believe the heir was a prince, not a princess!" Savenek's face was red, and he waved his hands around while he talked.

"I said to calm down. Now," Mako ordered. "Have a seat, so we can discuss this rationally, in a reasonable manner."

Savenek glanced at Rema, and then pulled the chair a good three feet away from her before plopping down on it. Mako leaned against his desk, facing them.

Savenek rubbed his hands over his face. "Are you absolutely certain it's *her*?"

"Yes," Mako answered. "Not only did I carry her out and save her myself, watching from a distance as she grew up, but she bears the royal tattoo."

"The royal tattoo?" Savenek sounded skeptical.

"Yes," Rema answered, her hand automatically going to the mark on her shoulder. "I bear the mark."

"Why didn't you tell me?" His eyes pierced into hers. Savenek looked so lost, desperate. It made her want to comfort him. She folded her hands on her lap.

"I just found out myself. Last night."

"So you didn't deceive me?"

"No."

"But you knew when I spoke with you earlier this

morning? When I asked you to be my wife?"

Rema nodded.

"Savenek," Mako said, "I specifically told you not to get close to or develop feelings toward her. This is why." He sighed.

"Of all the girls to fall in love with," Savenek mused, "I choose the one I can't have."

Rema had heard enough. "Regardless of my position, I wouldn't marry you."

"Why?" Savenek demanded, sitting on the edge of his chair.

"Has it ever occurred to you that my heart might already belong to another?"

It looked like he'd been slapped. "Is it Audek? I'll kill him."

"No, and Mako's right, calm down. This is getting us nowhere."

Mako looked lost in thought.

"Now, Mako, you were about to tell me about the Emperion ship and why our timetable has been moved up."

Mako's eyes bore into hers. She thought she saw understanding in them. Did he suspect she loved Darmik? Mako pushed away from the desk and walked over to the window, looking outside.

"This is absurd!" Savenek jumped up from his chair. "I haven't spent my entire life training—working day and night—to put some girl on the throne. She doesn't have a clue how to run the kingdom."

"Watch what you say," Mako said. "She is your sovereign."

"No, she's not! I haven't pledged anything to her."

This was insane. Rema hadn't even officially agreed to take her place and become queen. It felt like her choices were being taken away from her. Run— she needed to run. As Mako and Savenek stood there arguing, Rema got up and walked out of the room. There were two posted soldiers outside the doorway.

"Are we supposed to guard you, Rema—I mean, Your Highness?"

"No," Rema said. "I need some time alone."

She took off down the hallway, desperate to be out of this fortress, free from the confines of the walls and expectations.

She ran.

TWENTY-FOUR

Darmik

It had recently rained. The horse hooves pounded on the ground, tossing up mud as they thundered across the land. After hiking down the mountain for a week, it felt good to be riding on horseback across open land.

"Why do you think Captain and Lennek returned to the king's castle?" Neco shouted, riding neck to neck with Darmik.

Darmik was considering that very question ever since he borrowed horses from his soldiers in the small village town of Bovern, near the base of the Middle Mountains. His men had informed him that most of the army still roamed the island searching for Rema, but Captain and Prince Lennek were spotted heading toward King's City a couple of days ago.

"I fear they are searching the military compound for clues," Darmik said. "More specifically, my office."

"You don't have anything that would lead them to Rema, do you?"

"Not exactly," Darmik answered. "But I have a

map with rebel sightings. There were several near the base of the Middle Mountains. It's only a matter of time before Captain discovers their location."

"Or attacks another town," Neco added. "Why does Captain suspect you know Rema's location?"

"Call it intuition."

The city's wall came into sight. Darmik steered his horse toward the secret tunnel leading to the military compound. After stabling the borrowed horses, Neco and Darmik went to the barracks. No one was there.

"Lennek was only assigned one half of the Tenth, correct?"

"Yes," Darmik mused. "The Eighth Company should still be here. They are the only protection King's City has against an attack." They quietly walked down the corridor leading to Darmik's office.

"I want you to take a look around," Darmik told Neco. "Find out what's going on. Talk to castle servants and people in the city."

"I'm on it," Neco said. "I'll find you when I have something."

Darmik went inside his office. He looked on his desk to see if anything was out of place or moved. Everything looked as it should. Sitting on his chair, Darmik went through his drawers, again looking for anything amiss. Nothing appeared out of place. He leaned back and stretched out his legs. Where were Captain and Lennek? What were they planning? Darmik crossed his ankles, his toe hitting something. He crouched down and peered under his desk. A small piece of paper had fallen underneath. He pulled it out. It was a rough sketch of the island with all the major cities marked. Several towns were crossed off. The entire region of Jarko had an X through it. An area near the base of the Middle Mountains was circled with several marks around it.

Was this Captain's? Had he managed to narrow down the rebel's location already? If Captain had seen Darmik's map, then he certainly could have drawn that conclusion easily enough. Darmik had to find Captain and lead him away from the Middle Mountains. He needed to do something to indicate he knew where Rema was—and that she was near a bay town.

Darmik decided to head on over to the castle to see if he could find Captain or Lennek. Nearing the castle's wall, Darmik saw it was guarded by ten times the amount of usual soldiers.

At the gate, Darmik asked one of his men who had given the order for the additional soldiers on patrol.

"By order of the king, Commander."

Darmik headed straight to his father's office. Along the way, there were also twice as many sentries patrolling the hallways. The corridor where King Barjon's office was located was lined with soldiers.

Shoving the door open, Darmik saw the king with Captain Phellek and several other high-ranking officers, standing around the desk.

King Barjon's head snapped up. "I suppose you didn't locate the two-bit churl either?" he asked Darmik.

Lennek and Captain were nowhere in sight. "What's going on?" Darmik demanded.

"I've received reports that much of Jarko is burnt to the ground," the king said.

"Did Lennek tell you?" Darmik asked, standing next to his father.

"Yes," King Barjon responded. "Lennek told me Captain went ballistic searching for Rema. He'd been convinced she was in Jarko. When Captain couldn't locate her, he burned everyone's homes and land, trying to force someone to talk."

Darmik still didn't understand what his father was doing with Phellek and Darmik's other men.

"I'm taking it Captain and Lennek haven't located Rema either," Darmik said.

"No," King Barjon replied. "And I can't bloody well have an assassin from Emperion running around *my* kingdom destroying everything. Jarko is a farming region. Most of our food comes from there. Now what am I going to do?"

Darmik glanced at the large map spread out on the desk. "You know for certain Captain is an assassin?" Darmik asked.

"I'm not stupid," King Barjon said. "I played along with him, hoping he'd kill the girl and leave. If we don't find her soon, I fear more will come. And then what?"

"Has anyone else from Emperion arrived?"

Phellek cleared his throat. "Captain and Lennek showed up here a couple of days ago," he said. "When Captain returned, he met with a few dozen men—all rumored to have come off the boat Captain arrived on. I believe his men may be infiltrating the army."

"Yes," King Barjon said. "I ordered your men—*my army*—to the castle for added protection."

This was a side of his father Darmik rarely saw.

"Where is Captain now?"

King Barjon shook his head. "I have men following him, but he keeps slipping their notice."

"He's been spotted around King's City speaking with people," Phellek said.

"I believe he's preparing to leave again," a lieutenant said. "Food and other provisions have gone missing. I've been keeping track."

"What are your orders, Father?" Darmik asked.

"Find Rema, and bring her to me before she destroys my kingdom."

"Is the bet still on?" Darmik asked.

"Yes," King Barjon answered, "it is. But the stakes are higher now."

೩ఌ

What an interesting turn of events, Darmik thought as he walked down the corridor. His father feared Emperion would come in and take over the island—when Rema and the rebels planned to do just that. Unfortunately, the added soldiers would make it much more difficult for Rema and the rebels to infiltrate the castle. Unless Darmik could convince this company of soldiers to side with the rebels.

Darmik made his way to the entrance of Lennek's rooms. He knocked on the door, and Arnek answered.

"I'm here to see my brother," Darmik said, shoving past Arnek.

"Then you'll be disappointed to discover him occupied, Your Highness," Arnek said.

"Where is he?" Darmik demanded. He glanced around the sitting room, his brother nowhere in sight. The door to his bedchamber was closed, two soldiers standing on either side. "Is my brother sleeping?" Darmik asked. The midday meal already passed. Lennek might be lazy and enjoy sleeping in, but this was excessive even for him.

"As I previously told you," Arnek said, coming to stand before Darmik, "Prince Lennek is otherwise engaged." The mousy man smiled.

A thumping noise came from Lennek's bedchamber, followed by moaning. Realization dawned on Darmik—his brother was with a woman.

"Who?" Darmik demanded.

"I hardly see how that's relevant," Arnek answered, his nose in the air.

Darmik grabbed the man by his neck, slamming him against the wall. Arnek's legs dangled at least a foot above the ground. His face turned an ugly shade of red.

"Your stupidity astounds me," Darmik said through clenched teeth.

Arnek gasped for air. Neither soldier guarding Lennek's door so much as blinked. A girl's voice screamed Lennek's name.

"Who is in there with my brother?" Darmik demanded. If it were a noblewoman, Darmik wouldn't interfere.

Arnek clawed at Darmik's hands. Darmik slammed him against the wall again.

"Millet," Arnek squeaked. "A servant girl."

Darmik released his hold, and Arnek crumbled

to the ground. Darmik went to the door and threw it open. The soldiers standing guard on either side glanced at one another, unsure of what to do. Darmik gave them each a hard look, and they held their positions.

Storming into the bedchamber, he found a naked girl on top of Lennek. The girl screamed, pulling the silk sheet up against her body, covering herself.

"Come to see how it's done, little brother?" Lennek asked, smiling. He lay there completely naked, making no move to cover himself.

"Get out," Darmik said to the girl.

She looked to Lennek.

"I'm done," he said, waving his hand in the air, indicating for her to leave.

"Should I return later, Your Highness?" she asked.

Lennek sat up, reaching for his robe. "That won't be necessary," he said in a condescending tone. "You weren't that good. I need someone a little more…limber." He smirked.

The girl's eyes widened and glossed over with tears. She got up and ran from the room.

Lennek stood, pulling his robe closed. "Did you find Rema?"

"No," Darmik said.

"Because you already know where she is, don't you?"

Darmik stared at his brother. "What are you getting at?"

"Captain says you know where she is."

"If I knew, then I'd have her here."

"Perhaps." Lennek stepped around Darmik, going

to the vanity table and pouring himself a drink. "So you stormed in here to do what exactly? Catch a glimpse of a girl naked? Since you can't seem to get anyone to take their clothes off voluntarily for you?"

"I came here to ask you about Jarko," Darmik said, clutching his hands into fists. He couldn't hit his brother—at least, not yet.

"What about it?" Lennek asked, leaning against the table. He took a sip of his drink.

"How could you allow Captain to murder so many people? Burn all those farms? Those are *our* people!"

Lennek shrugged his shoulders. "Captain believed Rema was hiding in Jarko. It made sense. When no one would talk to us, I suggested we burn her out."

"That was your idea? Not Captain's?"

Lennek took another sip of his drink. "Does it matter?"

Darmik supposed it didn't. "I know there is a lot on the line to see who can get Rema first, but you can't destroy the island looking for her."

Lennek chuckled. "Why? Afraid people might revolt against Father? After all, he's the one who let the Emperion soldier roam the kingdom." Lennek tsked.

"You're trying to ruin Father?" Darmik whispered.

"I can't be king until he's gone, now can I, brother?" Lennek pushed away from the vanity table and came to stand before Darmik. "And right now, the *King's Army*, that you command, is destroying this island. It seems you're making this quite easy for me."

Darmik reached for his sword.

"Oh, I wouldn't do that, little brother. Captain

and I have reached an arrangement regarding Rema. You really have more important matters to tend to. I mean, you don't actually know where Captain is right now, do you? He could have Rema, and you wouldn't even know it because you're here with me."

Darmik released his sword. He had to find Captain and lead him toward the bay towns, away from the Middle Mountains. Darmik should have time on his hands. Captain wouldn't easily find the rebel fortress in the mountains. It was well concealed and had taken Darmik and Neco weeks to locate it.

Lennek raised his eyebrows, waiting for Darmik's response. Darmik pretended like he was going to leave. When Lennek laughed, his guard down, Darmik swung back and punched him in the jaw.

Lennek whipped his head around, fury in his eyes. "That was a very dumb move," he said, holding his hand to his jaw. "I will destroy you."

Darmik leaned in. "Not if I destroy you first."

"Guards!" Lennek shouted. "Arrest him."

The sentries glanced at one another, unsure of what to do.

"Touch me, and I'll kill you," Darmik said. The guards each took a step back, allowing Darmik to pass untouched. He hurried from his brother's room before Lennek summoned more guards to arrest him.

Darmik made his way to the kitchen for food. After, he packed some clothes and headed to the military compound. He grabbed all the weapons he could carry, and went to his office. He hoped Neco would be back with information. Darmik didn't have much time before men came looking for him.

After lighting a candle, Darmik went through his desk, packing maps and important papers. Glancing around, he realized this would be his last time in his office. He had pledged his loyalty to Rema, and it was time to join the rebels.

He really didn't know if Rema and her rebels had the forces and skill necessary to defeat King Barjon and Lennek. Regardless, Darmik intended to help them—no matter what.

The candle flickered. Darmik pulled out his dagger.

Neco slipped into the room. "We need to talk," his friend said.

"Not here. It's too dangerous."

"I know a place," Neco whispered. "Follow me."

Darmik grabbed his bags filled with provisions, and followed his friend out into the night. Trying to hide in the shadows, Darmik and Neco left the compound and headed to the narrow alleyways of King's City. Neco led the way to a nondescript, four-story building, where he pulled out a key and unlocked the door. They entered a short corridor and climbed two flights of stairs. Darmik followed Neco down a long hallway. Stopping before another door, Neco whistled, knocked, and then whistled again. The door cracked open, Neco said something, and it opened all the way to allow them entrance. Inside was a small room with several beds. It was empty except for the young man who answered the door.

The door softly closed. Neco hugged the boy. Perhaps he was a friend or relative Darmik was unaware of.

"Darmik," Neco said. "You remember Ellie."

The person removed their cap, hair spilling out around a familiar face. Ellie smiled up at Darmik. "Glad you're safe," she said. "We have a lot to talk about."

"So I've heard," Darmik responded.

All the windows in the small room were covered with blankets. Even so, Ellie only lit a small table candle, just as a precaution. The three of them sat on the beds.

"I've been staying here with Cassie," Ellie explained.

"It's one of the safe houses I use," Neco said, "when I'm doing spy work."

"Lennek was seen returning a couple of days ago with a small group of soldiers," Ellie said. "Shortly after that, a man with an odd accent started questioning people around the city. Rumors are flying about who he is and what he's doing."

"What sorts of questions is he asking?"

"Things about the rebels and Rema. He is saying he needs to find the girl who was supposed to be executed. He promises to keep her safe and pay a reward to whoever gives information on her whereabouts."

"Does he think she's here in the city?" Darmik asked.

"No, he doesn't," Ellie answered. "But he does believe that people here know where the rebels are. And he knows she's with them."

"But that's not all," Neco said. "Tell him the rest."

Ellie clutched her hands together. "He came here. One night. Banging on our door. I hid, like Neco told me to do. But Cassie…she answered the door."

"What happened?" Darmik asked, feeling sick in his stomach.

"The man knew who Cassie was—that she'd been a chambermaid for Rema. He wanted to know why she wasn't at the castle. Cassie said the baby was almost due, so that's why she'd left. The man took Cassie, kicking and screaming. I followed them. He has her in a building not far from here. There are several men guarding the place."

"First order of business, we need to leave. Now," Darmik said. Captain could have this safe house under surveillance.

"I checked the place. No one's watching," Neco said.

"You don't get it," Darmik said, standing. "These men are soldiers from Emperion. They don't play by our rules. They know tricks you've never seen before. We're not safe here."

Ellie jumped up and began packing her things. "I agree. Let's go."

Since Captain managed to find this safe house, Darmik had to assume all Neco's places were compromised. Darmik considered going to one of his soldiers' homes seeking shelter, but decided against it. They couldn't involve anyone else. And the less people who saw Darmik, the better.

The three of them left the safe house and wandered the city until Darmik was convinced no one was following them. After hiding their supplies in some bushes near a water fountain of King Barjon, Ellie led the way to where Captain was holding Cassie.

Ellie and Neco walked ahead of Darmik, pretending to be two friends returning home from an alehouse. Ellie swayed on her feet, as if she were drunk. Darmik followed behind them, hidden among the shadows of buildings.

When Ellie tripped, Darmik knew she was across from Captain's location. Ellie and Neco rounded the corner, out of sight. The plan was to rendezvous in fifteen minutes on the south side of the adjacent block.

Darmik quickly studied the building in question. Two stories, all the windows were black, no signs of life. He stayed very still, watching. In the moonlight, he could see down the alley next to the building. There were several heaps of trash. Darmik knew, without a doubt, Captain had men there guarding the perimeter. Perhaps there was access from the roof? Darmik needed to gain entrance into one of the adjacent buildings. Then he could have a better look.

Just when Darmik was about to cross the street, something made him glance to the front entrance of the building. He slid back into the wooden archway behind him. The door cracked open and a man came out, peering around. The entire street was eerily silent. The man nodded, and then two additional men came out, dragging a person between them. A burlap bag was over the prisoner's head. Her dress was torn and dirty, and her stomach bulging—it was Cassie. She thrashed her body, trying to break free, but she was no match for them. The two men proceeded down the street, dragging Cassie along. Darmik followed, careful to keep a safe distance. After three blocks, Darmik felt someone behind him. He unsheathed his dagger, spun around, preparing to throw it, but it was only Neco and Ellie. He put his weapon away, smiling, and the three of them continued together.

The men took Cassie up King's Street, which led to the castle. No one was about. When the men reached the soldiers on duty at the wall, they stated they had a prisoner for Lennek and were allowed in.

"Quickly," Darmik said, "before we lose them."

Darmik ran one hundred feet west to the secret door in the wall. It took him a moment to find it—it was well concealed and double the usual amount of sentries patrolled on top of the wall. Darmik had to push the stones just right in order to unlock it.

After his third try, the door opened. The three friends slipped inside and pressed against the wall.

"Do you see them?" Neco asked.

Darmik scanned the grounds, searching for the three figures.

"There," Ellie said.

"They're heading toward the barn," Darmik whispered. "Keep to the wall. When we near the tree, crawl to the bushes. Stay together now. Ready?" Ellie and Neco nodded.

They carefully kept to the shadows, trying to hurry without making any noise and alerting the guards on duty. Once they crawled to the shrubbery, they were able to stand and make their way to the barn.

"I don't understand why you're hiding," Ellie whispered.

Darmik stared at the girl.

"He's defecting," Neco said. "I'll explain later."

Ellie shrugged her shoulders, and they all crouched low, watching the two men drag Cassie inside the barn.

"Now what?" Ellie asked.

"You stop talking and stay here. If trouble arises, whistle two times," Darmik ordered. Ellie nodded.

Darmik pointed east, and Neco took off. Darmik went around the western side of the barn. He hid behind a bush that gave him a clear view of the inside. Several torches were lit. Only a couple of horses were inside the usually filled stables. The burlap bag was pulled off Cassie's head. One of her eyes and both cheeks had nasty, black bruises. There was dried blood at the corner of her mouth.

Nothing happened for several minutes. Ellie and Neco joined Darmik.

"What do you think?" Neco asked.

"They must be waiting for someone or something," Darmik whispered.

"I'll take the guy on the right; you get the one of the left. Ellie, you grab Cassie."

"No," Darmik said. "I want to know what's going on first."

"But we can easily recover Cassie right now. Who knows what the situation will be like later on."

"We'll grab her on her way back to Captain's," Darmik said. He needed to know why Cassie was being held, and if she knew any vital information about the rebels.

"Someone's coming," Ellie hissed.

The three of them froze, camouflaged in the

bushes. Two figures walked right past them, entering the barn. The torches inside illuminated the doorway, allowing Darmik to see Captain and Lennek standing before Cassie.

"My men tell me you're not speaking," Captain said, folding his arms across his chest.

Cassie's body shook.

"Where is Rema?" Captain demanded.

"I don't know!" Cassie cried.

Lennek grabbed Cassie's hair, pulling her head back. "You don't know?" he said, a scary calm to his voice. "Well, guess what? I don't believe you." Lennek pulled out a knife. He turned to one of the two soldiers holding Cassie. "Find the chambermaid Ellie. Bring her to me."

"Yes, Your Highness." The guard left.

Darmik turned to Neco. "You'll need to take Ellie away from the city. Hide her with Trell. She'll be safe there with my personal guard."

Neco nodded. Ellie's eyes were huge, her face white. For the first time since he'd met her, she appeared scared.

Darmik turned his attention back to the barn. Lennek rested the dagger against Cassie's throat.

Tears fell down her cheeks. "Please," she begged. "I don't know anything."

"You're every bit the whore Rema is," Lennek said. He moved the dagger to Cassie's protruding stomach. "Why did you visit my brother's bedchamber?" he purred.

Darmik froze. What was Lennek getting at?

Captain suddenly turned around, looking out of the barn, into the night.

"Is something the matter?" Lennek asked him.

"No," Captain answered. "I just thought I heard a noise. But all is still." He turned to face Lennek again. "Let's throw her in the dungeon. She may be of use later on."

Lennek chuckled. "I don't think so."

"Regardless, I'm sure Ellie has information that will be helpful."

"Assuming you can find her," Lennek said. "She wasn't at the safe house last time."

"True," Captain said. "But I have men watching it. We'll find her."

"I'm starting to doubt your abilities," Lennek said. "I thought you would've found Rema by now."

"I'm close," Captain said. "It's only a matter of time."

"You are aware Darmik returned today, yes?"

"With his personal squad?" Captain asked.

"Alone."

Captain rubbed his chin, lost in thought.

"As for you, my dear," Lennek said, turning his attention to Cassie. "I have no use for you." He pulled his arm back with the knife, preparing to strike.

Ellie sucked in a loud breath, about to jump up and run to Cassie.

"Get her out of here," Darmik commanded. Neco swung around, wrapping his arms around Ellie. He nodded.

Darmik jumped up, and charged into the barn. Lennek's hand came down. Darmik yanked out his dagger and threw it, hitting Lennek's knife and knocking it from his hand.

Lennek's head whipped around toward Darmik. "Brother. Fancy seeing you here." Lennek pulled out another knife and embedded it into Cassie's chest. She doubled over, falling to the ground.

"No!" Darmik screamed as he jumped at Lennek, his hands curling around his brother's neck. They tumbled to the ground, Darmik on top of Lennek.

Out of the corner of his eye, Darmik saw Captain's face. The hilt of a sword smashed into Darmik's forehead. There was an immense amount of pain.

Everything went black.

ॐ

Darmik came to. He was in a dark room. His arms were pulled tightly above his head, manacles surrounding his wrists. He tried moving his feet, but his ankles were chained to the floor. Two torches cast light in the small space. Darmik was in the interrogation room at his own military base. He blinked, heavy, thick blood covering one eye. His head throbbed with pain.

Someone chuckled. "Awake, are we? About time." Boots echoed in the dank room. Captain stood before Darmik. "Where is Trell?"

"Dead," Darmik answered, his voice raspy and barely audible.

Captain nodded to someone behind Darmik, and a whip hissed through the air, colliding with Darmik's bare back. White-hot searing pain exploded through Darmik's body.

"Where is Trell?" Captain asked again.

Darmik shook his head. The whip sliced through the air, hitting Darmik's back, ripping open his skin. Blood ran down his legs. Under normal circumstances, Darmik knew he could withstand about fifteen lashings before he'd pass out. Today, he'd be lucky to withstand five.

"Your personal squad is missing. Trell's body wasn't found." Captain nodded. The whip tore into Darmik's skin. Blood pooled on the ground at Darmik's feet. He clenched his hands into fists, wanting to fight back, but unable to pull free from the shackles.

"This is going to be a long night. If you're being this stubborn about Trell, I can't imagine how difficult you'll be about Rema," Captain smirked.

The whip sliced across Darmik's back again. He roared in pain.

"Get Prince Lennek," Captain said to a man standing by the door. "Tell him we're ready for him."

Darmik's vision swam, his head throbbing. He needed to think of a way out of this mess.

The door flew open, and Lennek stormed in. His face had a bruise on the side of it. "Brother," he said, seething with rage. He tossed his cape to the ground and rolled up his sleeves.

They stood facing one another.

"One day," Darmik panted, "I will kill you."

Lennek chuckled. "Bold words coming from someone locked in chains." He grabbed the mallet from the table.

"No," Captain said. "We need him alive and able

to lead the way to Rema."

"He doesn't need his arms or fingers to take us to the whore," Lennek hissed.

Captain replied, "No, he doesn't."

Lennek snatched a knife with a jagged edge, a wicked smile on his face. Darmik wanted to spit on his brother, but he didn't have the strength. His head throbbed as blood ran down his back.

Lennek's lips curled as he pressed the tip of the dagger against Darmik, just below his royal markings. Then he slid the weapon down and across, carving the letter "L" on his chest. The skin sliced open, blood gushing out.

Darmik ground his teeth against the pain.

"Where is she?" Lennek demanded.

"Why would I tell you?"

"So you can keep all ten fingers."

Darmik laughed. "I'll lose them anyway."

Captain stepped forward. "He knows where she is. I'm sure of it."

Lennek reached up, taking hold of Darmik's fingers. He started sawing one off. Darmik shrieked in agony.

There was a loud boom.

"What was that?" Lennek asked. Captain shrugged his shoulders.

Blood ran down Darmik's arm.

The wooden door in the ground flew open and half a dozen men rushed into the room. Darmik's vision blurred; he was about to pass out. Metal clanked and there were several grunting noises. Darmik tried to focus. Phellek was there, along with some members from Darmik's personal guard. Two of Darmik's men fought with Captain, another one had Lennek pinned down, two fought soldiers trying to come to Captain's aid, and another one secured the door so more of Captain's men couldn't enter.

Phellek fumbled with the key at the manacles around Darmik's ankles. Once he released them, he moved to Darmik's wrists. Finally, the metal clicked open, and Darmik collapsed to the ground.

"Quickly," someone shouted.

Phellek helped Darmik to the exposed tunnel in the floor. Branek, Traco, and Chrotek were there waiting for him. They grabbed Darmik and took him down the ladder. Darmik raised his head to thank Phellek.

"You're the son I never had," Phellek said.

Captain appeared behind Phellek, sword in hand.

"Behind you!" Darmik shouted.

Phellek twisted around just as Captain plunged the sword into Phellek's torso. Phellek's eyes widened, and his body slumped forward, covering the tunnel's entrance.

Darmik screamed and tried climbing the ladder to reach him.

"No!" Branek said. "It's too late. Don't let Phellek's sacrifice be in vain."

Hatred filled Darmik. Captain hadn't even hesitated—he killed Phellek without a second thought. Darmik vowed to repay the favor.

"Go," Branek ordered. "I'll stay here and guard the ladder." Chrotek and Traco each grabbed a hold of

Darmik's arms, pulling him down the tunnel.

"There isn't much time," Chrotek said. "We've rigged the tunnel to blow so we can't be followed."

Darmik understood that the rest of his men were sacrificing themselves to save him. He stumbled. "No," he said, "we have to go back and fight."

"There's too many of them," Traco said. "Captain has taken control of the Eighth Company."

They came upon boxes of dynamite. Chrotek stopped. "I've got this. You two hurry on."

Darmik and Traco rushed forward. Darmik's vision blurred. He felt like he was about to pass out. The exit was only a few feet ahead.

A rumble shook the ground, followed by a loud boom. Darmik and Traco were thrown from the tunnel. They landed facedown, on the dirt. When Darmik came to, he sat up and stared at the collapsed cave behind him. How many of his men died in order to save him? Darmik felt unworthy of their sacrifice.

Traco pulled Darmik to his feet. "Let's go."

Traco hoisted Darmik up on one of the two horses. "Go!" he shouted. Traco swung up on the other horse, and they took off toward Greenwood Forest.

TWENTY-FIVE

Rema

As Rema ran through the halls, people stepped aside. She flew through the corridors until she exited the fortress. Once outside, she located the door in the wall and left the safety of the compound, just like she had the previous night. Only this time, she was adequately dressed.

The soldiers on top of the wall obviously saw her. It was broad daylight, and she wasn't exactly concealing her appearance. Still, no one knew what to do. Allow her to pass? Or attempt to stop her?

At this point, Rema didn't care. She kept running, the cold air filling her lungs. After several minutes, she found what she was looking for—a cliff. Granted, there wasn't a body of water to jump into, but it afforded her a view of the astounding beauty. There were several other mountaintops eye level with her, all covered with snow. A dark green valley sat below. The wind was strong, wrapping around her body and tossing her hair every which way. She took the fur hat from her pocket and put it on.

Closing her eyes, she felt a rush of emotions from standing on the cliff with the wind gusting all around her. The past day was a whirlwind.

What was she going to do?

Pulling out the key necklace, Rema held it in her hands. It was a gift, given to her by her mother. A clue to her past. Rema was Princess Amer. But should she become queen? What right did she have to rule? Was it simply a matter of bloodlines and not qualifications?

Mako saved her life seventeen years ago, for the sole purpose of one day restoring her to the throne. Should she join this rebel movement, and kill King Barjon and Prince Lennek, as they had done to her family?

And what about Darmik? Would he really renounce his own father and brother to serve her?

He'd said he loved her. Rema's heart pounded just thinking about him saying those precious words. Although she was scared to admit it, she loved him too.

If she became queen, could she be with Darmik? There were so many unknowns; it was hard to think straight. She knew in her heart that stepping into the role she was born into was the right thing to do. She wouldn't make her mother's sacrifice for nothing. The journey ahead would be difficult. People would die. It was an enormous burden to carry—to be responsible for all the people here. But she would. And she would restore the island to peace and prosperity.

So she would be queen.

Even though Maya, Kar, and Mako had lied to her, their intentions were honorable.

The first step to restoring peace would be for

honesty. She would demand it from all her subjects. She would not, under any circumstances, be a figurehead for others to control or manipulate.

It was time to return to the fortress. Apparently, she had a coronation to plan.

❧

As soon as she neared the wall, a group of soldiers intercepted her.

"Your Highness," one of them said to her, "Commander Mako instructed us to find you. You aren't to leave the premises unaccompanied."

Rema allowed them to walk her back inside the compound. She'd have to address the matter of her supposed safety later. For now, she needed to tell Mako she'd assume her position and become queen. That way she'd be involved with all decision making from this point on.

Inside the castle, Rema dismissed the men. One of them looked concerned, like he was afraid to leave her alone. But Rema insisted she was safe now that she was inside. Walking to Mako's office, Vesha stepped out from a shadowed corner. "I need to talk to you," she said.

"I want to apologize for what you saw," Rema said. "I know you like Savenek. I have no interest in him other than as an instructor. I'm not even sure we're friends."

"I know," Vesha said.

Rema was relieved to hear that. She didn't want to lose Vesha, her one and only true friend.

"I want to say I'm sorry for not believing you."

Vesha stood a safe distance from Rema. She curtsied and turned to go.

"What are you doing?" Rema asked. She didn't want Vesha treating her any differently than before.

"Excuse me, Your Highness?"

"Oh, no," Rema said, shaking her head. "Don't you start that title stuff with me."

"But it's the truth."

"That may be," Rema said, "but we were friends before we knew my true identity. I expect our friendship to remain unchanged."

Vesha smiled. "I'd like that very much."

"Now, about Savenek," Rema said.

Vesha rolled her eyes. "That boy. I swear. He's a blout to fall for you. Although, I can't blame him. I suspected it all along."

"I'm not sure what to do about it," Rema admitted.

"You don't have any feelings at all for him?"

"No, my heart belongs to another."

"Who?" Vesha asked.

"I'd rather not say," Rema said. The friends walked down the hallway. "But it's no one here at the fortress."

"Now that you're going to be queen, I'm sure you could have any man you want."

"I'm not so sure about that," Rema admitted. Could she be with Darmik? She didn't think the people at the fortress would ever accept that. "I may have to marry in order to secure peace for the kingdom."

"No," Vesha said with authority. "That's one of the things your ancestors fought for—and why they founded this island. They wanted to marry for love. You will too."

Rema liked the idea of being able to marry for love. That meant maybe she and Darmik had a chance.

They arrived at Mako's office. The door flew open, and Mako stood in the doorway. "We need to talk," he said.

"Yes," Rema said, "we do."

∞

"The coronation will take place in two weeks," Mako said. "That gives us enough time to organize a celebration for afterwards."

"And still plenty of time to plan our attack on the king's castle," Savenek mumbled, studying a map spread out over the low table in Mako's sitting room.

Rema sighed. There was so much to do—learn the structure of the army, plan an attack to overthrow King Barjon, and be crowned queen.

"She'll need a dress," Vesha mused. "You can't crown her looking like that." She chuckled. "No offense, Rema, but you don't look like a queen wearing those trousers and tunic."

"Nor does she act like one," Savenek mumbled.

Rema wanted to tell him to shut the bloody heck up, but Mako interrupted her thoughts.

"That actually is a good point," Mako said. "Rema—you need to see the seamstress. Have her sew you a few dresses."

"The clothes she wears won't make a difference," Savenek said. "She's still just a commoner with nothing special or extraordinary about her."

"Is it really necessary?" Rema asked.

"Yes!" Vesha and Mako said at the same time.

"Rema," Vesha continued, "you need to look like a queen. Everyone here needs to know, without a doubt, that you were born to rule."

Savenek smirked.

Rema stood, walked over to him, and slammed her hand on top of the table. "You, perhaps more than anyone, need to understand and accept my position."

Savenek didn't look up at her. He kept his head down, focused on the map. "You are not my ruler."

"Savenek!" Mako shouted. "Rema is your sovereign. You will behave and address her as such."

Savenek stood and moved before Mako. "I have trained my entire life for this. Every day, every single minute. Complete dedication. For what? *Her?*"

"Yes," Mako said. "She is of royal blood. The true heir."

"She doesn't know anything."

"I know," Mako conceded. "It's our job to teach her."

"That's not my job. I am a soldier."

"And she will be your queen. In charge of you and the army. It will be hers to control. Not yours, not mine."

Rema had no desire to stand there listening to the two of them argue. "Mako's right," Rema said. "I need to be brought up to speed on all matters. I want to know everything."

They turned toward her, as if they forgot she'd been standing there the entire time.

"Of course," Mako said. He glanced at Savenek,

who shook his head and left the room. "I will bring you up to speed."

Mako agreed she'd attend all meetings starting tomorrow. Vesha agreed to see to Rema's wardrobe. Rema agreed that something was going to have to be done about Savenek.

⟨❧⟩

The following days flew by. Rema attended one meeting after another, trying to learn the captains and lieutenants of her army, trying to understand their plans to get everyone down off the mountain.

The days were long.

She still tried to train when she had the time. Of course, she no longer worked with Savenek. Luckily, Audek or Vesha were usually available and willing to train with her.

During the last meal of the day, Rema was sitting with Vesha when the horn sounded, indicating a threat was detected. The two soldiers who were assigned to escort her everywhere were immediately at her side.

"What's going on?" Vesha asked.

"I don't know," one of them answered. "We need to get Rema to a secure location."

"I'll see what's happening." Vesha took off running.

The soldiers escorted Rema through various corridors. They entered a section of the fortress she hadn't been to before. One of the soldiers slid open a black iron door, revealing a set of stairs leading up. Up she could do. If they had been down, like the dungeon's steps, it wouldn't have happened. One of her guards grabbed a torch. She quickly climbed the steps, no windows in sight. The stairs curved round and round and the light bounced off the walls, their bodies casting elongated shadows. This had to be in one of the corner towers. Finally, she reached the top. It was a small, circular room with four small windows evenly spaced. One of the guards ran to a window and looked out.

"There's some commotion in the main courtyard," he mumbled.

Rema went to one of the windows. There were three people in the center of the courtyard, a ring of rebel soldiers around them with swords drawn. Another group of rebel soldiers ran from the courtyard, through the gate, and outside the fortress.

Rema was too high up to make out any of the people. She assumed Mako was there, but she couldn't be sure. Who were the three captives? Soldiers from the King's Army? Or had random citizens managed to find the fortress?

There was a pounding sound, as if someone was running up the stairs toward them. The soldiers glanced at one another, and then one left to head off whoever was coming. Voices drifted up.

"Your Highness," a soldier said as he appeared at the top of the stairs, out of breath. "Commander Mako needs your help."

"Of course." Rema hurried after him, her two guards close behind.

They made their way down the stairs as quickly as possible without running. Then the soldier led her through a corridor and up to the second floor, down another hallway, and into an empty schoolroom.

"Over here," the soldier said, leading Rema next to a window. "Look to the courtyard below. Mako wants to know if you can identify the three prisoners."

Rema peered outside. Now that she was closer, she could see the three people in question—she recognized two of them—Ellie and Neco. The third, an older gentleman, she hadn't seen before.

She took off running.

Entering the courtyard, Rema sprinted toward the three prisoners. "Release them," she ordered.

Savenek didn't acknowledge her; he kept his weapon drawn on Neco.

"I don't know how they knew you were here," Mako said. "But they claim to know you."

"Yes," Rema stopped before Ellie. "This is my chambermaid and a soldier I met at the castle. They are our allies."

"How can you be certain?" Mako asked. "And what about the elderly man?"

"I'm sorry," Rema said, crossing her arms. "I could have sworn I ordered their release." She tapped her foot, impatiently. If they wanted her to ascend to the throne, then they needed to start taking orders from her.

"Yes, Your Highness," Mako said, lowering his weapon. Everyone followed his example. Savenek hesitated, but dropped his sword as well.

Rema hugged Ellie. "What are you doing here?" she asked.

"The island is in chaos. We came here for safety,"

Ellie answered.

Rema glanced to Neco. He stood staring at her. She needed to speak with him alone to make sure Darmik was well.

"Get them inside," Rema demanded. "See that they get hot food and drink."

"And what about this one?" Savenek asked, pointing at the old man.

"After they are fed and warm, we can ask him who he is, and why he's here," Rema said.

As the three were led inside, Savenek turned to Mako and said, "See, this is what I was talking about. She has no clue."

"Rema is your sovereign. And as such, you must obey her."

"She's going to get us all killed."

"I'm standing right here," Rema said. "And has it occurred to you that if they found us, others can, too? I want the watch doubled."

Savenek snapped his mouth shut. He blinked several times. "I'll see to it." He turned and left.

Mako chuckled. "I'll escort you inside."

❧

After the three guests were fed, Rema went to speak with them in one of the offices. Mako, Savenek, and a few other soldiers she didn't recognize were there. A circular table was center in the room, with everyone seated around it. A single chair was left empty. Rema slid onto it.

"Neco," Rema began, "why are you here?" she asked, hoping to ascertain something about Darmik.

He glanced at her. "I needed to get Trell to safety," he said, indicating the elderly gentleman.

"How did you find us?" Savenek demanded, leaning forward on the table.

Neco kept his focus on Rema.

"I will be the one asking the questions," she said, glaring at Savenek. Turning to Neco, she asked, "Why is Trell's safety so important?"

"He has vital information that will assist your cause," Neco answered.

"Do you plan to stay here? Or are you returning back down the mountain?"

"My orders were to bring Trell here, then return to aid where needed," Neco said.

Rema glanced to Ellie. The girl's head was down, her cheeks flushed. Rema looked back at Neco, raising her eyebrows in question. Neco gave her a half smile. Was something going on between him and Ellie? Rema would have to ask Ellie when they were alone.

"What makes you think we'd allow Trell to stay here?" Savenek asked, his voice low and angry.

Trell cleared his throat. "I thought this was the rebel army."

"It is," Savenek said, louder than necessary.

"I thought you'd welcome those seeking refuge. Those wanting to help your cause."

"We do," Mako answered, giving Savenek a hard look, silencing him.

"I have no intention of serving another monarch

just as evil and vicious as the one in power now," Trell said.

Savenek opened his mouth to speak.

"Leave, now," Rema ordered Savenek.

"What?" Savenek asked, stunned.

Rema looked to her two soldiers standing guard by the door. Both sets of eyes widened at the prospect of being ordered to remove their captain—soon to be commander—from the room.

"Won't be necessary," Savenek said, barely keeping his temper in check. He shoved the chair back, rose, and stormed from the room.

"He's a spirited one," Trell said.

"That's one way of putting it," Rema mumbled.

"I know who you are," Mako said, staring at Trell. "You came with Barjon."

Rema understood what Mako wasn't saying— that Trell was somehow responsible for the deaths of Mako's wife and child.

"Yes," Trell said, holding Mako's piercing gaze. "I came with Barjon. I planned the invasion, and for that, I am truly sorry."

"Why?" Rema asked, curious. Trell looked sad. But it could be an act, and Rema wanted to know and understand this elderly man before her.

His attention turned to her. "Princess Amer," he said, a small smile tugging the corners of his lips. "I was sent here for a single purpose—to establish the Empress's brother as king." Trell coughed. "You see," he continued, leaning forward, "the Emperor fears anything that threatens his position. Barjon was restless. Giving

Barjon his own kingdom, although small and remote, pacified Barjon and ensured one less threat."

"Surely the Emperor wasn't afraid of Barjon," Rema said. "The Emperor has to be protected at all times. What could Barjon do?"

"Barjon is deceitful, devious, and manipulative. The Emperor knew it would be far too easy for Barjon to slip some poison into the Emperor's food or drink. Or even place doubt in the Empress's ears. You see, placing Barjon in Greenwood Island accomplished many things."

"You still haven't answered my question. Why are you sorry?" Rema asked.

Trell leaned back in his seat. "You do understand you have a legitimate claim to the Emperor's throne, do you not?"

The entire room froze. Rema heard nothing but a dull ringing in her ears. She had a claim to the Emperion throne? How?

"When Nero left all those years ago, the true blood line shifted since he was an only child. You could go to Emperion and lay claim to the throne. You, my dear Amer, are the greatest threat to Emperor Hamen."

Rema hadn't thought of that. She was still trying to wrap her mind around being a princess, soon to be queen. The mere idea of being more was too much.

Trell continued, "So when you ask why I am sorry for my actions, my dear, you have to understand events from my point of view. I was sent here to ensure Barjon came into power. What resulted was a blood bath. And now, look at the state of the kingdom. What we did, killing your family, was wrong. And my hands are covered in blood for my part. I want to rectify that. I want Barjon gone, and you reinstated to the throne."

Mako cleared his throat. "And your motives?" he asked. "They simply can't be out of the goodness of your heart. I don't buy it."

Trell leaned forward on his elbows. "No," he said. "It isn't that simple. The fact of the matter is that I'm sorry for what I've done, and I'd like to rectify my actions. And yes, there is more to it. But until I can ascertain your plans, I have no intention of revealing more."

Rema liked Trell. There was something about his blunt honesty that she appreciated.

"Can you help us?" Rema asked. If he planned the invasion of a kingdom, surely he was well versed in military strategy. They could use all the help they could get.

"Rema," Mako said, "we need to speak in private on the matter."

She looked to Trell, awaiting his answer.

"What are your intentions?" he asked.

"To retake the throne and establish a prosperous, peaceful kingdom."

"Then yes, I will help you."

"Wait," Mako interjected, raising his hand.

"Excuse me," Rema said. "I am not fond of the lack of respect I'm receiving."

It looked like she'd smacked Mako across the face—he was so shocked by what she'd said.

Rema stood. "I am Princess Amer. Next week, I will be crowned queen. You will address me as such and show me the respect the title and position deserve."

Ellie smiled, nodding at her. Neco fought a grin. Trell looked deep in thought. Everyone else seemed stunned.

Rema raised her eyebrows.

"Yes, Your Highness," Mako said. Everyone followed suit.

"I'd like for our new recruits to be shown to their rooms."

"I will make the necessary accommodations," Mako said. "However, because I am the commander of your army, I need to address the matter of your safety." Rema nodded for him to continue. "Neco should remain here. It is far too dangerous to allow him to leave."

"Explain your reasoning," Rema demanded.

"We are weeks from attacking the castle. We can't afford for Commander Darmik to discover our location now. It would end our revolt before it even begins. Also, given Neco's stellar reputation, we could use him here."

Rema agreed. Even though Neco was rather stealthy, if there was an assassin here from Emperion searching for her, she didn't want to lead him right to her. And they really could use Neco's tactical skills.

"I concur," Rema said. "Neco stays."

Sitting on the ground in front of the roaring fire, Rema pulled her knees to her chest, resting her head on them. "What was Darmik doing when you last saw him?" Rema asked.

Ellie sat next to her. "Do you want me to brush

your hair?"

"No," Rema said, "I want to know about Darmik." Her friend had been carefully avoiding her questions since they returned from the meeting.

"I'm sorry; I'm not at liberty to say. You'll have to ask Neco."

They were alone in Rema's bedchamber. No one would overhear, so why couldn't Ellie tell her what was going on? Rema decided not to push the matter. She'd ask Neco the next chance she got.

"Thank you for volunteering to be my chambermaid," Rema said. "You don't have to help me though." Rema pulled at the hem of her dress. A string came loose.

"I know," Ellie responded. "I want to."

There was a knock on the door. Ellie jumped up and answered it.

"It's Mako," she said. "He needs to speak with you about an urgent matter."

Rema stood as he entered.

"Sorry to interrupt," Mako said. "But a scouting party has returned."

"Is everything under control?"

"Yes," Mako answered. "No additional threats were detected." He shifted his weight from foot to foot, appearing distressed.

"Then what's the matter?" Rema asked. She took Mako's hands in hers. "Please tell me."

"They found Kar and Maya in one of the caves."

Rema squeezed Mako's fingers. Were her aunt and uncle well? Or had something happened to them?

"The scouting party brought them back here. They are both fine, but Maya is suffering from an infection. She's been taken to the infirmary."

"I want to see them," Rema said as she released Mako's hands.

Mako took a deep breath. "I know you want to see them. However, Maya has been put in quarantine. No one is allowed to be around her until her infection is under control. I'm sorry."

Rema was afraid it was more serious than Mako let on. "Is her life at risk?"

"Nulea believes Maya will make a full recovery. In order to ensure the infection doesn't spread to others here at the compound, we are taking the necessary precautions. There is nothing to fear."

Rema hugged Mako. "Thank you for bringing them back safely, and thank you for telling me."

❧

After eating dinner in Rema's sitting room per Mako's request, Ellie and Vesha accompanied Rema to the gathering room. Rema wanted an opportunity to run into Neco—she needed to ask him about Darmik.

When they entered the room, it fell silent and everyone turned to stare.

"Um, maybe you should say something?" Ellie suggested.

"Good evening," Rema said in a loud, clear voice. "Please carry on." People looked to one another, clearly not sure of proper protocol around her. When she stayed at the castle, King Barjon was always announced before he entered a room, and people bowed. She'd have to discuss the matter with Mako and make sure they implemented the necessary procedures.

Ellie shrugged her shoulders. Rema spotted Neco playing a game of cards with some soldiers. He glanced up and nodded at Rema. She moved toward the tables and sat at an empty one, Vesha and Ellie joining her.

"Are we actually going to be playing a game?" Vesha asked.

"No," Rema said, "but I want it to look like we are."

Vesha pulled out a box of cards and divided them up.

Ellie picked up her stack. "This is quite the organization." She glanced over her hand. "And you're the queen." She smiled, her eyes sparkling. "Quite the turn of events since the last time I saw you."

"You better not treat me any differently," Rema said.

Vesha laughed. "I, for one, can't imagine you as queen. No offense or anything. But I'm just a healer's daughter. I shouldn't be socializing with royalty."

"Ugh," Rema moaned. "Promise me, both of you, to always be honest with me. I value your friendship, and I don't want that to change. Ever." Rema put her hand in the middle of the table.

Ellie and Vesha both reached forward with their left hands, taking hold of Rema's.

"I swear," Ellie said.

"Me too," Vesha added.

"Ahhh, how sweet," Audek said. He slid onto the

only empty chair. "Am I interrupting something?"

Vesha whacked Audek's arm. "No one invited you to join us."

"Do I need an invitation?" Audek laughed. "We're all friends. Well, except for you." He pointed at Ellie. "I don't know you, but I would sure like to!" He wiggled his eyebrows.

Rema couldn't help herself, she started laughing. "Audek, you are a piece of work!"

Neco appeared behind Ellie. "Everything all right?" he asked.

Turning to Rema, Ellie smiled wickedly. "I've been wanting to do this in public." She spun around, wrapping her arms around Neco's neck, kissing him on the lips. The tips of Neco's ears turned fire red.

"Well then," Audek mumbled, "I guess I won't like knowing her as much as I had hoped."

"What?" Vesha asked, confused.

Audek pointed to Ellie and Neco. "Another girl is taken. I'd like to know when it'll be my turn."

Vesha rolled her eyes. "Good luck with that."

Rema whispered to Vesha, "Would you mind getting Audek out of here?" Rema needed to speak with Neco about Darmik. And she definitely did not want Audek to know her involvement with Darmik just yet.

"On second thought," Vesha said, "come with me, Audek. I have some girls you need to talk to."

Audek's eyes widened. "You do?"

Vesha jumped up and grabbed Audek's hand. "Let's go, lover boy. Before I change my mind."

"Yes, sir! I mean, ma'am, I mean—"

ЯED

Vesha shoved him forward before he could get another word out. She glanced back at Rema and winked.

"Okay, you two," Rema said to the lovebirds.

Ellie laughed as she detangled herself from Neco and took a seat. Neco slid onto the other chair next to Rema.

"How are things off the mountain?" Rema asked, trying to keep her voice low, so no one could overhear her.

"Not good," Neco said, rubbing his face.

"And Darmik?" Rema asked, grabbing onto Neco's arm, fearful of his answer.

He looked at her, and their eyes locked. "Cassie is dead."

"What?" Rema asked, shocked by the news.

"Lennek murdered her," Ellie said.

"But that's not all," Neco added. "Lennek and Captain are now in control of a good portion of the King's Army."

"Who is Captain?" Rema asked.

"The assassin from Emperion."

Rema shivered. "Is that why Darmik wanted you to bring Trell here?"

"It is."

"And where is the assassin now?" Rema feared Darmik would get in Captain's way. She didn't want any harm to come to him because of her.

Neco avoided making eye contact, and Rema wondered if he was hiding something. Now that she was thinking on the matter, she realized he hadn't answered her question about Darmik.

"I'm not certain," Neco answered. "The plan

is for Darmik to lead Captain away from the Middle Mountains and to the bay towns. Once Darmik is certain it's safe, he'll return here to see you." Rema noticed Ellie's head jerk in Neco's direction. Again, she wondered if he was telling the entire truth.

At least Darmik was competent at what he did. He was definitely well prepared to handle an assassin.

"One last thing," Neco said, leaning forward. "I'll need to be able come and go from the compound, so I can check for Darmik on a daily basis."

"Of course," Rema said. "Please keep me apprised of the situation."

A shadow fell over Rema.

"What are you doing?" Savenek asked, towering above her.

Rema glanced up, wondering who he was directing his question to.

"Nothing," Neco answered. "We were just leaving." He stood, pulling Ellie up beside him. "Your Highness." He bowed. "Thank you for your time." He turned and strode away, Ellie at his side.

Savenek plopped down on the chair next to Rema. "We need to talk."

"We do?"

"Yes," he said.

"About what, exactly?"

"Your safety," Savenek said, clutching his hands together on top of the table.

Rema glanced around the room. Most everyone was occupied. Some played cards, others a dice game, some sat sewing, while others just talked to one another.

RED

At the entrance to the large gathering room stood the two soldiers now responsible for her safety.

She focused on Savenek. Why was he concerned for her well-being? Was it simply because he cared for her? Did he even still have feelings for her now that he knew her true identity? Or did he know of a specific threat?

"Please," Savenek whispered. "May I speak with you alone?"

"If you keep your voice low, no one will hear you here."

He finally looked Rema in the eyes. "Will you allow me to accompany you to your suite?"

Vesha and Audek had joined in a game of dice. Neco and Ellie were nowhere to be seen. "Fine." Rema stood. Savenek escorted her to Mako's rooms in silence.

With her two guards posted outside the door, Rema turned to Savenek. "What do you want?"

Savenek quickly checked the two bedchambers and privy, ensuring they were alone. He stood three feet away, staring at her. "You can't ascend to the throne."

Rema was tired of hearing him complain about her lack of qualifications. "I'm not going to stay here and listen to you. I may not be what you want or expected, but I'm it. I'm the only one left. Deal with it."

Savenek jerked his head back, eyebrows bent inward. "That's not what I meant," he said, shaking his head.

Rema started to walk toward her room.

"Wait," Savenek said, grabbing her arm. "Please just listen to me for a moment before you run away, like you always do."

Savenek infuriated her sometimes. Did he not realize what he said? Or how he was always insulting her? "Fine," she said, glancing at his fingers curled around her arm. He released her.

"What I meant was that if you become queen, Emperor Hamen will kill you."

"It makes no difference," she said.

"Being dead will make a huge difference." Savenek ran his hands through his hair, appearing agitated.

"He'll have me killed whether I take the throne or not. The emperor already knows I'm alive."

"How?" Savenek demanded.

"I'm not sure," Rema admitted, "but he's already sent an Emperion soldier here to hunt me down and kill me."

Savenek stood staring at her. "How do you know this?"

"Neco told me what's going on around the island. He's from the King's Army and has access to vital information. You might know this if you'd give him a chance." She still wanted to keep Darmik out of this. She knew Savenek would never trust him.

"And you believe Neco?"

"Yes. I spent enough time in the castle to know Neco is trustworthy."

Savenek nodded. "You do realize the emperor won't stop with one assassin."

Rema avoided using that word. "I know." She'd spent a lot of time considering her options. "That's why, when we've taken back the kingdom and established peace,

I will send an envoy to Emperion to open negotiations for a peace treaty."

"You think that will work?"

"If I can convince Emperor Hamen I want no part of his kingdom and that my sole interest is in Greenwood Island, he'll leave me alone. I'll sign whatever he wants to denounce any legitimate claim I hold to the mainland."

Savenek sat on the chair. "Who will be part of the envoy?"

"I don't know yet. I need to discuss the matter with Mako and Trell." And Darmik. He had been to Emperion and would know what to do. "So you see, it will all work out. I already have two soldiers that escort me everywhere. I am completely safe here. Once we retake the castle, I will have my own royal guard."

Savenek nodded his head. "Okay. I'm glad you take your safety seriously."

"Thank you for your concern." She turned to go to her room.

"One more thing," Savenek said. Rema turned back to face him. "I, uh…I still care for you."

Rema had no idea what to say to that.

"I want the opportunity to court you." He stood and came before her.

"But Mako said—"

"Mako's not in charge. You are. And I want you to give me a chance." He reached out and took Rema's hands in his. "Please."

One minute he was yelling at her, and the next he was declaring his love. Rema never met anyone so confusing before. What should she say to him? Her heart belonged to Darmik, but she liked Savenek as a friend—most of the time at least. She valued his knowledge and hoped he would be part of her army, not necessarily in charge, though. With his temper, she didn't want to hurt his feelings and have him do something stupid.

"Savenek," Rema said. "Now is not the time. We're about to go into battle."

"I know, but—"

The door opened. Ellie walked in and froze. "Am I interrupting?" she asked.

"No," Rema said, pulling her hands free. Without looking at Savenek, she turned and went into her bedchamber, Ellie right behind her.

♻

Rema yawned, staring out the window. She'd been stuck in yet another meeting. This one started shortly after breakfast, and it was already dark outside. Her back ached from sitting all day.

"Rema," Mako said, gently touching her shoulder. "Do you have an opinion on the matter?"

She was daydreaming, again. She had no idea what Mako, Trell, and about a dozen other soldiers had been discussing. Mako insisted she didn't have to attend every meeting, but she wanted to be involved—and she wanted to be taken seriously.

"I'm sorry," Rema said. "What are the options again?"

Trell shifted the map on the table, so she could see it better.

"Once all of our forces are in position," Mako said, pointing to several marked locations around King's City, "do you want to send in a small, elite team to kill Barjon and his sons, or do you want a full-scale attack?"

"What is your opinion?" Rema asked Trell.

"Send in an elite team first. I fear that if we attack all at once, King Barjon and Prince Lennek could slip away."

"I agree," Mako said, "but the issue is Commander Darmik. He most likely won't be in King's City. We'll still need to take him out."

Trell raised his eyebrows, looking at Rema. She knew she'd need to explain the situation with Darmik. "I need a moment alone with Mako and Trell," she announced. After everyone else left the room, Rema turned to Mako. "There is something you don't know." She shifted on the chair, not sure how to explain her relationship with Darmik. "Commander Darmik has pledged allegiance to me."

Mako sat very still. After several moments of utter silence, he said, "Explain."

Rema quickly outlined how she and Darmik met, how they formed a friendship, about Darmik's discovery of her identity, how he allowed her to escape, and his visit to see her when he gave her his oath to serve and protect her.

Mako rubbed his face. "Why have you not told me any of this sooner?"

"I feared you wouldn't believe me, and I was afraid you'd harm Darmik."

"How can you be certain of his intentions? That

he isn't going to double-cross you?"

"All she says is true," Trell answered. "Darmik is trying to keep the army away from the Middle Mountains. He is trying to buy us time to finalize our attack. When the opportunity presents itself, he will openly join our cause."

Mako stood and went to the window, staring outside. "I always wondered why he allowed me to escape with you."

Rema hoped that by having Darmik on their side, it would ensure a swift victory.

"The people here will not take kindly to this information."

"I know," Rema admitted. "That's why I haven't told anyone. I know how people here feel about him. But he really is a brilliant man, and he is quite kind and loving—despite his reputation."

"This certainly changes things," Mako said, turning around to face her. "Does he still control the army? Will they follow him? Or is their loyalty to the king?"

Trell shook his head. "I don't know."

"Nor do I," Rema said.

"Let's keep Darmik's involvement quiet for now. When the right opportunity presents itself, I'll tell our people. With the coronation tomorrow, let's resume our planning after the celebration."

When Rema exited the room, her two guards stood waiting for her. "Where are Vesha and Ellie?" she asked.

"In the training room," one of the soldiers answered.

"Then that's where we're going."

When they arrived, the sight was not at all what Rema expected. Instead of everyone working with their small groups running through drills, all fifty people present worked together. Rema stood at the entrance watching.

The room was utterly silent. A group of men were stealthily crouched down and moving forward. Every five feet, one soldier threw a knife at a straw dummy. Realization dawned on her—they were pretending to travel down a makeshift corridor, and the straw dummies were the enemy soldiers.

The group stopped before a wooden stick, which served as a faux door. On the other side, two dozen men stood with blue marks on their chests. There was also a bed with a sleeping person on it.

The group stormed into the room and a hand-to-hand battle ensued. It seemed chaotic. The person on the bed rose and fled the room.

"Stop!" Savenek said. "We failed. Again."

"Maybe we need to try a different formation coming through the door," Neco said.

"What are you doing?" Rema asked.

"Her Royal Highness, Princess Rema," Neco shouted, dropping to a knee. Everyone followed suit, except for Savenek.

"Why, we're killing King Barjon, Your Royal Highness." Savenek smiled and bowed.

"I sure hope you intend to kill Lennek at the same time," Rema said, coming further into the room.

"That's the plan."

"Excellent." Rema motioned for everyone to stand. "Make the bastard pay."

"With pleasure."

❧

Ellie finished braiding the ribbon into Rema's hair.

"Just like old times." Rema smiled, watching Ellie in the mirror.

"If I had pins, perhaps. It's near impossible to do what I want with your hair without the necessary items." She tied off the ribbon. "This will have to do."

"I think she looks beautiful," Vesha said, coming into the room carrying a dress.

"Is that what she's wearing for the coronation?" Ellie asked.

"It is." Vesha grinned as she held up the dress.

Rema was at King Barjon's court long enough to know this dress wasn't in fashion, yet, it was beautiful.

"There weren't many fabrics to work with," Vesha said. "However, I think this turned out quite well."

"It's perfect," Ellie said. "Put it on!"

Rema removed her robe and slid into the dress. Ellie laced up the back, and turned her to face the mirror.

Rema could not believe what she saw before her. The dress was deep red, matching the ruby from her key necklace. It was form fitting on top, with long sleeves. The bottom contained several layers of fabric that bowed out. But what made the dress stunning and unique was the gold embroidery covering the red material. The seamstress must have stitched the entire thing by hand.

Vesha came up behind and draped a cape over her shoulders. The cape was lined with white fur, the outer fabric gold. Rema's family crest was stitched on the back.

"You truly look like a queen," Ellie whispered.

For the first time ever, Rema felt like one.

"You're timeless," Vesha whispered.

There was a knock on the door, and Mako entered.

When Rema turned to face him, he had tears in his eyes. "You look just like your mother."

Rema didn't expect that. She took hold of her key necklace—the one from her mother. "I wish I'd known her," Rema said. She wanted to add that she wished her family and Mako's hadn't been killed, but she couldn't bring herself to say the words aloud.

"We'll see you there," Vesha said. She and Ellie left.

"Are you ready?" Mako asked, his voice gruff.

No, Rema thought, *I'm definitely not ready.*

Mako held out his arm to escort her to the courtyard where the ceremony would take place. What was she doing? She was just a child. She had no experience leading or ruling people. Everyone had such high expectations of her. She was supposed to overthrow King Barjon and bring peace to the kingdom. What if she couldn't accomplish these tasks? What if she disappointed everyone? Peoples' lives were going to depend upon her.

"Rema?" Mako asked, recapturing her attention.

"Of course I'm ready," she said, smiling. Rema took hold of Mako's arm, and they began their journey to the courtyard.

"I do have one question for you," he said. "Your given name is Amer. Shall I crown you Queen Amer? Or Queen Rema?"

"Rema is my name," she answered. "Amer sounds so foreign to me. But like you said, it is the name my parents gave me, the name I was crowned princess with as a baby. Can we use both?" she asked.

They descended the stairs to the ground level. It was strange to see the corridors so empty. Rema assumed everyone was already in the courtyard.

"Do you mean both names put together?"

"Precisely. Queen Amer Rema of Greenwood Island."

"And shall you always be called both names?"

No one used two names. Rema sighed. "No," she said. "Whenever my title is used, I will go by Amer. However, informally, around family and friends, I will go by Rema."

They stood at the entrance to the courtyard. Mako glanced down at her. "Your father would be so proud of you."

Tears threatened. Rema did not want to cry in front of everyone. She swallowed the lump in her throat. The sound of a horn filled the courtyard. Mako and Rema walked out onto the platform situated at the northern end. Someone had placed flowers all around the edge of the stage. In the center sat a high-backed chair covered with red fabric that matched her dress. She assumed she'd sit there while everyone came up individually and pledged their loyalty to her.

The music stopped.

Rema stared out at the hundreds and hundreds of people crowded together in the courtyard and on the balconies.

Mako thanked everyone for coming and gave a short speech. Rema couldn't concentrate on what he said—instead her focus was on Kar and Maya. They both stood before the stage with huge smiles on their faces. Rema hadn't seen them since their return. Maya had lost weight, but other than that, she appeared healthy. Kar looked as he always did. Pride radiated from him, and Rema stood a little taller.

Behind her aunt and uncle, stood Ellie and Vesha. Both girls appeared overly eager. Behind them stood Neco, Savenek, and Audek. Savenek, as usual, looked stern and serious. Neco had a blank expression that reminded her of Darmik. Audek, of course, wore a goofy grin.

Mako turned and stood before Rema. He held a ring with a ruby on it.

"I, Mako, Commander of King Revan's Army, do hereby grant and name Princess Amer as Queen Amer Rema of Greenwood Island, sole surviving heir of the royal family, to hereby lead, rule, and govern our great kingdom." He slid the ring on her finger.

A child came forward carrying a wooden box. Mako reached down and opened it. He pulled out a gold crown encrusted with rubies. He placed it upon her head, and knelt before her. Mako pulled out his sword and laid it on the ground at her feet. "I, Commander Mako, do hereby pledge my life to you." He stood and sheathed his sword.

"I give you Her Majesty, Queen Amer!"

Rema stepped forward, toward the edge of the platform. Everyone dropped to one knee, bowing their heads.

"Rise," Rema commanded her subjects.

Everyone cheered and clapped.

The weight of the crown sitting atop her head was heavier than she had anticipated.

TWENTY-SIX

Darmik

armik peeled his eyes open. He was in a dark cave, a small fire next to him. How had he gotten here? He remembered the explosion in the tunnel, being thrown on the ground, and mounting a horse. He must have blacked out after that.

Looking across the fire, Traco was sitting there staring at him. "Try not to move," he said. "You've lost a significant amount of blood. I patched you up as best I could."

Looking down at his chest, Darmik saw the bandages covering the "L" Lennek had carved onto him. He could also feel his back was wrapped as well.

"How long have I been out?" Darmik asked, his voice hoarse.

"Days."

He needed to get up the Middle Mountains to Rema. He had to protect her.

"I sewed your back shut," Traco said. "Also stitched your finger and that nasty mark on your chest. I don't think anything is infected."

Traco came around the fire, holding a steaming cup of liquid. "Here, you need to drink this." He lifted Darmik's head, holding the cup to his lips. Darmik tried to swallow as much of the pungent-smelling drink as he could. It burned going down.

"Thank you," Darmik said. His eyelids became heavy, and he drifted back to a dreamless sleep.

When he awoke, everything looked the same.

"Did anyone else from my personal squad make it?" Darmik asked.

Traco shook his head. "I'm afraid not."

"We need to get back to the compound to see if Captain managed to capture any of my men." Darmik carefully sat up. His head pounded, and his back stung with excruciating pain.

"Neco gave orders that no one was to be taken alive."

The decision made sense. It was what Darmik would have ordered, too. Still, the thought that Darmik lost almost every single member of his personal squad was almost too much to bear. He'd known these men for years. Had fought side by side with them. How could they be gone? Tears filled his eyes.

"I swear I will avenge their deaths," Darmik said. "Captain will pay."

Traco nodded. "I will help you."

A plan started to form. "Traco, I need you to do something for me."

"Anything."

"I need you to find everyone in the King's Army who is still loyal to me. If they are willing to denounce

ЯED

King Barjon and Prince Lennek, and instead, follow the rebels, and me, tell them to amass in Werden. Then I want you to go to Werden and organize them."

"You want me to organize them to do what exactly?" Traco asked.

"Prepare for battle."

⁘

Even though Darmik's wounds were not fully healed, he couldn't wait any longer. He had to get to Rema and protect her. The rebels needed to strike now before Captain or Lennek gained control over a larger portion of the army.

Traco left the cave to amass an army loyal to Darmik. Darmik journeyed up the Middle Mountains alone. He couldn't travel very fast on account of his wounds. However, he kept picturing Rema—her blonde hair and blue eyes, riding a horse, free and wild. Her image was enough to keep him on his feet.

After twelve days of complete and total exhaustion, Darmik exited the black tunnel. He went to the cave he and Neco had previously stayed in near the rebel fortress. After making a small fire, he settled down for the night.

⁘

"Darmik," a familiar voice said. He opened his eyes. Neco was sitting next to him. "I'm glad you made it."

"You and me both," Darmik mumbled. "Thank you for the rescue."

Neco handed him bread and water. Darmik wondered where he got the supplies. The rebels? And where was Ellie? Was she safe?

Neco chuckled. "You look like death, but I can tell your mind is still in commander mode."

Darmik sat up and took the water, gulping down the ice-cold liquid.

"I arrived here safely with Ellie and Trell. We made contact with the rebels, and have been staying with them inside the compound. I've been coming here two to three times a day, hoping you'd show up."

Darmik coughed. His ribs ached and lungs burned.

"We need to get you to a healer," Neco said. "Can you walk?"

"Obviously," Darmik said. "I did manage to make it here, didn't I?"

Neco opened his mouth to say something else, but Darmik raised his hand, stopping him. "Is it possible to speak to Rema before I enter the rebel compound?"

Neco nodded. "I'll get her." He stood and added a few more logs to the dying fire.

"How is she?" Darmik asked.

"Good." Neco smiled. "She's quite stubborn and feisty. I like her."

Darmik raised his eyebrows, questioning his friend.

"She'll be good for the island," Neco clarified before leaving.

Darmik awoke to the sound of voices and commotion. He removed his cape—the fire had warmed the place up. When he stood, his vision blurred and he swayed on his feet. Darmik closed his eyes and took a deep breath, steadying himself.

"I know perfectly well where he is," a familiar voice said. "I've been to the cave before."

Darmik smiled. She was here.

Neco and Ellie entered, followed by Rema. Her eyes locked with Darmik's. It felt like time froze. She ran to him, a huge smile plastered across her face. Rema threw her arms around his neck, their bodies slamming together, and they kissed.

All Darmik's aches and pains vanished, and all he could see, smell, and think of was Rema. Darmik vaguely heard Ellie laugh. Neco said, "Uh…we'll give you two a minute alone."

Darmik wrapped his arms around Rema's back, pulling her even closer. Her hands lifted his tunic over his head. He untied her cape, and it fell to the ground with a soft thud. Darmik's lips moved to her ear, her neck. Her smooth skin was soft and inviting. Rema's fingers slid under Darmik's shirt and up his back. He gasped, a searing pain burning his skin.

"What?" Rema asked, her fingers gently exploring the bandages. "Are you hurt?"

Darmik nodded.

Rema lifted his shirt, revealing his bare torso. She gasped. "What happened?"

Darmik shook his head. He didn't want to think

about being tortured—he wanted to lose himself in Rema again.

"Tell me," she demanded. Her hands gently touched the bandage covering the "L" carved onto his chest, just below his royal markings. Dark blood had soaked through most of it.

"Lennek and the assassin, Captain. They captured me when I tried saving Cassie."

She gasped. "How did you escape?"

"Phellek," Darmik said. "He's dead." A pain, different from what the cuts in his skin caused, shot through him. Phellek was more of a father than King Barjon had ever been.

"I'm so sorry." Rema's eyes glistened. Her hands cupped Darmik's cheeks. She reached up and kissed his lips.

Soft.

Hot.

Wanting.

Needing.

Darmik led Rema closer to the fire. He took their cloaks and spread them out. Then he gently pulled Rema down.

"I don't want to hurt you," Rema said, her eyes darting to his wounds.

Darmik smiled. "I was thinking the same thing."

Rema lay down, her blonde hair cascading against the black fabric, her potent blue eyes penetrated into his. Her fingers went to the ties at the top of her dress.

"Allow me," Darmik said. He undid the laces, her dress slipping down her shoulders. Her skin was silky, smooth. Lowering himself next to her, his lips touched each shoulder.

Rema's hand trailed down his bare chest, igniting a fire inside of Darmik.

"I love you," he said, looking at her beautiful face.

"And I love you," Rema said, smiling. "Now shut up and kiss me. I've missed you."

Darmik lowered himself on top of Rema, kissing her lips. He propped himself up with one arm so his weight wouldn't crush her. His free hand slowly pulled the fabric of her skirt up.

Darmik heard voices. He hoped Neco and Ellie weren't returning so soon. He ran his hand down her leg. "We better stop before someone sees us."

"I know," Rema sighed. "But I really don't want to."

He kissed the tip of her nose.

"What in the bloody hell is going on here?" a young man demanded. All color drained from Rema's face.

"Sorry," Neco said, appearing behind the man.

"Yeah," Ellie added, coming next to Neco. "We tried to stop Savenek, but you know how impertinent he can be."

Carefully watching the man, Darmik helped Rema tie the top of her dress. He looked furious, and Darmik wondered why. Was Rema not allowed to be out of the fortress?

Savenek's hand rested on the hilt of his sword. His eyes darted between Darmik and Rema.

Darmik helped Rema stand. She adjusted her dress and shook her head, throwing her loose hair away from her face. "What are you doing here?" she demanded, a hard edge to her voice.

"Who is this?" Savenek pointed to Darmik.

Darmik reached down, grabbing his shirt and tunic. He quickly put his clothes back on.

"This is Commander Darmik," Rema answered.

Savenek's body went ridged, and his face reddened. "The enemy?" he said, seething with rage. He unsheathed his sword. "Is he trying to capture you? Are there others here?" Savenek pointed the weapon toward Darmik.

Neco stepped forward but Darmik shook his head, wanting him to hold his ground.

"No," Rema said. "Put that away, you idiot."

"Then why are you here with him? Alone?" Savenek pointed to her dress, like he wanted to say more.

Savenek acted as if he was jealous. Was this man in love with Rema? Darmik looked at her. She didn't have feelings for Savenek, did she?

Rema put her hands out, trying to calm Savenek down. "Watch yourself," she said. "You will not forget your place."

Darmik wondered what she was talking about.

"Clearly, you are confused," Savenek said. "Because you, Your Majesty, certainly wouldn't be fraternizing with the enemy."

Your Majesty?

Rema's eyes sliced over to Darmik. "I was crowned queen," she explained.

"And this Savenek," Darmik said, "who is he, and why is he here?"

"He's a captain," Rema answered. "I don't know

why he's here." She put her hands on her hips. "But he is leaving. Now."

"I'm not leaving you alone with him." Savenek shook his head. "I'm placing Darmik under arrest."

Under normal circumstances, Darmik knew he could easily disarm Savenek, but with his recent wounds, he wasn't so sure. Neco moved forward. "Wait," Darmik said. Everyone froze. "I'll go. It's fine."

"No," Rema said. "I'm queen. I will not allow Savenek to arrest you."

"You may be queen," Savenek said, leaning toward Rema, "but you are out of your mind."

"Enough!" Darmik shouted. "You will not speak to Rema that way, remember her position. You treat her that way again, and I'll pommel you to the ground."

"Really?" Savenek moved to stand toe-to-toe with Darmik.

"Really," Darmik said.

"Stop." Rema slid between them.

Savenek looked down at her. "Is this why?" His shoulders were moving up and down from breathing heavily.

"What?" she asked.

Darmik took a step back, bringing Rema with him and away from Savenek.

"Why you won't marry me?" Savenek jerked his head at Darmik.

"Neco," she said, "restrain Savenek."

"That won't be necessary," Savenek said, moving past them and storming out of the cave.

Savenek had asked Rema to marry him? At least

she'd said no. But still, Darmik didn't want another man looking or thinking of her that way.

"Let's go," Rema said. "We need to get back before it gets dark." She grabbed her cloak and made her way out of the cave, Ellie right behind her.

"That was interesting," Darmik said to Neco.

Neco smiled. "You have no idea. Here, lean on me. I'll help you."

When they neared the fortress, several dozen soldiers stood waiting for them, bows and arrows trained on Darmik.

"Lower your weapons!" Rema shouted. "Now."

"Keep them raised!" Savenek yelled, standing among the soldiers. "That is Commander Darmik."

"If my orders aren't obeyed, I'll have you all arrested," Rema said.

Darmik had never heard Rema speak so forcefully before. The soldiers all looked torn, unsure of what to do.

"Rema," Darmik said, "it's fine. Let's just get inside." He was getting weak and feared he might pass out.

"No," she said. "I won't have one accidentally shoot you."

She stood her ground, chin raised—the expectation of being followed clear on her face. Pride filled Darmik. The men lowered their weapons.

"Let's go," Rema said. She slipped her small hand into Darmik's and led him forward. Neco stood in front of them, Ellie behind. As they passed the soldiers, all lowered their heads, bowing.

Except for Savenek.

TWENTY-SEVEN

Rema

Neco led them to the barn. Rema glanced back, trying to be discreet, to see who followed. Savenek was right behind Ellie, sword in hand. Audek and Vesha hovered behind him. Rema didn't notice anyone else, not even her usual two guards.

She assumed Neco knew where to find Mako. When they entered the barn, Mako was standing toward the back, brushing one of the horses. Kar was with him.

"What's going on?" Mako asked, focused on Darmik.

"Uncle Kar," Rema said, "I would love to chat with you, but I have an urgent matter to discuss with Mako. You're welcome to stay, if you want."

"No," Kar said, shaking his head. "I need to get back to Maya." Her aunt's health was steadily improving each day, but Maya still required extra attention and care.

Savenek glanced in the stalls, making sure no one else was there. Rema thought about dismissing everyone except Darmik and Mako, but decided against it. She needed to make Savenek understand why Darmik was there—and she wanted to ensure his safety, which would best be accomplished with everyone present.

"Commander Darmik," Mako said, putting the brush down and coming before him. "We meet again."

Confusion filled Savenek's face.

"Darmik," Rema said, "this is Commander Mako."

Darmik reached forward to shake his hand. Mako hesitated, put his hand out, and shook.

Savenek opened his mouth to speak, so Rema hurried and beat him to it. "Darmik has sworn loyalty to me. He is here to join our cause."

"I thought we were going to wait," Mako said. "We decided the people weren't ready."

"Events have unfolded, making it necessary," Rema said.

"What is going on?" Savenek demanded. "I deserve and explanation."

"You do," Mako agreed. "But now is not the time, nor the place. We will speak in private, later."

"Darmik is the enemy," Savenek said.

Rema glanced at Darmik. He had little color and didn't look steady on his feet. She glanced to Vesha. "Get your mother," she ordered. "Darmik needs medical attention. Have Nulea meet us in my room."

Vesha nodded and hurried from the barn.

Savenek stood staring at Rema. "Have you gone mad? Completely lost your mind?"

Darmik's hand shot out, grabbing Savenek's tunic. "I thought I told you not to speak to Rema in such a manner?"

Savenek glanced at Mako. "Don't look at me,"

Mako said. "I've been telling you to watch yourself."

"You're siding with him?" Savenek said.

"I'm not siding with anyone. Just behave yourself."

Darmik released Savenek. Both stood staring at one another, neither backing down.

"Darmik," Mako said. "Can you tell me what's changed, and why you're here?"

"Yes," he said, finally breaking eye contact with Savenek. "The Emperion assassin has taken control of a portion of the army. I believe he and Lennek are in league with one another. If you are prepared to strike, now is the time."

"An Emperion assassin is here for Rema?" Mako asked.

"Yes."

"So Trell was right," Mako murmured.

"We need to move quickly, before he gains control of a larger portion of the army," Darmik said.

"Why are we trusting him?" Savenek asked. "How do we know he's not here to kill Rema himself?"

Everyone stood staring at Savenek. Rema knew Darmik wouldn't be happy with what she was about to do, but she had to do something.

"Audek," she said, "please help Darmik to my room. He can use my bedchamber while Nulea looks at and tends to his wounds." She avoided Mako and Savenek's glares. She was queen and could do as she pleased.

"Savenek," Rema continued, "I'd like a word with you. In private."

"No," Darmik said. "Absolutely not. He can't be trusted."

"I understand your concern," Rema said, "but this is something I need to do." She kissed his cheek, and then left out the back of the barn.

A few seconds later, gravel crunched under boots as Savenek came to meet her.

Rema turned to face him.

"Don't," he said, taking a step back, away from her. "I don't want to hear any explanation you have."

"Darmik and I, we—"

"No!" He placed his hands on her arms. "Please," he said, more gentle now, "I can't bear to hear you talk about another man. Especially *him*."

Rema wanted to tell Savenek that they could at least be friends.

"I can tell just by the way you look at him that you love him." Savenek turned away from her. "I've dreamed of you looking at me that way." His voice was gruff. Rema had no idea what to say to him.

"I'm sorry," Savenek continued. "This is difficult for me. I never imagined finding someone I could love, that I'd want to spend my life with. Then I met you. You turned my world upside down. You made me look at life differently. Made me see new possibilities. When I finally came to terms with it and understood that I loved you, I learn you're the heir to the throne. As if that wasn't bad enough, you're in love with someone else. Only, now I know he's not just anyone. He's the commander and prince of our enemy. It seems unbelievable. A cruel, sick joke."

Savenek turned to face her, his eyes red.

"Now I know," he said. "You'll never love me. At

least, not the way I love you."

He turned and left.

Rema was too stunned to say anything. She'd never even heard Savenek talk that much before. Although she didn't feel any better about the situation between them, at least she knew he wouldn't hurt Darmik out of anger. The fire inside Savenek was put to rest. For now.

◎◎

Word quickly spread through the compound that Prince Darmik had defected from the King's Army to join Queen Amer and the rebels. Rema feared people would be weary and distrusting. However, that was not the case. Wherever Darmik went, people swarmed around him, eager to express their appreciation.

"I can't believe people are so accepting," Rema said to Vesha. They were sitting at one of the long tables in the mess hall, eating.

Darmik had offered to get Rema's breakfast for her. Only, he'd gotten stuck in line talking to several people.

"I know," Vesha said, shoving a biscuit in her mouth. "But look at him."

Rema was looking, along with the dozen or so men and women surrounding him.

"I mean, Savenek's handsome, but Darmik…well, there's just something appealing about him." Vesha sighed, lost in thought. Presumably about Darmik.

"Vesha," Rema said, claiming her friend's attention. She didn't want other women looking at him like that.

Vesha jumped. "I was simply observing why so many women are talking to him. And, as for the men, well, Darmik's reputation is reason enough."

Ellie chuckled. "You have nothing to worry about, Rema. Everyone here knows you two are together."

"Why would I be worried?" she asked. "I'm not worried." Rema just wished he'd hurry and bring her breakfast already. She was starving.

"Here," Savenek said, sliding a plate in front of Rema. "You look hungry." He left before Rema could thank him.

She certainly hadn't expected that. Tearing off a piece of the bread, Rema quickly devoured her food.

Darmik finally made his way to her table. "My apologies," he said. "There are more people here than I anticipated. I want to get to know everyone."

"How are you feeling today?" she asked.

"Much better, thank you. Nulea is well skilled."

"Yes," Rema said. "She is."

Vesha stood. "Speaking of which, I promised Mother I would help her today."

After Vesha left, Neco walked over. "Ellie and I have some things to tend to this morning. We'll see you later at the meeting with Trell."

"We do?" Ellie asked, her face scrunched in confusion.

"Yes," Neco grinned. "Let's go."

Rema was glad they two of them had some time alone.

"So," Darmik said with a wicked grin. "Are you giving me a private tour of the compound?" Rema could think of nothing better than being alone with him.

Savenek appeared next to Rema. "Ready?" he asked.

Darmik's body went rigid.

"For what?" she asked.

"Our training."

He wanted to train now? After days of ignoring her? She couldn't remember the last time they'd worked together. Besides, she wanted to be alone with Darmik.

"We have a meeting on the final details of the attack," she said.

"I know," Savenek said. "But that's not until later. We have time."

Rema glanced over at Darmik. He sat staring at her, no expression showing.

"Unless you're afraid to be around me," Savenek teased, nudging her shoulder.

The sad, depressed Savenek from the barn was gone, and the arrogant, cocky Savenek was back. Rema rolled her eyes.

"You need the practice," he said. "Especially if you're going into battle with us."

Darmik raised his eyebrows. Her involvement in the attack was still being debated.

"Fine," she said. "But I was planning to work with Darmik."

"Sorry," Darmik said. "I have orders to take it easy today. I don't want to reopen my wounds. I need to heal quickly so I can be ready for the attack."

Savenek smirked, leaning against the table. "Then it's just the two of us," he said. "Let's go." He held out his hand for Rema to take.

"Not so fast," Darmik said. "Just because I can't physically train, doesn't mean I can't watch and offer advice." He got up from the table, holding out his hand.

Rema couldn't believe the two of them. She stood and left the mess hall, not looking back to see if either followed.

Instead of going to the small, private room she and Savenek usually used, Rema went to the main training room. She figured it was safer there with several dozen people around.

"Not in there," Savenek said as he grabbed her arm, pulling her back into the hallway. "I want to practice in one of the main corridors."

"Excuse me?" Rema said.

"You need to practice what to do in an actual real-life situation."

"Good idea," Darmik said, joining them.

Savenek smirked.

"Fine." Rema sighed. "Lead the way."

Savenek took them up to the third floor where most of the offices were located.

"Now what?" Rema asked. Men were going about their business.

"Most likely King Barjon will be in his office," Darmik said. "The corridors are heavily guarded right now."

Savenek blinked several times.

"I told you he was here to help," Rema said.

Savenek shrugged his shoulders. "So what do you suggest?"

"That Rema be nowhere near the castle. If my father gets his hands on her, he will destroy her."

Rema shuddered. The king was a cruel, heartless man. She hoped she'd never see him again.

"Then let's prepare for that," Savenek said.

Darmik agreed.

Rema was confused. They were getting along? "I'm not following you," she said.

Savenek turned to her. "Let's assume Barjon has gotten a hold of you."

"He'll have you brought to his office," Darmik said. "Is there an unoccupied room we can use?"

Savenek nodded and then led them down the hallway and into an empty room. There was a desk, two chairs, and a rug.

"It's a little small," Darmik mused, "but it'll do."

"I suggest you pretend to be your father," Savenek said.

Rema remembered King Barjon's cruelty—the way he ordered the horse to be whipped to death without even a second thought. She didn't want Darmik to even pretend to be that man.

"No," she said. "Please don't. Just tell us what he'd do."

Darmik nodded in understanding. "If Rema is captured," he said, "my father will have her brought before him. I doubt she'll be bound—my father is too arrogant. He won't perceive her as a threat."

"Good," Savenek said. "She'll have the element of surprise." He came up behind Rema and took hold of her arm. "Assume I'm a soldier, and I've captured you."

Rema allowed him to lead her to the desk.

"My father will come before you." Darmik stood in front of Rema. "He'll want to get close to intimidate you."

Rema nodded. "And if Lennek is present?" she asked.

"I have a feeling he'll be elsewhere."

Rema wondered what Darmik meant. She'd have to ask him later, in private.

"The first thing will be to break free from the guard, and then go after Barjon," Savenek said.

"Excuse me? You've always taught me to get free and run."

"You won't be able to run this time," Darmik said. "There will be too many guards."

"Your only chance is to kill the king," Savenek said.

"Me?"

"You'll be our only hope at that point."

She let what Savenek said sink in. "Very well, then. I'll try." Perhaps if she had a weapon, she'd be able to kill Barjon before he murdered her. But she would be killing Darmik's father. She peered up at him. Darmik wore his mask—no expression on his face whatsoever. When they were alone, she'd have to talk to him about it.

Savenek nodded. "Assuming the king is standing before you, and I'm a guard, you'll need a plan. And you'll have to be fast and quick about it."

Rema nodded.

"Your best bet will be to start talking to distract them," Savenek said.

"I can do that."

Darmik laughed. "Just say something to upset my father."

"Anything I say upsets him."

"The king will be focused on you, not your hands," Savenek said. "Your guard will most likely have a dagger either here, or here." Savenek pulled her fingers back, patting his arm and side.

"Under clothing?" she asked as she felt the knife sheathed under his sleeve.

"Yes," Savenek said. "He has to be able to access the weapon quickly, so there will be a way to pull it free, if you're careful."

Rema didn't want to be feeling around Savenek's body, trying to unsheathe his dagger. "Show me," she said.

"When Barjon and you are talking," Savenek said, "move your hand back. If I'm holding your arm here, then you can slide your fingers under my tunic and pull the weapon free."

Rema did as he said, but she couldn't get the dagger out. She fumbled with the fabric, unable to pull the weapon free.

Frustration boiled up inside of her. "This isn't working."

"It's right here," Savenek said, guiding her hand to the knife. "Try again."

"I have a different idea," Darmik said, coming next to Rema. "When Barjon's attention is diverted, take a step back, like you're scared."

She leaned back, touching Savenek's chest.

"Good," Darmik said. "Now put your entire body against his."

"Um," Savenek said, his lips close to her ear, "exactly what are you doing?"

Darmik ignored him. "Then with both hands, reach back and grab onto the soldier's tunic, like you're afraid for your life."

Rema did as he said.

"No, lower," Darmik instructed.

Savenek jumped. "That's really close to my, uh—"

"I know." Darmik smiled.

Rema felt a strap around Savenek's thigh. She grinned. "I understand."

"The opening will be about one half to one inch above the top. You'll need to move fast."

Rema slid her hands higher. She felt Savenek tense behind her, his breath fast and heavy. Two of her fingers slid into the opening. As soon as she felt the metal, she whipped the dagger out while stomping on Savenek's foot and shoving him backwards. Caught totally off-guard, he lost his balance and fell.

"Perfect," Darmik said. "Now the key will be striking the king hard and fast, before anyone understands what happened and grabs you."

"Bloody hell," Savenek said, standing. "You could have warned me."

"Where would the fun have been in that?" Rema teased him.

Savenek ran his hands through his hair. He still seemed a little rattled to her. She tried to hide her smile.

"You'll want to plunge the dagger here," Darmik said, showing her where to strike. "And then use the king's body as a shield. It may be your only way to get out alive."

"Yes," Savenek added. "Excellent idea. Now if you'll excuse me, I have some errands to tend to before the meeting with Trell." He hurried from the room.

"Well done." Darmik chuckled. It was good to see him laugh.

TWENTY-EIGHT

Darmik

Rema and Darmik entered Mako's office where about a dozen men were seated, waiting for them. There were two empty chairs—on opposite ends of the table. One, at the head of the table, had clearly been reserved for Rema. However, Savenek sat next to that particular empty chair.

Darmik was no fool. He leaned down close to Rema and whispered in her ear, "I'm feeling a bit faint. I need to sit and rest. I may need your assistance."

The corners of her lips rose. "Savenek," she said, "please help Darmik to your chair. He is recovering from wounds and will remain at my side."

Savenek's eyes narrowed. Darmik smiled at the man. Shoving away from the table, Savenek did as Rema asked and took a seat at the other end of the table, away from her. In all honesty, Darmik's wounds were healing nicely. The salve the healer gave him worked wonders. Aside from a sore head, and several bruises and scabs, he was well on his way to a full recovery.

"Darmik, my boy," Trell said. "It's good to see you.

I feared for your life when word came that you'd been captured."

Savenek said, "Am I the only one who—?"

"Don't even say it, Savenek," Rema said. "I trust Darmik, and I'm queen. Understand?"

Savenek raised his hands in surrender. Everyone else looked slightly uncomfortable.

Darmik couldn't help but smile. He loved Rema. She was quick minded, feisty, and had a beautiful heart. Darmik wanted to ask her to be his wife as soon as the occasion arose.

"Things aren't as simple as we hoped," Rema said. "Darmik brings us new information we must consider."

Darmik was given the opportunity to explain that an Emperion assassin was here hunting Rema, Lennek and Captain were working together, security at the castle was tripled, and Captain had control of a portion of the army. He also explained that he believed Lennek played a larger role than anyone suspected.

"In conclusion," Darmik said, "not only do we need to deal with King Barjon, Lennek, and Captain, we must also address the matter of Emperion. If Captain fails, they will send another assassin. At least right now, we know what Captain looks like."

"I agree," Trell added. "We must deal with Emperion. But we can only do so much."

"Yes," Mako added. "Let's put Rema officially on the throne, ridding the island of Barjon and Lennek. Then we can look to Emperion."

Darmik enjoyed the opinions offered by everyone. Mako had a good, honest system in place.

"So long as Emperion is not forgotten," Savenek added. "Like Darmik said, once we kill Captain, they will only send another to replace him."

"I do have one question," Mako said, looking at Darmik. "I know you claim allegiance to Queen Amer, but can you honestly kill your own father? Your own brother?"

Darmik leaned back on his chair. "I've been contemplating that very question. Honestly, I'd rather imprison them. I've seen enough killing."

Savenek smirked. "And you claim to be loyal and want to help us."

"I'm simply being honest," Darmik said. "If it comes down to them or us, I'll choose us."

Trell stood. "I, for one, am glad Darmik is here," he said. "He will only help us succeed."

"Yes," Rema said, standing. "And I am appointing Darmik as the Commander of my personal Royal Guard. That is, if he will accept the position."

Darmik was shocked. Everyone stared at him. Head of the Royal Guard was an honor. Only the most proficient and loyal were selected. But he was used to commanding an entire army. Still, the position would keep him at Rema's side.

"I accept," he said.

"Thank you," Rema answered. "Now, if you'll all excuse me, it's been a long day. Darmik?"

He stood, eager for the opportunity to escort her to her bedchamber. For the chance to be alone with her.

⁂

Rema stood in the sitting room of Mako's quarters. Darmik closed the door. They were finally alone.

"So," Darmik said. There were many things he wanted to say to Rema, but he didn't even know where to begin. And all he could think about was kissing her soft, red lips.

She smiled up at him. "I love when you look at me like that," she said, taking a step toward him.

"Rema."

"Yes?" She took another step, closing the distance between them. Darmik wrapped his arms around her waist, her hands resting on his biceps.

"I—"

"Shh." Rema held a finger up to his lips. "There will be plenty of time to talk—later. Right now, talking is not what I have in mind."

He wanted to ask her to be his wife. Darmik probably needed to discuss the matter with Kar and Maya first. Even though they weren't technically her aunt and uncle, they were the closest people to family she had. Any negotiations on the marriage contract would have to take place between them. Although, Mako seemed to have also taken a protective position. Maybe Darmik should just ask Rema directly then.

He'd think about that later. Right now, well, right now, Rema was in his arms. He lowered his head, kissing her. Rema's hands went to Darmik's shoulders, pulling him closer. He couldn't get enough of her. His hands fumbled with the tie at the back of her dress. The fabric around her torso loosened, and she gasped.

Darmik murmured against her lips, "I want to feel your soft skin. Every inch of it. But if you're not ready, or want to wait, just say the word."

He looked into her piercing blue eyes.

Reaching up, she removed Darmik's tunic. He helped her pull it over his head, tossing it to the ground with a soft thump. Sliding her hands down and taking hold of his undershirt, she pulled it off. He stood before her, nervous. What did she think of him? He had a hideous "L" carved onto his chest, and his back was covered with white scars and healing wounds.

Rema stepped forward, her hands lightly trailing along his royal tattoos and down his stomach, no thought to his imperfections evident on her face. Darmik reached for her shoulders, gliding her dress off them. Rema bit her lip, staring up at him. Lowering his head, he kissed her soft lips. Their tongues met and tangled, breaths mingling. He wound his hands in her blonde hair, the smell of lavender engulfing him. His lips trailed from her mouth to her bare shoulders, causing Rema to gasp. Taking hold of the fabric of her dress, Darmik prepared to remove it.

"I love you," he whispered.

"I love you, too." Rema grinned a beautiful, heart-stopping smile.

Darmik never felt like this before. Content, peaceful, loved. Darmik started to lower her dress. He was so nervous that his hands were shaking.

Rema jerked her head up, her eyes widening at something behind him. She grabbed her dress, pulling it tight against her body.

Darmik spun around. Savenek stood in the doorway, his mouth hanging open.

"I...uh...I...didn't," Savenek stuttered.

"It's fine," Rema said. "Darmik, we should go to my bedchamber."

Darmik grabbed his discarded shirt and tunic off the ground.

"What?" Savenek said, raising his voice. "You're taking him to your bedchamber?"

His face was red, furious. The door was still open, and Rema's guards were probably outside hearing every word of what they said.

"Lower your voice." Darmik pulled Savenek into the room and closed the door. "Have a little discretion."

"Me?" Savenek said. "You're the one standing in the sitting room half naked. And Rema. I didn't think you'd stoop so low."

Rema looked as if she'd been slapped.

"Watch yourself," Darmik said. "No matter what your feelings are, you will treat her with respect." He was tired of Savenek's jealousy.

"Treat her with respect?" Savenek hissed. "Like you?"

"Both of you, cut it out!" Rema screamed. "I am sick of your behavior. Can't the two of you find a way to get along? This is ridiculous!" Rema turned and stormed into her bedchamber, slamming the door behind her.

Darmik had no intention of apologizing to Savenek. He was an arrogant prick in love with Rema. Darmik faced him—giving him the opportunity to apologize if he so felt the need.

"Do you even love her?" Savenek asked.

"More than anything," Darmik answered.

"What's going on?" Mako asked, coming into the room.

Darmik put his undershirt back on.

Mako closed the door. "Are the two of you arguing, again?"

Neither answered.

"We are going into battle in a matter of days. *Days.* The two of you need to put your differences aside," Mako said.

"Of course," Darmik answered. He wanted to go into Rema's room, but he felt awkward with Mako standing right there.

"Fine," Savenek mumbled.

"I want both of you to focus on the upcoming battle and winning. Understood?"

They nodded.

"Rema is our priority right now—putting her on the throne and keeping her safe. After that, the two of you can argue over her. But until then, I want a truce."

Darmik stood staring at Mako. He liked him. He was a wise man.

A loud thump came from Rema's room. Darmik ran to the door, throwing it open without knocking.

The room was empty.

"Rema?"

Darmik went inside the bedchamber, searching for her.

Twenty-nine

Rema

Rema slammed her door closed. Savenek and Darmik were being ridiculous. She was sick and tired of their fighting. She stood, staring at the door. Would Darmik join her soon? She should probably prepare for him. Taking off her dress, she tossed it over the chair and slid on her nightgown.

She shivered. It was rather cold in her room, considering the fire blazed in the hearth. Going to the windows, she noticed one wasn't closed all the way. She hadn't even been aware the windows opened—especially since she was on one of the higher levels.

Rema pushed the window closed. She heard voices coming from the sitting room. She wished Darmik would leave Savenek alone and just get in here already.

Going over to her bed, she pulled back the blankets. Her face flushed remembering Darmik's strong hands on her shoulders, his warm lips devouring hers.

A shadow at the corner of her room flickered, catching her attention. Rema turned to look. The curtain next to the window shifted. Was another window open?

She went to investigate. Moving the curtain aside, she inspected the window. It was closed. An arm reached out from behind the curtain, wrapping around her upper body. Fabric was shoved over her mouth and nose. A foul smell engulfed her. She tried not to breathe it in. She screamed, but no sound escaped her lips.

Rema clawed at the arms encircling her body. She tried stomping on a foot, hitting the groin. Anything to break free.

She felt light-headed.

Her vision blurred.

Rema's world went black.

Thirty

Darmik

armik frantically searched the room. Where did she go? A window was open. He ran over and looked outside. Nothing.

Glancing around the room, he saw a knife protruding from the wall, something dangling from the tip. Darmik ripped off the paper.

Thank you for the hunt.
Although it was a little tedious, you led me right to her.
-C-

Darmik crushed the calling card Captain left behind.

"What?" Savenek asked as he stepped into the bedchamber.

"He has her," Darmik fumed. Red-hot rage boiled inside of him.

"Who?"

"The assassin."

"Is she dead?" Savenek asked, all color draining from his face.

"Not yet. But we don't have much time."

"I'll raise a search."

"You won't find her." Darmik balled his hands into fists. He needed to leave immediately if he wanted to try and stop them.

"I will if we hurry," Savenek said, rushing to the doorway.

"No, you don't understand." Darmik grabbed his traveling sack and cape. "He's taking her before the emperor to kill her. They're going to Emperion."

End of Book 2

Acknowledgements

I wouldn't have completed my fourth book without you, my readers. I want to personally thank each and every one of you for taking the time to read my books, enjoy the worlds I've created, and fall in love with my characters. Your support and encouragement exceed my wildest dreams. Thank you!

Writing a book is an enormous undertaking. I am so blessed to have a wonderful husband and three beautiful children who know and understand my obsession with reading and writing. Thank you for allowing me to do something I'm passionate about, and giving me the chance to soar.

My wonderful sister, Jessica, and my mom, Shirley, have been my own personal cheerleaders throughout the entire process. I love you both dearly.

Rebecca van Kaam—where would I be without your red pen? You are the best beta reader ever!!!! I'd also like to thank Amber McCallister, Jan Farnworth, Hope to Read, Allyssa Adkins, Elizabeth Nelson, Angelle LeBlanc, Kristy Hamilton, Lauren Dootson, Sara Kaiser,

Kimberly Russell-Shaw, and Stacie Buckingham for your help making ЯED what it is today. You guys are the best!

My talented critique partner, Karri Thompson, you have been invaluable with offering constructive criticism. I'm so thankful to share this journey with you.

I have an endless amount of gratitude for the ever-fabulous Jamie Kimok. I'm so glad to have you in my life. Really, I'm much more organized with you watching my back!

To everyone at Clean Teen Publishing—thank you for believing in this series and bringing it to life. I would especially like to thank Dyan Brown, Rebecca Gober, Marya Heiman, and Courtney Nuckels. I am proud to be a part of your team. You truly are publishing ninjas! Also, a special thanks to Cynthia Shepp for doing a fantastic job with editing.

There are a few other people that deserve a special thank you: Melissa Lynn Simmons, Mayra Arellano, LC Helder, and Dvora Gelfond. Your advice, support, and help mean the world to me. Thank you for all of your encouragement.

And last, but not least, Brooke, Jennifer, Natalie, Cheer, Heather, and Amber, you girls help me more than you'll every realize! Thank you for spreading the word about my books!

About the Author

Jennifer graduated from the University of San Diego with a degree in English and a teaching credential. Afterwards, she finally married her best friend and high school sweetheart. Jennifer is currently a full-time writer and mother of three young children. Her days are spent living in imaginary worlds and fueling her own kids' creativity.

**Visit Jennifer online at
www.JenniferAnneDavis.com.**

CPSIA information can be obtained
at www.ICGtesting.com
Printed in the USA
LVOW12s2043240716

497224LV00002B/14/P